SIZE
MATTERS

SIZE
MATTERS

ALISON BLISS

FOREVER

NEW YORK   BOSTON

Copyright © 2016 by Alison Bliss
Excerpt from *On the Plus Side* copyright © 2016 by Alison Bliss
Cover design by Elizabeth Turner. Cover photography by Claudio Marinesco.
Cover copyright © 2016 by Hachette Book Group, Inc.

Forever
Hachette Book Group
1290 Avenue of the Americas, New York, NY 10104
forever-romance.com
twitter.com/foreverromance

First Edition: November 2016

Forever is an imprint of Grand Central Publishing. The Forever name and logo are trademarks of Hachette Book Group, Inc.

The publisher is not responsible for websites (or their content) that are not owned by the publisher.

The Hachette Speakers Bureau provides a wide range of authors for speaking events. To find out more, go to www.hachettespeakersbureau.com or call (866) 376-6591.

ISBNs: 978-1-4555-6802-4 (mass market), 978-1-4555-6803-1 (ebook)

Printed in the United States of America

OPM

10 9 8 7 6 5 4 3 2 1

To women everywhere,
of any size or shape.
You're all beautiful.

Acknowledgments

I have heard that writing can be a lonely endeavor, but I'm lucky enough to never feel alone. No matter how many books I write, the amount of love and support I receive from the people in my life is immeasurable. I can never thank you all enough for what you do for me, though I'm going to try.

Thank you to my mom, my dad, my four sisters, my nieces, my mother-in-law, my aunt Deborah, and especially my amazing husband and our two wonderful boys. You all mean the world to me!

Special thanks to my critique partners, Carol Pavliska and Samantha Bohrman, for always being ready to read when needed and providing awesome notes that tickle my funny bone and make my books better. Thanks to Sonya Weiss for our impromptu brainstorming sessions. You crack me up, woman! And a special shout-out goes to The Floozies. You girls are the best!

Big hugs and a warm thank-you to all the members of the Pure Bliss Street Team for helping me spread the word about my books and sharing a piece of yourselves with me every day. You guys have my heart.

As always, big thanks to my superwoman agent, Andrea Somberg, for being there for me when I need her. Your support, guidance, and friendship mean so much to me!

To my remarkable editor, Alex Logan, thank you! Your expertise and wisdom know no bounds. I appreciate everything you do for me. I'm thrilled to be one of your authors!

As with every manuscript, there are a team of people who work behind the scenes, but make all the difference in the world. So thank you to the art department for the fantastic job they did with the cover, as well as anyone else at Grand Central who helped turn this manuscript into a shiny new book. You all amaze me!

Last but not least, thank you to my readers! You don't know how many times a simple message from one of you has touched my heart or lifted my spirits when I've had a rough day. I hope you will continue to read and enjoy my books, but most of all, I hope you will live to the fullest, love with your whole heart, and laugh often.

SIZE
MATTERS

Chapter One

Leah Martin nearly choked on her beer.

"What do you mean *just pick one?*" Her eyes scanned the entire bar before settling back on her friend. "Pick one what?"

"A guy, of course."

Yeah, because it was just that simple. For Valerie maybe. Even though they were close in size, Valerie always wore her weight better and turned heads everywhere she went. It probably helped that she had expressive blue eyes, wavy platinum blond hair, and looked more like a cutesy toy poodle any guy would give their right testicle to take for a walk.

"I hate to tell you this, Val, but that only applies to women who look like you." If Leah had to classify herself in that same frame of reference, she'd accurately describe herself as a bulldog. Not only did she have the breed's innate stubborn streak, but she also had the matching broad shoulders, wide hips, large chest, and—if she didn't lose a few pounds—probably the same short life span. "Hippy brunettes with body image issues and smudged eyeliner don't get the luxury of *just pick one*."

"Oh, shut up," Valerie said, rolling her eyes. "Your eyeliner looks fine."

Yep, that about sums it up. My eyeliner is the only thing that looks decent on me tonight.

The little black dress she wore was just that—too little—and was slowly squeezing the life out of her. Especially after packing on ten extra pounds in the last few months. The sheath of fabric clung to every curve, as well as every bulge. Thank God they lived in Texas instead of Alaska or an Eskimo might've mistaken her for a seal and tried to skin her.

"So what's your pleasure?" Valerie asked, not giving up. "Plenty of gorgeous men in here tonight."

"Sure, if I squint."

"Okay, stop being negative. You're gorgeous, and lots of men love curvy women. I should know. Now pick one."

No point in arguing with her. Once Valerie set her mind to something, she didn't stop until the mission was accomplished. But the only time Leah had ever had her pick of anything was when she stood in front of the doughnut case at work, deciding between a chocolate éclair or a cream cheese Danish.

"How am I supposed to know who to pick? It's not like they wear signs on their foreheads saying, I DIG FAT CHICKS."

Valerie shot her an exasperated look. "We'll just establish a baseline for the kind of guy you want."

"The kind of guy I'd want wouldn't be hanging out in a bar called Rusty's Bucket. In fact, I wouldn't be here either if you hadn't forced me to come."

"Leah, you got dumped. Happens to all of us sooner or later." Valerie's voice softened as she reached for Leah's hand. "It sucks, I know. But you're always at work or up-stairs in your apartment, which means you never leave that damn building. It's not healthy. You can't hide out forever."

"I'm not *hiding*. I've just...been busy. I never imagined I'd be this swamped only a month after grand opening, and I've had to put in a lot of extra hours." Leah caught Valerie's *I'm not buying it* expression. "Come on, Val. The wedding is tomorrow night. Everything has to be perfect because...well, you know."

Valerie rolled her eyes. "Why does it even matter?"

"Because my reputation is at stake. It's *my* cake the happy couple will be stuffing into each other's mouths. They can choke on it for all I care, but it's going to be the tastiest damn wedding cake they've ever eaten while keeling over. Every-thing has to go as smoothly as possible, and I have a million things to do before tomorrow night. I still need to—"

Valerie raised her hand to stop her from continuing. "What you need is a break. Let's find some guys to dance with and have a few hours of fun before you lock yourself up in the cave again. Just humor me, okay? Now, what would say your dream guy's most attractive quality would be?"

Leah sighed. "A pulse."

"No vampires. Check. What else?"

"I don't know. This is stupid." Leah caught the disap-pointment in Valerie's eyes and groaned. "Okay, fine. I guess I'd want..."

Her gaze sifted through the crowd, landing on two men at the bar. While the one standing motioned to the bartender, the other rolled up the sleeves of his blue button-down shirt, drawing Leah's attention to his tanned, muscular forearms. When he finished, he bumped his elbow against the other man's ribs and said something that made them both laugh. The warm, amused smile he wore sent a zing of pleasure through Leah, like she'd been given an intravenous shot of serotonin. *Him. I'd want him.*

Leah smiled. "I guess I'd want someone who could make me laugh."

"That's great and all"—Val groaned with annoyance—"but you're killing me here. What would he *look* like? That's what I want to know."

"Tall, dark brown hair, well-toned forearms, killer smile, a bit of scruff on his face, and a light blue shirt," Leah said automatically, still eyeballing the man across the room.

"Um, okay, wow. That's pretty specific."

Leah gazed back at Valerie, shaking her head to clear the man's image from her mind. "Sorry, it just sort of…popped out."

"No, no, it's good. Gives us something to go by. At least now we have a starting point. Okay, so let's see," Valerie said, peering around the crowded room. "Ah, there's a guy in a blue shirt." She nodded toward a man sitting four tables away.

He wasn't looking in their direction so they waited for him to turn around. Then they both cringed.

"Well, I guess two out of seven isn't bad," Valerie said, crinkling her nose.

"Two? The blue shirt is a given, but I doubt he has a pulse. Definitely pale enough to be considered a vampire, though…well, if he had any teeth."

"Okay, what about…*that* guy?"

Leah glanced in the direction Valerie pointed. "Oh, come on! Give me a break. Even I'm not that desperate."

"What's wrong with him? He's exactly what you described. I'm all for being picky, Leah, but you're just going to dance with him, not marry the guy."

The man at the bar noted their attention and swiveled his

stool around to get a better look at his captive female audience. He took an extended pull from his longneck, swept his thick tongue across his bottom lip, then set it down before giving them a not-so-sexy wink.

"I'm glad you think the best I can do is a guy who actually has teeth, but I never said I wanted a guy in stained overalls and white rubber boots. If you like Shrimper Bob so much, then *you* go talk to him."

"Wait. What? No, not him." Valerie grasped Leah's head and turned it a fraction of an inch to the right. "Him!"

Leah didn't know why she was surprised. She'd given Valerie his basic description, which was the equivalent of placing a flashing neon sign above his head with an arrow pointing down.

Granted, she'd left out some of the other noticeable details. Like how his large hand wrapped strongly around his beer, yet brought it to his mouth slow and gentle, as if he were touching his lips to a woman's breast. Or how the muscles in his back bunched beneath his shirt while leaning over the bar, as if a satiated woman lay limply beneath him.

Leah wouldn't have minded being that woman. But when he shifted on his stool and his eyes met hers, then darted away, she got the message loud and clear. *Not interested.*

"You're totally eye-humping him," Valerie shrieked, smiling at the new mission in which she was about to partake.

"No, I'm not."

"Yeah, right, Leah. I can see the drool dribbling down your chin."

Insecure about whether her friend was telling the truth, Leah nonchalantly wiped the back of her hand across her face.

"See?" Valerie said, laughing. "You *do* think he's hot.

Know what else? It wouldn't surprise me if you had described him from the start."

"Shut up, Val."

She laughed again. "God, I love it when I'm right."

"I didn't say you were right."

"No, but you always get defensive when I am. Why didn't
you just point him out to begin with?"

Leah shrugged. "Not my type."

"Oh, please. A guy like that is every woman's type. What
you're actually saying is that you don't think you're *his*
type."

"It's the same thing, no matter how you put it. Either way,
he's not interested."

"Oh, so now you're a mind reader, I guess. How do you
know what he's interested in? Maybe he's waiting for you to
ask him to dance."

Leah grimaced. "You've seen me dance, and it's not
pretty. If he isn't interested now, he definitely won't be after
seeing *that*."

Valerie giggled and leaped out of her seat. "Guess we're
about to find out."

"No, Val. Don't go over—" *Damn it.*

* * *

Sam Cooper wasn't about to turn around.

In the mirror behind the bar, he watched as the yappy
blonde in his ear made a play for his buddy Max. Not only
had she flirted with him, but she'd touched his biceps—
Max's second favorite part of his anatomy—and cinched
the deal. Within seconds, she had him promising to join
their table, offering to buy her and her brunette friend a
drink, and eating out of her slick little hands. The lady

was damn near professional. *The sonofabitch never had a chance.*

After she finally walked away, Max turned to Sam. "I need you to stay a little longer and be my wingman."

"Nope. You're on your own, *Rico Suave*. I told you I was leaving after this beer."

"Yeah, but that was before the dark-haired girl caught you checking out her rack and her friend invited us over to join them."

Sam grinned. He had noticed the well-endowed piece of real estate on the pretty brunette across the room, but that wasn't what grabbed his attention the most. It was the way her expressive eyes flickered over him as she licked her pouty lips. That alone did more for his libido than her oversized breasts—not that those weren't nice to look at too.

But..."I'm not interested."

"Even though you're single now?"

"Doesn't matter," Sam said, shaking his head. "I just broke up with one crazy broad. Last thing I need is another one breathing down my neck."

"Oh, come on. You only dated Sylvia for a month. How much damage could one chick do in such a short amount of time?"

"She wanted to get married."

Beer spewed out of Max's mouth as he burst into hysterics. He reached for some bar napkins and wiped at his tear-filled eyes before cleaning up the spray on the bar. "Sorry to hear that," Max said, still chuckling.

"Yeah, the sympathy is rolling off you in waves."

His buddy suppressed his lingering smirk by running a hand over his face. "No, I mean it. I really am sorry to hear that. But I'm a little confused. Just last month, you said it was time for you to settle down. It's fast, but if she wants the same thing... well, I guess I don't see what the problem is."

"I told you. She's crazy."

Max shrugged his brows suggestively. "Like crazy-in-bed kind of crazy?"

"No, crazy as in crazy-as-a-loony-tune. She had the whole thing planned out. First she'd meet Mr. Right—which apparently was me—and then she'd marry him and have a white picket fence, a dog named Spot, and exactly two-point-five kids. The woman had goddamn charts."

"Fuck."

"Yeah, tell me about it. That's why women are off my radar for now. I don't need or want the complication. The hell if I'm going to marry someone because they have a schedule to keep."

Max motioned for the bartender, ordered four beers, then turned his attention back to Sam. "Look, I'm buying this round. Come on, take one for the team. You know I'd do it for you."

"I wouldn't need you to."

"You cocky bastard," Max said with a laugh. "I just need you to entertain her friend while I make my move."

"I'm surprised you're even interested in the blonde. I thought you only liked women so skinny you could pick your teeth with them?"

Max grinned. "Let's just say I'm willing to make an exception on a case-by-case basis. Now, come on. Do a good deed for your buddy. You know you want to."

Sam groaned and glanced at his gold watch. "One hour. If you haven't worked your magic by then... Well, you're going to owe me. Big time. By the way, you're buying my beers the rest of the night too."

Max paid the bartender, picked up two beers, and headed

across the room with a smile on his face and an eye on the blond yapper. *Poor bastard.* Against his better judgment, Sam grabbed the other two beers and followed.

The women had their heads together whispering but stopped talking the moment they approached. The blonde smiled up at them, but the brunette kept her gaze lowered, and her cheeks blushed fiercely. It almost made Sam want to check and see if his zipper was down.

While introductions were being made, he forced himself to keep his eyes on hers because staring at her glorious chest or that delicious mouth implied a strong sexual interest he preferred to avoid. But when her glistening green eyes lifted to his, he decided her forehead was a safer bet.

Sam hadn't even gotten out a single word before the blond Chihuahua beckoned his friend toward the dance floor with a sexy come-hither wiggle of her hips and a crook of her finger. Max smiled and glanced over at Sam, who shrugged and took a seat across from her friend. Hell, maybe an hour was generous. At this rate, he'd be heading home in twenty minutes. *Thank God.*

He slid a beer across the table. "So, Leann…"

"Leah," she said, her brow wrinkling a little. "My name's Leah."

Shit. "Sorry."

"It's okay," she said, though her tone conveyed otherwise.

Sam ran his fingers through his hair. "Well, I guess the two of them didn't waste any time ditching us."

"Yeah, I guess not." She hesitated but then continued, "You'll have to excuse Valerie. She's not very subtle."

"That's okay. I like when a woman goes after what she wants." *Damn. Why did I word it that way?* He made the mistake of glancing at Leah's mouth, which curved into a delighted smile.

Disturbed by the pleasant sensation it gave him, he fastened his eyes back to her forehead and kept them there. But he couldn't stare at her head for an hour straight. If he didn't do something soon, his eyes would eventually work their way back down to her face. Or worse, her cleavage.

"Maybe we should go out on the dance floor and show them how it's done." When she didn't respond, he said, "Well?"

"I, uh...I can't dance."

"Everyone can dance."

"No, I mean I *really* can't dance. Last time I tried, someone called 911 because they couldn't figure out if I was possessed or having a seizure."

Sam laughed and accidentally lowered his gaze again. Her wide eyes and pinked-up cheeks told him everything he needed to know. The girl was terrified of embarrassing herself again, and for some strange reason, the desire to relieve her of that mental anguish washed over him. "If you can walk, then you can two-step. I'll teach you." He rose to lead her to the dance floor, but she didn't move. "Come on," he said, coaxing her out of her chair. "I promise not to let anyone call an ambulance...or a priest."

She stood and smoothed out the wrinkles in her dress by running her hands over her curves. Sam shifted his gaze and blew out a breath. *Don't look at her, you idiot, or you won't be going home alone.*

He held out his hand—one she reluctantly accepted—and then pulled her onto the crowded dance floor. He settled her left hand on his right shoulder and wrapped his free hand around her waist.

She stiffened.

"Relax," he said, offering her a comforting smile. "This is supposed to be fun." He quickly explained which leg to start on and the tempo of the dance, while she sighed nervously and forced her body to loosen. "Okay, ready?"

She nodded hesitantly, and he moved toward her, dancing her backward to the beat of the music. At first, she stumbled to keep up. She bit her bottom lip and concentrated intently on her foot placement, but she didn't quit. Sam liked that about her, even if her jerky movements were throwing him off as well.

To help her keep the rhythm, he pulled her closer, forcing her to look over his shoulder instead of down at her feet. Then he lowered his mouth to her ear and whispered, "Quick, quick, slow. Slow."

She improved instantly, and her movements lined up with his, matching the pace he'd set to the music as they glided across the dance floor. He was sure she was chanting the mantra over and over in her head and probably still wore a tense look of concentration and determination, but he hesitated to pull back to see for himself. Mostly because her soft skin emitted a sweet, delicious aroma, and he couldn't get enough of it. Like the woman had bathed herself in vanilla-scented sugar. *God, she smells incredible.*

Her unexpected laugh had him wondering if he'd spoken out loud, but then he noticed her friend across the dance floor with a huge smile, giving them a thumbs-up. Not only was Leah dancing, but she was doing a fairly decent job at keeping up. Sure, her form could use a little polish, and she stepped on his foot every now and then, but he had to give the girl some credit.

"Your friend seems nice," he said, making small talk to pass the time as well as smooth out the awkward silence.

"Valerie's great, even under all that toy poodle cuteness."

Sam let out a hearty laugh. "A poodle—that's it! I had her

pegged more as a Chihuahua, but I think you nailed it. All she needs is a large, obnoxious pink bow in her hair."

"She stopped wearing hair ornaments after I made the reference last year," Leah said with a giggle.

"She keeps staring over here. Why does she look so surprised to see you dancing?"

"Because I can't dance," Leah said evenly.

"Oh, really?" Placing his hand on her hip, Sam pushed her out, spun her around twice, and pulled her back to him in one smooth motion. "Looks like you're doing a fine job to me."

"It's you," she said, looking him square in the eyes with a heavy-lidded gaze that stole his breath. "Y-you make me look good."

The song ended, and although they stopped moving, they didn't separate. Silently, he stared at her face, taking in her features one by one. Emerald jewels stared back him, glistening under the strobe lights. She licked her plump, ripe lips nervously, coating them with a glossy sheen of moisture. Rosy cheeks, heated by the spike in body temperature, clearly had nothing to do with dancing. For a moment, Sam lost his wits.

"I don't know about that," he said, allowing his eyes to drop lower for a delicious view of her nicely rounded curves. "I think you look pretty damn—"

"Excuse me," someone interrupted, tapping his shoulder. "Do you remember me from the other night?"

Sam and Leah both turned toward the black-haired beauty standing behind him. The young woman's red leather pants clung low on her waist, displaying a midriff pierced by a sparkly diamond on a silver chain. Her top—if you could call it that—resembled a sexy push-up bra with rhinestones.

"Sorry to interrupt," she said, glancing at Leah and then

back to him. "But I saw you when I walked by and couldn't help myself." She giggled and blushed a little. "After all, it's not every day a girl gets picked up and taken home by a stranger."

Sam knew she referred to the innocent ride home he gave her when he found her on the side of the road with a flat tire and no spare, but he stiffened a little anyway. Anyone—including Leah—could easily take the girl's comment out of context. And judging by the irritated expression on Leah's face, she had done just that.

He could've told the truth. Hell, maybe he should have. But remembering what he was about to say to Leah made him rethink his position. The interruption had to be some sort of divine intervention. Otherwise he'd have his mouth trailing all over Leah's body until morning. And that couldn't happen. He meant what he'd said to Max. *No women. Not even this one.*

"Amy, right?" Sam asked the young woman and waited as she nodded in confirmation. "Would you like to dance?" Out of the corner of his eyes, he monitored Leah's reaction. Her green eyes widened, and her mouth fell open before she snapped it closed. "You don't mind, do you, Leah?"

"No, of course not." She smiled briefly, but the disappointment was apparent in her lackluster eyes. Without another word, she pivoted and marched away, leaving an overwhelming amount of guilt in her wake.

"Give me a second," he told the young woman and then rushed to catch Leah before she vacated the dance floor. "Leah, wait!"

She spun on him, her fierce eyes punching him straight in the gut. She was pissed and rightfully so. And that only made him feel more like a heel than he already did.

"Leah, it's just that…" He should explain it all, if only

to keep her from thinking he was a jackass. But he couldn't. Not without leading her on, which wouldn't be fair to her. The last thing he wanted was to get involved with her—with anyone, for that matter. And as cowardly as it was, the simplest solution was to let her think whatever horrible scenario she'd conjured up in her mind was true. "I'm sorry. You're just not my type," he blurted out.

Leah glanced across the floor, her eyes scrolling up and down Amy's skin-baring, leather-clad figure. Then she peered down at her own voluptuous body and pursed her lips. "It's okay, Sam. It's not like I didn't see it coming." Then she turned and walked away.

He cringed. Not only was what he said the farthest thing from the truth, but the thoughtless brush-off sounded more like a fucked-up insult. *Smooth, asshole. Real smooth.*

Chapter Two

Leah sank into her chair.

It wasn't the first time she'd been turned down because of her weight, and she doubted it would be the last. It was, however, the first time a man had been honest about it though. *Not his type. Hmph.*

As Sam danced with the girl, he occasionally glanced over, as if he were expecting Leah to burst into tears at any moment. Okay, so maybe she did feel like crying a little. But she wouldn't. Not in public anyway. That sort of thing usually snuck up on her when she was lying in bed alone in the middle of the night, wondering if she'd ever meet a nice guy who didn't care she had love handles and wasn't a size two.

Even her ex-boyfriend had tried to force her to lose weight by ordering her salads and convincing her to join the gym. If he'd been a health nut, then it might not have been so insulting. Instead, he'd boasted about his great metabolism, ordered himself a bacon cheeseburger, and said he didn't have time to work out. Yeah, he was a jerk too.

Leah sighed, motioned for the waitress, and ordered five shots of tequila. Her plan was simple. She'd show Sam there were no hard feelings by buying the next round, including one for the stripper wannabe he was dancing with. Because she was mature like that. She stole another glance at him dancing with the midriff-baring brunette. *Dickhead.*

Why couldn't he have just fed her a line of bullshit like other guys always did? *I've sworn off women for good. I think I'm coming down with something. What's your friend's name?* She wasn't his type because he obviously preferred younger, skinnier girls. Why was she surprised? He hadn't even committed her name to memory two seconds after they'd exchanged them. And he'd barely looked directly at her. That alone spoke volumes.

Leah rubbed at her forehead, wondering if the word *pathetic* had somehow appeared without her knowing. Because that's exactly how she felt after Sam blew her off to dance with another woman.

The waitress brought the shots to the table, and Leah became even more depressed. Five shots of tequila sat in front of her reminding her that she was now the fifth wheel. *Just great.* And she was doing what she always did... pretending it didn't bother her. But it did bother her. No, actually it annoyed the hell out of her.

So she developed a little crush on an inaccessible guy who wasn't into shapely women. So what? Story of her life. No need to torture herself this way. Then she made the mistake of checking on Valerie. Unsurprisingly, she was in Max's arms on the dance floor, engaged in conversation as they exchanged flirty eye contact and subtle glances.

Leah sighed. She didn't begrudge Val for having a good time, but she would give anything to know the girl's secret. How was it possible Leah struggled to find a single date, while a full-figured Valerie attracted every man who crossed her path? Maybe the old saying was true after all—blondes had more fun.

But then she glanced back to Sam dancing with the skinny brunette and narrowed her eyes. *No. Apparently only blondes and thin women have more fun…*

Well, not anymore. *Screw him.* She would make her own fun.

For the first time in her life, Leah was going to be bold. She picked up one of the shots of tequila and plucked the lime wedge off the side, tossing it onto a napkin. She didn't need a sissy-ass lime wedge chaser. She was proving to herself how daring she could be. This was for her. Then she downed the shot in one gulp.

Oh God. She cringed and shuddered, then quickly reached for the lime wedge and bit into it, neutralizing the nasty tequila flavor. She knew she had made horrible faces but couldn't help herself. The taste of the tequila was terrible. *Thank goodness no one saw…Crap.*

Wearing a grin, Sam stared at her from the dance floor.

She squirmed in her seat as irritation transformed into anger, and the sudden need to wipe that stupid smile off his face took over. So she lifted a second shot glass and quickly tossed it back, forcing herself to keep a straight face. He continued to watch closely so she lifted a third glass. That had him raising a brow and his mouth collapsing into a thin, straight line. Guess he didn't approve.

Like I care? Hardly.

Leah wanted to laugh, but instead she lifted the next shot higher, toasting Sam's asshole behavior, and threw that one back as well. The shots were getting surprisingly easier—and better tasting—by the minute, so she finished off the other two. That made Sam frown, and he squinted at her, as if he were trying to figure out what the hell she was doing. Like it was any of *his* business.

She ignored his questioning glare and again searched the room for Valerie, who had vanished. *Great.* Leah still hadn't spotted her when a broad figure blocked her view of the dance floor. She gazed up to see Shrimper Bob leering at her with his eyeballs dangling out of their sockets and halfway down her cleavage.

"Whoa! I'd do a body shot off your chest any day," he said.

"Excuse me?"

He gestured to the five empty shot glasses. "Tequila tastes better when you lick salt off each other. Why don't we try it and have a little fun?"

Leah cringed. No way was she licking anything off someone she'd dubbed Shrimper Bob. "No thanks."

"Aw, come on," he slurred drunkenly. "I don't bite. At least not unless you want me to." He chuckled and stepped closer.

Leah shot out of her seat to move away from him but swayed and gripped the back of her chair, dizzy from the five shots that had apparently hit her when she rose. Shrimper Bob gripped her arm and pulled her into his chest, which reeked of beer and sweat.

"It's okay, babe. I've got you."

"Let go. I don't want your help."

He sniffed her hair and tightened his grasp on her arm, while wrapping his other brawny arm around her waist. "Why don't I take you out to my truck and you can lay down on my lap for a while?"

Yeah, like that was the least bit appealing. "Why don't you get lost?" Leah jerked away, freeing herself from his grasp. "Like I said, I'm not interested."

A drunken, lopsided grin widened his face. "I bet I could change your mind."

And I bet I could kick your nuts halfway across the room. "Sorry, it's not going to happen." She started to stagger away, but he reached for her again and laughed, as if this were some fun game they were playing. "Stop touching me!"

"Oh, come on, I'm just playing around," he said, holding his hands up in mock surrender and winking. "You know, just copping a little feel."

"Touch her again and the only thing you're going to feel is my fist in your face."

* * *

Sam had known this guy would cause trouble before the night was out.

When the big man had sat near them at the bar, Sam heard some of the crude comments he made to the bartender about various women who passed by. Since the man hadn't spoken directly to any of them, Sam let it go, chalking it up to the alcohol. But putting his hands on a lady, when she'd already asked him not to, was going too far.

"I can handle this," Leah said, stepping up beside Sam.

"Looks like your boyfriend wants in on the action." The man laughed and squared his broad shoulders, daring Sam to intervene.

A searing heat traveled through Sam's body as he clenched his fist. He was only seconds away from losing his temper completely. "Why don't you walk away before someone gets hurt?"

The other guy's eyes lit up at the challenge. "What? Afraid your little bitch found herself a real man?"

Sam shook his head. "Should've listened to the warning, dipshit."

In a lightning-fast move, he swung and cracked his knuckles against the other man's rock-hard jaw. The solid punch knocked him out cold, and his big body crumpled into a heap on the floor. Sam stood over him, shaking his fist and rubbing his sore knuckles.

"What the hell did you do that for?" Leah yelled.

Sam looked at her stupidly. "He insulted you."

"And?"

"And...he insulted you."

"So what? You think it's the first time I've been insulted by some asshole?" she scolded him with an accusatory glare then paused and lifted one finger in the air. "Oh, I get it. You probably don't think I get many offers."

"What? No, of course I don't think that. I was just—"

"Uh-oh," Leah said, glancing over his shoulder.

A bald-headed bouncer in a black shirt barged over, pointing to the exit. "Out!" he demanded. "Both of you."

Leah's eyes widened. "But my friend is in here some—"

"I don't care," the bouncer sneered, unsympathetic to her situation. "Get out. Now."

She scowled at Sam then huffed as she wobbled toward the door. He followed behind her, amused by the way she focused all her attention on walking so she wouldn't fall over. Served her right for slamming back five shots, one after another.

Once outside, she rounded on him with glazed eyes of fury. "This is all your fault," she slurred, swaying on her feet. "If you would've just stayed out of it, then everything would've been fine. You didn't have to punch him."

"He had it coming."

"I was handling it."

"You can barely walk straight, much less fend off some offensive asshole."

She narrowed her eyes, obviously still pissed off. "Oh yeah? Well, he wasn't the first offensive asshole I crossed paths with tonight."

Sam had a sneaking suspicion she was referring to him, probably from the way her eyes shot flaming daggers at him. "What the hell is that supposed to mean?"

"What happened? Did you draw the short straw? Lost a bet with your buddy, Max, and got stuck with Large Marge?"

Sam blinked, stunned and completely clueless as to who she was talking about. "Bet? What are you talking about? And who the hell is Large Marge?"

"Like you don't know?" Leah shook her head with disgust and sighed. "Now, thanks to you, I have to walk home. Valerie was my ride."

"I'll take you home," Sam said, pulling his keys out of his pocket. "You're in no condition to walk anywhere."

He wasn't sure why the comment upset her even more, but she practically growled out, "I guess you don't think I can walk that far."

Sam shrugged it off. "No, actually, I don't. You'd face-plant before you even got out of the parking lot." He led the way over to his red truck nearby and opened the passenger door as she mumbled incoherently behind him. "Do you need help getting in?"

She climbed clumsily into the cab without his assistance and heaved out a breath. "What were you planning on doing...greasing my whale ass to fit through the door?" Then she slammed the truck door closed.

Only then did Sam understand. Obviously, he had somehow offended her about her weight, though he wasn't sure what he did wrong. Then he remembered his comment on the dance floor. *You're just not my type. Oh, hell.*

She must've thought that was what he meant. God, she didn't know how wrong she was. It was Max who liked his women sleek and thin as a rail, not Sam. In fact, most women his buddy dated were one sandwich shy of being hospitalized for malnutrition. Their bones jutted out of their shoulders, and the majority of them shopped in the kids' clothing department to find something that fit their tiny frames. To Sam, that wasn't a sexy woman—it was a pre-pubescent child.

He had never been fond of the anorexic, always-on-a-diet type. And he sure as hell didn't want to sleep with a bag of bones either. Sam appreciated the sensual rounded curves of a feminine body, a girl with some meat on her hips. The soft contours of a woman's thighs, large shapely breasts, and a gently rounded ass he could grab on to with his hands—that was what he loved about a womanly figure. All the things Leah possessed.

But somehow she'd misunderstood. Had he known she pictured him at the helm of a boat with a harpoon in his hands, he would've gladly corrected the assumption. Leah was not a whale, by any means, and it was almost laughable she would think of herself in that manner. Especially since he was so attracted to her that he had to maintain a slight distance while dancing to keep from rubbing the hard bulge in his pants across her abdomen. It had taken all his strength just to keep from adjusting himself in front of her.

Some dickhead had obviously done a number on her self-esteem because there wasn't a damn thing wrong with the way she looked. *Whoever told this woman she's fat should be shot and strung up by his testicles.*

Actually, she looked better than any of the women he'd

seen in the bar in the last month. Hell, he wanted nothing more than to find out what she was wearing under that tight little black dress that hugged her curves so deliciously. Every time his eyes landed on her tonight, he'd imagined what it would be like to have her unravel beneath him while he thrust into...*No. I can't go there. Take the girl to her door and forget about her. It wouldn't be right.*

He wasn't ready to get involved with another woman after the drama with his ex-girlfriend. Hell, a psychiatrist could make a year's fucking salary off Sylvia in just the first session alone. Sam needed to be single and allow himself time to regroup, to figure out what he wanted in a life partner. He'd been serious when he'd told Max he was ready to settle down, but he wanted to do so with the right person. Sylvia definitely wasn't that person. And he doubted that the pissed-off, inebriated woman in his truck was the right one either.

He strolled around the hood and climbed into the driver's seat, keeping his eyes straight ahead, not wanting to ogle her any more than he had to. "Okay, where to?"

Leah didn't answer him.

He asked again, but all he heard was the soft sound of snoring coming from the passenger's seat. He dared to glance over. Her eyes were closed tight, and her head lolled to the side. He pushed on her shoulder, but she only snored louder. Sam couldn't help but grin at the way her head leaned so far back against the seat that her mouth hung open.

"Leah?" he said, nudging her again, "you have to wake up so you can tell me where you live."

No movement. No opening her eyes. She was out cold. So Sam did the only thing he could. He started the truck, shifted into gear, and drove out of the parking lot.

Chapter Three

Sam poured the steaming coffee into the mug and carried it toward his bedroom. He wasn't sure how Leah took her coffee—or if she even drank coffee—so he made it as strong as usual and hoped she liked it black.

Still asleep, she was lying on her back with one arm above her head, the cock-eyed pillow forcing it into a weird, break-neck position. She had kicked the comforter onto the floor, leaving her luscious, full-figured body covered only by a lacey black bra and matching panties. Unfortunately, those meager scraps of lace did nothing to hide her hard nipples.

Fuck me. He tried his damnedest not to stare, but the mere idea of her lying in *his* bed, with her hair cascading down *his* pillow, already had his dick twitching in delight.

Her mottled skin was broken out in gooseflesh, possibly from the combination of the cold air conditioner and the fan circling on high over the bed. It probably hadn't helped that Sam had undressed her to make her more comfortable. If she hadn't been passed out cold, he doubted he would've been such a gentleman and kept his hands to himself. It definitely wasn't the first time he'd undressed a woman in complete darkness, but it *was* the first time he'd slept on the couch afterward.

He tapped her on the shoulder, hoping the alcohol had worked its way through her system. Maybe he'd be able to actually wake her this time.

Slowly, Leah stretched as her body and mind came into a conscious state. She sighed as her eyelids fluttered gently. She must've sensed she was in an unfamiliar place and panicked or something though because suddenly her eyes shot wide open and she arched her body off the bed, oddly clutching at her back.

The quick movement startled him, causing him to tilt the mug and splash hot coffee onto his hand, burning him. "Sonofa—" He wiped the side of his coffee-splattered hand on his jeans. "What's wrong with you?" Sam asked.

"I . . . uh, was just checking."

"For what?"

"M-my kidneys?" It sounded like a question.

He squinted at her, not sure what she was talking about.

"I was freezing. I guess I just thought . . . Well, you hear stories about people waking up in tubs of bloody ice water and missing a kidney."

Sam blinked and shook his head. "You've got some serious issues."

Leah lay back with both arms above her head and laughed. Then she must've realized she was not just in his bed but wearing only her bra and panties. She shrieked and immediately covered her chest with her arms, then sat up and drew her legs in to hide the rest of her as well.

He grinned lightly. "Too late. I've already seen it."

"Oh crap. What did I do last night?"

"Nothing your mother would be proud of," Sam said easily.

Her eyes widened. "Are you saying that we...um, I mean, did we...you know?"

"Settle down. I was talking about getting drunk and kicked out of a bar, not having sex."

"So just to be clear, we didn't..."

"Of course not. Why kind of pervert do you take me for? I wouldn't take advantage of an unconscious woman."

She was quiet for a second, probably trying to recall the events that led her to this very moment. He doubted she'd remember much more than climbing into his truck before the lights went out on her memories. "How did I get here?"

"You fell asleep in my truck, and I couldn't wake you. I didn't know where you lived or what to do with you so I brought you here."

"Did you drag me inside by my ankle or something?"

He gave her a puzzled look. "No. I carried you in."

"You must be pretty strong then."

Sam frowned. She was dogging her weight again, and it was starting to piss him off. Some jackass had really given her a very unhealthy image of herself. "You're not nearly as heavy as you think you are," he said, looking directly into her eyes to show how serious he was.

Leah blushed a little and stammered, "Um...why am I naked?"

He glanced down at her partially covered body. "That's hardly what I consider naked." The words rumbled out, low and breathy, like he was turned on.

And if he was being completely honest with himself, he was. She was just as attractive out of her clothes as she was in her clothes, and Sam was enjoying the view.

"I thought you'd be more comfortable out of that tight-ass

dress, but don't worry, I left all the good parts covered," he said. When she cringed and tightened her arms across her chest, Sam realized how that must've sounded. As if nothing else about her body was good, except her most private areas. "What I mean is—"

"Can I please have my dress back?" She spoke with a cool tone, obviously meant to end this particular conversation.

He stared at her for a second longer then tossed her the dress that had been lying on a chair across the room. To be a gentleman, he kept his back turned, allowing her time to slip into it.

Sam cleared his throat. "So I guess you don't sleep in the nude?"

"Of course not."

"You say that like it's not normal for people to sleep naked. Lots of people do, you know."

"Well, not me."

"And why's that?"

"Because I . . . well, I'm fat."

He turned to look at her, just as she finished zipping up her dress. "Who the hell told you that you were fat?"

She sat on the bed and slipped on her heels one at a time. "Well, if we're talking most recently . . . you did."

"Leah, you misunderstood—"

"Look, I don't want to talk about it. To answer your question, I don't take my clothes off unless I absolutely have to, and sleeping doesn't require it."

Sam eyed her tight dress and then met her gaze head-on. "That depends on who you're sleeping with."

* * *

Leah didn't know what to think.

After his remark, they'd both just stood there as a moment of awkward silence passed between them. His comment had sounded like a flirty come-on, and his brown eyes had done this funny, smoldering thing like he was picturing her naked or something. But then he'd completely shut down again. *Damn him and his mixed signals.*

Now he was giving her a ride home—a dreadfully quiet one, at that—which was way more awkward than it should've been for two strangers who'd spent the night together but *hadn't* had sex.

"Turn right when you get to Market Street," she told him.

He nodded but didn't say anything. Just kept his eyes forward and tightened his grip on the steering wheel. The knuckles on his right hand were still swollen and red from the punch he'd landed on Shrimper Bob's jaw.

Without thinking, Leah reached over and rubbed a finger gently over the bruising, making him tense up. "Does it hurt?"

Sam shrugged. "Probably not as much as his jaw does."

"I guess I should thank you," she said, pulling her hand back and placing it in her lap as he took a right turn.

"But you won't." He looked over and cracked a smile.

She gave him a teasing smirk back. "Hey, I told you I could handle it. But I will thank you for taking care of me last night."

He gave her a quick wink. "No problem."

"And for being such a gentleman."

"Oh, that was the easy part."

Leah cut her eyes over to him. *What the hell is that supposed to mean? I'm so obviously unattractive that he had no problem keeping his hands to himself?* She sighed inwardly. "You can drop me off in front of the bakery on the right."

He ran a hand through his hair. "Yeah, I guess I should've offered you some breakfast before we left. Sorry about that."

Great. Now he thinks he should've fed the Goodyear Blimp before giving her a ride home. Jesus. What's wrong with this asshole? Could he make it more plain that he thinks I'm a cow? Whatever. No sense in working herself up. Besides, she still had her decorations up from the pity party she threw herself last night. Nothing like getting ditched in the middle of the dance floor for a thinner girl who barely looked old enough to be in the bar in the first place.

Sam pulled up at the curb under the Sweets n' Treats sign and stopped to let her out. "I'm running late for work, but I can wait…unless you're going to be a while."

"Okay, that's it!" she yelled, unbuckling her seat belt and swinging open the passenger door. "I've had enough of your snide remarks."

His eyebrows shot up in surprise. "What'd I say?"

As she stepped out, she slammed the truck door and turned to face him through the open window. "Don't play stupid. It's not cute. You've made it painstakingly obvious that you aren't attracted to me—which is fine, by the way—but you don't have to make fun of me."

Sam shook his head. "Leah, I'm not making fun—"

"Oh, really? Well, then why am I surprised you didn't pull into the weigh station on the way here?" The moment she said it, she wished she could take it back. But once the flood gate was open, she had a hard time closing it. "For your information, I'm not here to eat. I'm here to work. This is *my* store. I know, such a cliché, right? Fat girl owns a bakery." She turned to walk away.

"Leah, wait…"

She stopped in the middle of the sidewalk but didn't turn around. "Thanks for the ride, Sam." Then she hurried inside.

The aroma of fresh-baked cinnamon raisin bread and vanilla-scented sugar glaze smacked her in the face. It was their top-selling item, and already a line of customers waited to get their share. Valerie wasn't at the counter, which meant she was most likely filling orders in the kitchen.

Though Leah knew Valerie would need help, she continued to stand near the door, wondering why Sam was still parked out front and hadn't driven off. For a moment, she thought he might even come in after her. But then he shifted into gear and pulled away from the curb. Leah shook her head, disgusted with herself. *Stupid. Guys like him don't chase after girls who look like me.*

Valerie came out of the kitchen through the swinging door. She carried two small, white pastry boxes that she set on the counter as she caught a glimpse of Leah. "Hey, you! I've got an apron back here with your name on it."

Leah hurried around the counter past Valerie. "Five minutes," she called out, then did a mad dash through the kitchen and up the creaky back stairs leading to her home over the bakery.

Thankfully, Leah had lucked into leasing a building that came with an overhead apartment, which meant she only paid one rent instead of two. The one-bedroom was small and had been furnished by every garage sale in the neighborhood, but it was hers. A much better option than living with her parents at her age—not that twenty-seven was old or anything.

Leah stripped off her dress and jumped in the shower, hurrying to make it back downstairs before the morning rush was over.

Valerie hadn't seemed upset that Leah was running late, but she didn't want to press her luck. Mornings in a bakery were always the busiest time of the day, and although Val was a capable employee and a good friend, Leah wouldn't allow herself to abuse their relationship.

Sweets n' Treats had been open for only a month in Granite, Texas, but word of mouth had proven to be a powerful advertising weapon. From the beginning, Leah had realized she needed to sprout another pair of hands to keep up with the demands. That's when she'd hired Valerie.

By the time she threw on jeans and a T-shirt, pulled her wet hair into a ponytail, and made it downstairs, the line at the counter had already diminished.

Valerie continued filling the last few orders while Leah grabbed a clean apron from the back and jumped right in, restocking the nearly-empty glass display counter with parchment-lined metal trays of apple fritters, custard-filled doughnuts, and maple-glazed cinnamon twists.

Once the last customer exited the bakery, Leah turned to Valerie. "I'm sorry I was late. I don't know what I'd do without you."

"Actually, all that prep work you did yesterday saved me a lot of trouble. I know I told you not to worry about it, but I'm glad you didn't listen. It made the morning run so much smoother." Valerie sat down on a stool, wiping her brow. "And boy, I was swamped."

"Hinting for a raise?" Leah asked with a laugh.

Valerie smirked. "Right now, I'd settle for some intel about last night."

Leah blew out a breath, shrugged, and turned to wipe the counter. "Nothing to tell."

"Bullshit."

"No, really. Nothing happened."

"Shovel, anyone?" Val yelled out to the empty bakery. "Come on, Leah. You can't seriously expect me to believe that you went home with Sam and nothing happened."

"It's true," she said, continuing to wipe a clean counter to avoid facing her friend.

"Oh." Valerie paused. "Well, it's probably for the best anyway."

She looked over her shoulder at Valerie. "Why do you say that?"

"Max said he has a small penis."

Leah laughed. "Max has a small penis?"

"No. Sam does."

She stopped laughing. "That's not funny, Val."

"Who's laughing?"

"Why is Max talking about Sam's penis with you? And how would he even know?"

"I don't know. That's just what he told me when I asked him why Sam was dancing with that other girl and you were sitting alone. Max said for me to tell you not to worry about it and that you weren't missing out on anything."

"So you saw all that?"

"Yes. A jerk move on Sam's part, I might add. Max and I were going to come sit with you, but I got stuck in a long line for the bathroom. By the time I came out, you and Sam had both disappeared. I was a little concerned, but I ran into a girl who comes in the bakery almost every morning. She said she saw you leaving with a guy who fit Sam's description."

"We were thrown out by the bouncer. Sam punched Shrimper Bob."

Valerie blinked, then threw her head back and laughed. "Oh no! Why'd he do that?"

"It was one of those macho things, I guess. You know, checking to see who had the bigger dick." *Shit. Wrong choice of words.*

That made Valerie laugh even more. "I take it Sam and his micropenis must've lost."

Leah rolled her eyes, then summed up the rest of the story—well, what she could remember of it—as quickly as she could, but Valerie continued the hysterics. Finally, Leah had enough and sighed. "Stop laughing. It's not funny."

"Oh, come on. It's a little funny."

"Not really," she said, pushing open the swinging door and heading into the back room with a scowl on her face.

Valerie stopped laughing and trailed behind her. "Whoa! You really like him, don't you?"

Why do I have to be so damn transparent? "Doesn't matter. He doesn't return the sentiment."

"Then Tiny Tim is a jackass and doesn't deserve you."

"Well, how did you and Max get along?" Leah asked, waggling her brows suggestively.

"We didn't go home together, if that's what you're ask—" A noise sounded from the front room. Valerie stepped over to the swinging door and peeked out the window. "Shit. Incoming."

Leah tossed her cleaning rag onto the counter. "Great. Just what I need right now. Don't worry, I'll go head her off at the pass."

"I'll just stay back here out of the way."

"Yeah, right. Coward," Leah called out as she shoved open the door and stepped into the front room.

A slender woman with a flawless ivory complexion, mauve-painted lips, and wavy brown locks—at least a shade lighter than Leah's—rounded the display counter.

"Hi, Mom. What's happening?"

Her mother swept a glance over her. "Definitely not that outfit. And you didn't even fix your hair today. How are you going to attract a good man looking like that?"

Here we go again. Leah rolled her eyes. "Dad says I'm perfect just the way I am."

"Your father's a liar. Besides, mothers are always right." She stood in front of the swinging door just as Leah turned toward her and propped a hip against the counter. "Don't slouch, honey. Good posture makes you look thinner."

Leah sighed but didn't say anything. *Not like it would do any good anyway.*

Just then, Valerie's head appeared in the window of the swinging door behind Leah's mother. She put a gun-shaped finger to her own head and pulled the trigger, pretending to blow her brains out.

Leah cleared her throat to keep from laughing. "So why'd you stop by, Mom?"

"I wanted to check on the cake for tonight's wedding. I ran into Mrs. Newman at the supermarket and…frankly, she seemed worried. I think she's afraid you might sabotage Gavin's reception by doing something to ruin their cake."

Valerie's head appeared again in the window as she mimed hanging herself with an invisible noose. Leah bit her cheek to keep from smiling. "Well, then maybe Mrs. Newman should've thought about that before ordering her son's cake from his ex-girlfriend's bakery."

"Honey, please don't do anything to embarrass me. I have to sit on the City Council with that dreadful woman, and it would make for some very awkward town hall meetings." Mom shifted slightly and almost caught Valerie sticking her finger down her throat, but Val ducked just in time.

"Believe it or not, Mom, my reputation is important to me. I wouldn't do anything to mess up Gavin's wedding. Especially since this business arrangement is going to bring lots of new clients who happen to be friends with the Newmans. That's the only reason I agreed to make Gavin's wedding cake in the first place."

"Good. Then it's settled. No mishaps tonight." Her

mother maneuvered around the counter, mission apparently accomplished. "Oh, and don't forget to dress nice. Something black and slimming. There'll be some available, well-endowed men at tonight's party," she said, swishing out the door without looking back.

The moment her mom left, Valerie poked her head out of the back room. "Well-endowed, huh?" she said, waggling her eyebrows.

"Yeah, I think my mom wants me to find a guy with a good income so he can pay for my Lap-Band surgery."

"God, that sucks. Why is she always so critical of you?"

"I don't know. I think it's in the genes or something. Dad says her own mother was overbearing in much the same way. My mom spent her whole life trying to gain her mother's approval. I don't think she's trying to be mean, but I guess she gets it honestly. Her mother wanted her to marry someone well endowed too."

"Wonder what she would say if I told her you spent last night with a guy who has a pencil for a dick."

Leah smirked. "Don't make me fire you."

Chapter Four

He must be a glutton for punishment.

What other reason would Sam have for going back to the bakery to talk to a woman he couldn't look at without getting a hard-on and couldn't speak to without unintentionally insulting?

And why had he run home to shower and put on something decent before stopping by, rather than just heading straight over after work all sweaty and covered in sawdust? *Christ. What the fuck am I doing here?*

He was apologizing, that's what. No matter what her reaction would be, he couldn't stand by and let Leah think he wasn't interested because of her weight. Especially since that wasn't the case. *Just a quick apology, then I'll be on my way.*

Sam pushed open the bakery door and stepped inside. The sweet scent of warm chocolate overpowered his senses, and he breathed deeply, letting the delicious aroma permeate every pore in his body. *Damn, that smells good.* Yet he was alone in the bakery. The lights were on, but there were no customers. Hell, there weren't even any employees. Nothing.

Figuring someone forgot to lock up for the night, Sam turned to leave, but a strange gurgling noise drifted from the back room and stopped him in his tracks. Worried that someone, possibly Leah, might be hurt, he moved quickly around the counter toward a swinging door. "Hello?"

A weak, strangled voice came from the back. "I'm c-closed."

Sam recognized it as Leah's and pushed the swinging door open anyway.

He found her standing in front of a long, stainless steel table wearing a shimmery black cocktail dress that easily rivaled the tight, sexy one she wore the night before.

Surprised, Leah looked up with tears streaming down her cheeks before blushing and quickly turning away. "I...I said I'm closed."

"You okay?"

She sniffled a little and swiped at the tears in an effort to hide them. "I'm f-fine."

"You don't look fine." It slipped out before he realized how she might take it. *Damn, I have a knack for saying the wrong things to this woman.*

Leah cleared her throat, lifted her head, and turned to face him. "What do you need, Sam?" Her tone wasn't particularly friendly.

If she wants to pretend everything is okay, then who am I to argue? "I stopped by to apologize for this morning and...well, for last night. I think you misunderstood some things I'd said, and I wanted to clear the air between us."

"Fine," she said, her voice still cool. "Apology accepted."

He stepped farther inside the room and hooked his

thumbs into his front belt loops. "Strange, since I haven't given you one yet."

"Look, I appreciate you coming by, but I really don't have time for this right now," she snapped.

Damn, this woman has the temperament of a stray dog— one minute she's eating out of my hand and the next she's biting at me. "What's your problem?"

She sighed heavily with defeat. "My air conditioner just went out in my car, and I have to figure out how to deliver a wedding cake without the heat melting the icing all over the place."

I didn't mean the actual problem. I meant...Christ. Never mind. "That's what has you this upset?"

"Yes."

"Doesn't seem like much of a problem. It's just a cake."

"Just a cake?" She gawked at him. "I'll have you know, I use only the best ingredients in each of my creations and make everything from scratch. It's my ex-boyfriend's wedding, and I spent weeks planning out every detail of this cake, down to the last edible flower."

"Your ex, huh?" His lips curled involuntarily. "And someone's eating flowers? Real ones?"

She sniffled. "Yes, real ones. Some flowers petals are edible, you know. And they'll complement the cake's Bavarian cream filling."

Sam chuckled softly. "So let me get this straight. You need to deliver your ex-boyfriend's wedding cake, topped with plants, and filled with something that sounds like a venereal disease...and people are actually going to eat it?"

"Well, I suppose, if that's the way you want to look at it, but—"

He stood up straight and clapped his hands together. "Okay, let's go then."

"Huh?"

"You need a ride, don't you?"

"Yes, but—"

"Well, then what are we waiting for? I wouldn't miss this for anything."

* * *

Everyone was watching.

But that wasn't why Leah's hands were shaking. No, her hands were shaking because *he* was watching. Sam's laser-beam gaze pinpointed her every move as she added the finishing touches to the now-assembled wedding cake. *As if I'm not nervous enough already?*

Shortly after they'd arrived at the reception hall, a steady stream of people had begun trickling in, awaiting the bride and groom's grand entrance. Most were still gathered around her, ooohing and ahhhing over her intricately designed creation.

When the applause started, Leah knew it wasn't for her. She was out of time, and the happily wedded couple were now in the building. Thank goodness she'd just scattered the last of the rose petals. If it hadn't been for Sam giving her a ride and helping unload all the cake boxes, she'd never have finished on time.

Leah took a step back and admired her work, her chest swelling with pride. The white, six-tiered round cake looked magnificent with all the carefully applied edible pearls and black curlicue piping. Organic red rose petals lined the perimeter of the base cake, as well as each tier. As far as she was concerned, not only had she outdone herself, but she'd created an artful masterpiece.

Then she heard a shriek behind her and turned to look.

The bride—a thin, little waif of a woman—came running from across the room, dragging her reluctant groom behind her. "Our cake, Gavin! Oh, isn't it gorgeous?"

Leah smirked. *Well, at least she has good taste in some things.*

"Yes, dear. It's great." Clearly uncomfortable, Gavin adjusted his collar with one finger. "Now why don't we go say hi to—"

"Are you the cake designer?" the bride asked in a syrupy-sweet voice, looking straight at Leah.

"Y-yes, I am," Leah replied, catching a glimpse of Gavin as he stood next to his bride holding his breath. "I'm a... friend of the family."

Gavin let out the breath and relaxed his posture. "Sweetheart, this is Leah Martin. She owns the Sweets n' Treats bakery over on Market, where my mother ordered the cake."

Still getting Mommy's approval on everything, I see. "I'm so glad you like the way it turned out," Leah told the bride, offering her hand. "By the way, your dress is stunning."

The bride cocked her head, allowing light to glint off her tiara, and smiled. "Oh, thanks. It cost almost as much as the wedding did."

Leah grinned but didn't take the comment negatively. There was no mean-spiritedness in the bride's tone, just a shallow, gum-popping, valley girl vibe. As Leah started to open her mouth to respond, something caught the bride's attention. She released another girly squeal and ran off to join a group of girls all wearing the same short red dress. Apparently the bridesmaids were more entertaining than Leah. *Thinner too.*

Gavin stepped closer and smiled at Leah. "Thanks for not telling her that we used to date. It would've upset her."

She glanced over her shoulder at the bride twirling in

circles amid her friends. "Nah. Your bride has the personality of a cocker spaniel and the attention span of a goldfish. She would've gotten over it in seconds." Then she gave him a quick wink to show she was teasing.

Gavin smiled. "Still, I appreciate it. Especially since I know we didn't leave things on the best of terms."

She shrugged. "I'm over it." *And you.*

"Good. I'm glad to hear that. So how do you like owning your own bakery? You always said you wanted to open one."

"It's great, although it's impossible to work a single shift without wanting to eat my way through the menu. It's no wonder I'm overweight." *Oh God. Why'd I say that? And to him of all people.*

An awkward silence followed so Leah let her gaze wander, searching for Sam, in hopes of using him as an excuse and a way out of this conversation. But he was standing off to the side about ten feet away, staring at her with a scowl on his face. *Hmm. Maybe not.*

"Well, be careful," Gavin said, chuckling a little. "Or you won't retain your girlish figure."

Leah gave a nonchalant wave of her hand. "Oh, you know me. The only thing I retain is water." *Jesus. What the hell is wrong with me? Do yourself a favor, Leah, and stop talking!*

It was like seeing Gavin again caused all her insecurities to unleash at once, triggering all the conflict and stress behind her low self-esteem. He obviously hadn't liked her body when they were dating since he'd repeatedly tried to coerce her to lose weight. And when she hadn't lost the excess pounds, he'd dumped her, only to turn around and marry Miss Anorexia.

As if that wasn't bad enough, Leah had also gained ten pounds since she'd last seen him eight months ago, which only added to the embarrassment. She lowered her head, not wanting to meet his gaze.

"Leah, you look really great," Gavin said.

"I agree," Sam said out of nowhere. "You look fantastic, honey."

Honey? Leah's head jerked up just as he stepped in front of her, blocking her view of Gavin. Without warning, Sam threaded his warm fingers into her hair at the nape of her neck and lowered his mouth to hers.

Leah stiffened, immobilized by the sudden invasion of her senses. *What the hell is he doing? Why is he...kissing me?* But a man like Sam didn't need a reason to do anything. The moment his tongue parted her lips, she stopped caring about *why* and worried more about *how*.

He manipulated her mouth with his, diving into her depths enthusiastically, as shivery delight rippled through her. The mellow flavor of his lips was irresistible. Slightly tangy, yet heady, like a perfectly aged muscadine wine.

The moment she began to kiss him back, his hands gravitated to her waist, pulling her closer until their bodies connected. Rough fingers clenched her sides. Noses bumped angrily as they changed the angle of their heads.

It was an impolite kiss. One filled with power and frustration. The kind of kiss two people share in the privacy of a bedroom while lying naked together between sweat-soaked sheets. This was not the way you kiss someone in front of a crowd of strangers.

But who gives a shit?

Leah didn't. And apparently Sam didn't either.

Chapter Five

Sam couldn't take it any longer.

He'd watched Leah stand there in front of her ex-boyfriend, blushing and stammering uncomfortably as she cracked fat jokes about herself. He was sure it was some sort of defense mechanism, but he didn't feel sorry for her. Nope, he was too pissed off to feel bad. He vaguely remembered thinking, *Okay, that's it!* before he'd marched over and planted a kiss on her, hoping to give her a reality check.

But as his mouth moved over hers and he tasted the sugar-sweet vanilla flavor of her warm lips, Sam realized his plan had backfired. He'd expected her to pull away in surprise, not open her mouth and allow him further access. The moment her tongue tentatively touched his, a frantic mania tore through him, traveling the length of his spine before settling painfully in his groin.

Sam pulled her closer, delighting in the feel of his hands on her and the way her body fit perfectly against his as she thrust her hips forward. But it still wasn't close enough. Somehow, he knew it would never be enough. *God, I need to be inside this woman.*

And with that revelation, his entire existence shattered. As if he'd just walked barefoot over hot coals and tripped, falling face-first into the raging fire that was currently consuming him. But there was no pain, only pleasure, in those rising flames, and apparently Leah was the accelerant.

He needed to stop this. Now.

Ending the embrace took more strength than Sam imagined, but he managed to pull back, though his mouth still lingered near hers. Leah steadied herself with one hand on his chest, looking every bit as flustered and disturbed as he felt. Her eyes glazed over, and her soft, full lips were swollen. Sam ran his thumb along the crease, noting the discoloration around her mouth. It was a warm recollection of the long, searing kiss they'd just shared.

Sam may not have heard the tinkling of small bells when he kissed Leah, like people sometimes do in movies, but the electric sparks zinging through him were demanding his full attention and definitely trying to tell him something.

Breathless, Sam tried to articulate his thoughts into words, but the only thing he managed to do was lick his lips and say, "Good stuff." Then he cringed at how dumb he sounded. *Good stuff? Who the hell says that?*

When a voice cleared next to them, Sam remembered her ex-boyfriend's presence. Leah must have too because she blushed beet red, probably realizing she now sported a just-bedded, tousled look. She quickly combed her fingers through her hair, taming the strands Sam had mussed, as though trying to reclaim a small shred of dignity.

"Gavin, this is Sam. He's my—"

"Fiancé," Sam said, cutting her off. Leah blinked, as if

she hadn't heard him right, but Sam just smiled and kept talking. "It's nice to meet you. Heard a lot about you."

They shook hands, but Gavin seemed a little lost for words. "Oh, I...uh...I hadn't even heard Leah was with anyone new, much less engaged. Leah and I used to date, but split up last year."

Sam gave him a megawatt smile that was anything but sincere and put his arm around Leah's tense shoulders. "I'd say I'm sorry to hear that, but I'd be lying." *Well, at least that part was genuine.*

Gavin glanced at Leah, then back to Sam. "Well, uh, congratulations. You're a lucky man."

Sure, buddy. We'll see how lucky I am when you walk away and Leah rips my head off my shoulders and shoves it up my ass. "Thanks. We appreciate the sentiment," Sam said while mentally rolling his eyes. He gave Leah's shoulders a little squeeze. "Don't we, sweetie?"

"Y-yes, of course. I...um...Gavin, I need a minute alone with my...*fiancé*."

"Sure. I need to go find my new bride anyway. You two stick around for a while and enjoy the reception."

"Thanks," Leah said, clearly fake-smiling until he walked away. Then she turned back to Sam with a grimace planted firmly on her face. "What the fuck was that?" she asked quietly, keeping her voice low so the other guests couldn't hear her.

"What? The kiss or pretending to be your fiancé?"

She crossed her arms and glared at him. "Both."

Sam ran his hand through his hair, not the least bit surprised that she was upset. "Look, I was trying to help. You were saying such awful things about yourself. I didn't want him to—"

"To what? Think I'm pathetic? I'm not your charity case.

And what about tomorrow when he learns I'm suddenly no longer engaged? What then, huh?"

"I guess I didn't think it through that far."

Leah sighed. "Look, I know you were trying to help, but Gavin's mother is the town gossip and sits on the City Council with my mom."

"Maybe he won't tell her."

"Are you kidding me?" Leah snorted. "Gavin lives and breathes by his mother's opinions. If I didn't know any better, I'd swear the woman still bathes him. Although I'd love to see her face when he tells Mommy Dearest I'm engaged to someone other than her precious baby boy, I need to figure out what I'm going to tell *my* mom. She's going to flip out when she hears this."

Sam cringed. "I'm sorry. I just didn't want him to make you feel bad about yourself."

She shook her head. "That's funny seeing how the only guy who keeps making me feel bad about myself is *you!*"

"Leah, I—"

"Darling, there you are," a voice rang out behind him.

Leah peered around him and sighed. "Oh great. Just what I freaking need right now."

Sam turned to see an older brunette woman wearing a shimmering black, floor-length gown approach from a few tables over. "I've been looking for you." Her scrutinizing gaze landed on Sam. "And I see you brought...a friend? Or is it possible you actually have a date?"

He didn't like the way Leah winced, nor did he appreciate the prying woman standing there eyeing them with a rude smirk on her seemingly perfect face. *Gavin's busybody mother, I presume.*

"Actually, I'm Leah's *fiancé*," Sam corrected, grinning ear-to-ear.

He didn't know whose gasp was louder—Leah's or the older woman's. Both stood there blinking at each other for a full minute before Leah finally spoke up. "Mom, it's not what you think!"

Mom? Shit! Wrong mother.

Sam waited for Leah's mother to break into a tearful display or, at the very least, purse her lips into a disapproving grimace. But she didn't. Instead her eyes lit up and her face broke out with a full-on smile.

"Fiancé? When did this happen? I didn't even know you were seeing someone, sweetheart. Why didn't you tell me?"

What the fuck? Why is this woman smiling? When Leah said her mother would flip out, Sam hadn't expected that her mother would be happy about the news.

"It's not like that, Mom. Last night, Sam and I—"

"He proposed last night?"

"Well, not exactly. I…um…" Leah looked at Sam helplessly.

"And to think I was trying to set you up with Chad Howard, the building inspector," her mother said. "I was planning to invite him to come with us next weekend on our annual trip down to the shore."

"Oh God. Mom, please tell me you didn't."

"Well, no. Not yet anyway. I wanted to make sure you didn't mind sharing a room first."

Just hearing that had Sam cringing. Not only was Chad Howard the asshole who delayed all of Sam's building permits, but he was also a chauvinistic dick. It was a well-known fact he never bedded the same woman twice, and the thought of Leah sleeping with that man…

Sam's hands clenched into fists, and a rising heat seared his insides. *Over my dead body.*

"Well, I guess you'll have to forget that idea," Sam said,

smiling at her mother. "I proposed to your daughter this morning."

* * *

Leah knew her exit wasn't graceful.

She marched past Sam, bumping his shoulder as she did, and kept going out a side entrance that led to the parking lot.

He caught up to her as she reached the truck and spun her around. "Are you mad?"

"Mad? Oh no. I'm not mad, Sam," Leah said as he sighed prematurely in relief. "I'm furious! What the hell were you thinking?"

He stepped back, giving her some room. "I'm sorry, okay? I was just trying to . . . to . . . I don't know what."

"Damn it, Sam! Now my mother thinks I'm engaged." Leah stood by the passenger door with her arms crossed as Sam unlocked it and swung it open.

"It's okay. You can tell her we broke up. In fact, you can even say you broke things off with me."

"Oh, so I can be the bitch who breaks my mother's heart and makes her cry? I don't think so."

"Then I'll break up with you."

"Before Friday?" Leah stared blankly at him. "God, you're such an ass." After Sam's big announcement, she had stood there like an idiot, dumbstruck and silenced by her guilt, while her mother chatted with her fake fiancé, inviting him to join them on their weekend trip so he could meet the rest of the Martin clan. "First you agree to go on vacation with my family, and now you're going to cancel on them?"

"Okay, so I'll go on the trip with them then."

"And lead them on? What the hell is wrong with you?" She climbed into the cab and pulled the door shut.

Sam walked around and slid into the driver's seat. But instead of starting the engine, he rested his arm along the back of the bench and stared at Leah. "Maybe you should tell me what it is you expect me to do."

"I expect you to not tell people we're engaged when we aren't."

"Too late."

"Exxxxactly."

Sam shook his head and started the truck. He probably thought she was acting crazy—and hell, maybe she was—but it was all his fault that she was in this position with her mother. *Why should he get away scot-free and leave me to deal with the shit-storm he created?*

As he drove toward the bakery, Leah tried to think of a way out of this mess. But it was no use. She'd be mortified if anyone ever found out the whole thing was a sham. It was embarrassing enough that Sam felt the need to do her a "favor" by giving her a toe-curling, spine-tingling kiss. A kiss that obviously meant nothing to him. *Jesus. It was a pity kiss. And a damn good one too.*

After a minute of driving in silence, Sam finally spoke up. "If you're interested, I have an idea."

At least one of us does. "I'm listening."

"Why don't we continue the ruse? Let them believe we're engaged for a little while longer...say, two weeks?"

Leah considered his words, then shook her head. "What's the point? I still have to tell them the truth afterward."

"Not necessarily." The corners of his mouth twitched. "What if they hate me? Then when we break up, they'll be relieved."

"Why would they hate—" Leah stomach clenched as his suggestion sank in. "You're going to be mean to my parents?"

He glanced over, giving her a "get real" look, then shifted

his eyes back to the road. "No, I'm not going to be *mean* to them. I'm just not going to give them a reason to like me. Then they'll beg for you to break things off with me, and you won't have to tell them the truth."

She squinted at him. "Why would you do that for me?"

He pulled up to the curb in front of the bakery and turned off the engine. "I did get you into this situation to begin with. Besides, I figured we could work out a little horse trade on the side. If I do this for you, then you have to do something for me."

Leah sat a little straighter in her seat. "Something as in…"

"Well, you are an expert in oral gratification, aren't you?" His brown eyes were doing that weird smoldering thing again.

Leah rolled her eyes and opened her door. "Good night, Sam."

His hand shot out and gripped hers. "Calm down. I'm just kidding with you. Well, sort of. I *do* want something." Wary, she cocked her head and lifted a brow, awaiting his response. He chuckled a little. "What does a guy have to do to get some dessert around here?"

She smiled. Now *that* was a problem she could do something about. "I, uh, have some leftover cupcakes in the fridge from earlier today, if you're interested."

"I'm in," he said, opening his door and stepping out.

As he rounded the front bumper, Leah met him on the sidewalk. She unlocked the bakery door, flipped on the lights, and Sam followed behind her as they made their way to the back room. Leah walked straight to the walk-in cooler, grabbed a cellophane-wrapped platter and a gallon of milk, then carried them back out, kicking the metal door closed behind her with her heel.

When she returned, Sam was examining a softball-size hole in the wall behind the metal swinging door. "What happened here?"

She shrugged. "I don't know. The hole was there when I leased the place. Not sure what caused it."

"Are you going to fix it?"

Leah set the platter and milk down on the stainless steel table, not bothering to look up. "Probably not anytime soon. I don't know how to fix it myself, and repairs like that aren't in my budget."

Sam joined her and sat on a nearby stool just as she peeled back the plastic wrap covering the platter. His eyes brightened, and his mouth quirked into a smile. But as he gazed at the confections, he suddenly frowned. "No chocolate?"

"Always the first to sell out," she said, turning to grab two glasses from a cabinet behind her. She poured them both a glass of milk.

Sam lifted a red velvet cupcake, pulled back the paper from around the edges, and took a large bite. He licked the white cream cheese frosting from his lips and grinned. "Never mind. This will do."

Leah pushed the glass of milk toward him as he shoved the other half of the cupcake into his mouth, then immediately reached for another. She watched him eat most of it before asking, "Well, what do you think?"

Sam held up one finger as he polished off the second cupcake. He took a drink of milk, then pulled the entire platter closer to him. "I think you need to fix the hole in the wall," he finally said.

"I was talking about the cupcakes."

"So was I," he said, grinning. "I think we could work out one more trade, if you're interested."

She lifted one brow and stared at him curiously as he ripped the paper off another cupcake and stuffed most of it into his mouth. "Go on…"

He chewed, swallowed, then downed the rest of his milk in one gulp. "I'm a contractor. It's what I do for a living—build and remodel houses. If you want, I can fix the hole in your wall, and you can pay me…in dessert."

Leah glanced at the small pile of decorative cupcake wrappers he'd accumulated in less than five minutes and shook her head. "I don't think I can afford you."

Sam grinned and picked up another cupcake, this time choosing one with toasted coconut scattered across the top. "Well, think about it. You can let me know after I finish these off."

She laughed. "You're not going to eat eight cupcakes."

"You're right, I'm not. I'm going to be a gentleman and save you one. But I call dibs on the other seven."

She smiled and grabbed one for herself, opting for the carrot cake with the vanilla icing. "Fine. Go ahead. But you're going to make yourself sick."

"Nah. I could eat these all day and never get sick. It's a good thing I don't work here or I'd weigh five hundred pou—"

He stopped talking, and his gaze met Leah's. She felt the familiar heat in her cheeks and looked down. *God. Why do our conversations always circle back to my weight?*

"Leah, I didn't mean—"

"Can I ask you something, Sam?"

When he didn't answer right away, she lifted her eyes to his. He was sitting a little straighter than before and pursing his lips, as if he expected her to ask something he didn't want to answer. So it surprised her when he nodded.

"Does size really matter all that much?"

"To men...or to *me?*"

She shrugged. "You're a man, aren't you?"

"Yeah, but if you want me to speak for all men, then you're going to get a vague answer. If you're asking me for my personal preference, then you'll get a more direct response."

"What's the difference?"

"The difference is...well, it's like asking if someone prefers vanilla or chocolate. There are plenty of men who have a preference for vanilla, but there are probably just as many who'd choose chocolate. Then there are some who just don't care—chocolate or vanilla."

"So you're saying it doesn't matter to you?"

"Hell no. I'm a guy who'd choose chocolate over vanilla any day."

Leah sighed inwardly. *That didn't answer my question.*

An awkward silence followed before Sam shifted nervously on the stool. "Can I speak frankly?" he asked.

Oh. Here it comes. "Of course."

"It's not just men. Size matters just as much to women, if not more."

Hmm. Not quite the response I expected. "You mean a guy's..."

"Yeah."

She kept her eyes glued to his to stop herself from looking down at his crotch. *Damn it, Val! Why did you have to go and tell me something so personal about him? Like I needed to know he was lacking in the penile department.*

She didn't want him to feel self-conscious so she smiled and said, "Not *all* women are impressed by a man's...er, size."

Sam rolled his eyes. "Bullshit. That's the biggest crock I've ever heard."

"No, I'm serious," Leah said softly, hoping she came across as sincere and genuine. And she meant it. Mostly. "You know what they say, *'It's not the size of the boat, but the motion of the ocean.'*" She shrugged her brows suggestively to lighten the mood...and hopefully keep from hurting his feelings.

Sam leveled a gaze at her. "Leah, I'm not naïve. I've been with enough women to know most will choose a yacht over a dinghy any day."

Poor guy. How many times has his dinghy been passed over or deserted for something a little more seaworthy? Leah shrugged, not wanting him to feel worse about himself than he already did. "I find it's often the man who is obsessed with his size, more so than the woman."

"Touché." Sam nodded in agreement. "But I never much saw the point in worrying about whether some other guy was bigger than me. I have what I was born with, and that's all there is to it."

Holy shit! It can't be that small. Can it?

Chapter Six

After a long day on the construction site, Sam pulled up in front of the bakery and dragged himself out of his truck and onto the sidewalk. Once he'd polished off the rest of her cupcakes the night before, he and Leah had parted ways, but he hadn't gotten any sleep.

He'd tossed and turned all night thinking about Leah and her body-image issues. Sam couldn't fix that for her, but there was one thing he could help her with. That damn hole in her kitchen wall. It was bothering him...almost as much as Leah did.

He grabbed a toolbox, a small tub of joint compound, and a leftover section of sheetrock from the back of his truck and carried them toward the Sweets n' Treats entrance. The neon sign was off, but that didn't stop him from turning the knob and letting himself in. It was only fifteen minutes after closing, and he figured Leah would still be puttering around inside. The loud music and God-awful singing coming from the back room confirmed his suspicion.

As he pushed open the swinging door, he saw Leah and smiled.

Ignorant of his presence, Leah shoved a push broom across the room in the opposite direction, singing off-key and bobbing her head to the beat of the music. When she stopped suddenly, Sam thought she'd heard him come in and expected her to turn around.

But no. Instead, she began singing into the broom handle and dancing—if that was what he'd even call it—with an abnormal amount of enthusiasm.

Clearly enjoying her time alone, Leah was oblivious to her environment, much less him. She strutted a few more steps, making jerky movements with her arms and odd patterns with her feet, like she was practicing dance moves in front of a mirror.

Sam gave her points for creativity, but the flapping of her arms and the strange way she lifted her feet resembled a weird bird's mating dance rather than a graceful white swan gliding across water. But in truth, her movements were surprisingly innovative to be so heartwarmingly dorky, which only made him grin wider as he lurked in the doorway.

He started to call out her name, but before he could, she stopped midstride and spun around to face him, eyes closed as she belted out the final lyrics. His silent patience was rewarded with an overly exuberant jiggle of her hips, one that made her ample breasts bounce beneath her tight T-shirt. The feminine flare she put into the movement defined her womanly figure and caused a strong sensation to grip Sam from deep within.

That sexy ass. Those sensually curved lips. Her well-proportioned, voluptuous body. Striking, like some sort of domestic goddess.

The *"under the influence"* effect she had on him was

mesmerizing, as if her sheer magnetism had reached down into his pants and stroked him intimately. Then an image flashed through his mind of taking her on the nearest flat surface, pumping hard and fast into that soft, sweet body until they both collapsed from exhaustion.

It left him unsettled.

Leah was quickly becoming a kink in his woman-free lifestyle. It didn't help that his brain had taken a momentary leave of absence, which only compounded the problem. If he had a lick of sense, he'd get the hell out of there before she saw him. And he'd stay as far away from her as possible.

But a shriek filled his ears. *Shit. Too late.*

With wide eyes, Leah lurched forward, clutching her chest in surprise and breathing so hard he thought she might faint. She stepped over and turned off the music. "Damn it, Sam! You scared me. What the hell are you doing here?"

Sam grinned and leaned against the doorjamb. "You mean besides watching you show off your skills with that performance?"

The blood drained from her face, then her cheeks bloomed bright red. She turned away from him and lowered her head, using her hair as a curtain to hide behind as she gathered her composure.

Oh, hell. He hadn't meant to embarrass her. Now he was the one who felt like a fool. "I'm sorry. I didn't mean to barge in or anything."

She lifted her head slightly and peeked at him through her strands as she twisted them together. "I told you before...I can't dance."

"You can't sing either." Sam gave her an exaggerated wink, trying to make her laugh. When she did, his grin widened. "I came to fill your hole."

She stopped laughing and blinked. "Excuse me?"

Sonofabitch. Why'd I say it like that? He laid the section of sheetrock on the table and rapped on it with his knuckles. "The hole in your wall."

"Oh, I... um, okay."

"So what's for dessert?"

"Well, if I'd known you were coming by tonight, I would've saved the rest of the pecan bars I sent home with Valerie. But since you didn't bother mentioning it, I guess I'll have to figure something else out."

"Might want to get to figuring then because I'm not touching your hole until you do."

She stood motionless, gawking at him, as she inhaled a large breath.

Jesus. Why do I keep referring to it as her hole? I sound like a fucking pervert. Use a construction term or something, damn it.

Leah thought for a moment. "How about some bran muffins?"

"How about I leave?"

She giggled. "Okay, fine. Um, well, I have a great recipe for a sour cream pound cake."

"Uh-uh. You can't convince me to eat something by telling me it's rotten. Try again. This time with the word *chocolate* thrown in."

Leah grinned at him. "I can make a chocolate pie from scratch in about twenty minutes, but it would need to set up and chill in the cooler for at least an hour."

He nodded and flipped open his toolbox. "Works for me. That's about how long it's going to take me to spackle your hole."

Ah, shit.

* * *

Leah carefully measured the flour and the unsweetened cocoa while Sam pulled off his red flannel shirt. Her mouth
went dry as the white T-shirt he wore underneath tightened
against his firm abs with every movement. She kept her
eyes focused in his direction, waiting to see if he'd pull the
undershirt off too.

Unfortunately, he didn't.

Probably a good thing though. The last thing Leah needed
was to see him without a shirt. Her mind was already running amok over his massive biceps and the way his jeans fit
snugly against his ass. As it was, she'd never get that image
out of her head.

She added water to the powdery mixture and whisked
it in a double boiler until it formed a smooth paste, then
glanced up to check his progress. Sam had just finished cutting a squared-off section around the hole in the wall with a
utility knife. He pulled the damaged drywall loose, making
white dust rain down onto his work boots.

"Shouldn't you be filling in the hole, not making it bigger?"

He eyed her playfully and raised a brow. "You wanna do
this yourself?"

A giggle tickled her throat. "Nope."

He pulled out a tape measure, marked the new piece of
drywall he'd carried in with him with a pencil, and cut it.
Even eyeballing it, Leah could see that it was way too big to
fit in the now-square hole. *What the hell is he doing?*

"That's not going to fit in that hole. It's too big."

"No shit, Sherlock." He grinned as he sliced the new
piece down the sides and peeled the back of the drywall off.
"I'm doing what we call a butterfly patch. It's where we
cut the new section two inches bigger in diameter, score the
sheetrock along the border, pull out the chunks of plaster,

and just leave the paper edge that'll hang over the wall to secure it."

He lifted the new piece and fit it against the hole, tapping to squeeze it into the tight space. Two inches of paper overlapped the wall on each side, just as he said it would.

"Why do you do it like that?" Leah asked as she added some sugar and beaten egg yolks to the paste she'd made.

"Because you don't have a stud here...well, unless you count me, of course." Sam gave her a quick wink that made her stomach twirl. "This is the easiest way to fix a hole in the wall when there's nothing to nail to."

He bent down and opened a tub of something that looked like whitish-gray frosting while Leah added milk and a touch more water to her chocolate concoction and whisked it all together.

"What's that?" she asked, turning the stove's heat down low.

Sam breathed out heavily. "You sure you don't want to fix this yourself?"

"Sorry, I'm just curious." She headed to the walk-in.

He laughed and called out, "You know, I'm not breathing down your neck and asking you why you're baking a pie on top of the stove rather than in an oven, am I?"

Leah found what she was looking for and stepped out of the cooler with an already prepared piecrust in her hand. "I never said anything about baking a pie. I said I'd *make* a chocolate pie. The only thing I have to actually bake is the piecrust...which I'm about to do."

"So, in other words, I got screwed?" Sam asked, chuckling to himself.

She tossed it in the preheated oven and whisked the chocolate filling again, making sure it had started to thicken. Glancing up, Leah froze when she saw what he was doing.

"You? I think I'm the one getting screwed here. Why the hell are you smearing that crap all over my wall?"

Sam pursed his lips. "Sweetheart, if I was screwing you, you'd know it. Trust me on that."

He glanced over at her, and his eyes did that weird smoldering thing again, causing a shot of pure lust to run straight down Leah's center. *My God. One look from him and I'm a puddle.*

"It's joint compound," he explained. "This mud will seal the paper to the wall and hide the seams."

"Oh," she said softly, then busied herself—and her hormones—by adding butter and vanilla to her chocolate pie filling.

Sam continued swiping mud on her wall with a funny-looking spatula that made a weird scraping noise. He put it on thick but ended up scraping most of it off before he was through. She didn't really see the point, but Leah couldn't ask him why. Mostly because she was still trying to steady herself after his remark about screwing her.

With an oven mitt, she pulled the golden brown piecrust from the oven and then poured in her chocolate filling. After placing it in the cooler to chill, she cleaned up the mess she'd made and loaded the dishwasher.

Once the mud on the wall dried, Sam sanded the seams and applied another thin coat. Quietly, she watched him work. The way his muscles bunched and flexed under his thin undershirt. The way his capable hands gripped the spatula with strength and endurance, yet smoothed over the wall with a soft, delicate touch. The room would've been completely quiet if it wasn't for the sloshing sound of the dishwasher and the scraping of metal along the wall.

By the time the pie was chilled and had set up marvelously, Leah had already retrieved two plates, forks, and a piping bag filled with whipped cream. She cut them both a slice and topped each with a white dollop. "Ready for dessert?" she asked.

Sam turned, wearing a wide grin. "Just finished," he said, dusting his hands on his jeans. "All you have to do is paint the patch job to match the rest of the wall. Mind if I borrow your sink to wash up?"

"Not at all."

As Sam washed, Leah looked over his handiwork. Not only was the hole completely gone, but she couldn't see the seams anymore either. If it hadn't been for the different colors of the patched wall, she wouldn't have known there had ever been a hole there. "Wow! Sam, you did a fantastic job."

He walked up behind her. "Still feel like you got screwed?"

Her cheeks heated. "Um, no...not yet." *Oh, jeez. Did I have to say that?*

"Good. Now let's get on with it."

She blinked. "Get on with *it?*"

"The pie," he clarified. "Are we going to stare at the wall all night or are we going to eat?"

Knowing her cheeks had grown hotter, Leah hurried to the counter ahead of him and sat down on one of the stools as he took another. She slid a piece of chocolate pie toward him and waited for him to take his first bite. As he did, his eyes closed, and his mouth turned up into a smile.

"Sooo," Leah said, "do you feel like *you* got screwed?"

"Oh yeah. In all the right ways too," Sam said on a moan. "Jesus. This is almost better than sex."

God. His penis really must be small if he thinks pie is better than sex.

Leah sighed. She needed to change the subject or she would be thinking about Sam's Slim Jim the rest of the night. "I wanted to talk to you about this Friday. I know we had an agreement, but I don't really expect you to keep your end of the deal and go on this trip with my family. I can just call my mom and—"

"No, Leah. Like you said, I got you into this whole mess. It's only fair that I get you out."

"That's sweet, Sam. Really. But it's not going to work anyway. No one in my family is going to believe we're dating, much less engaged. We hardly even know each other."

"I already thought of that." He grinned and shoveled another big bite into his mouth. "Debriefing session. Tomorrow night. You come to my house this time."

"Why your house?"

"It'd be a little strange if my fiancée doesn't know where I live or remember anything about my house," he said with a chuckle. "You were pretty hungover the last time you were there. Besides, it's just one less lie you'll have to come up with. The truth is always easier to remember than lies. Less chance that one of us will mess this up."

Leah picked at her pie with her fork. "I don't know. I just don't think it's going to work."

"Trust me," he said with a wink. "Your family is going to hate me."

Chapter Seven

You've spent almost every night with her this week," Max said. "What happened to being single?"

Sam shook his head. "I *am* single. Leah's just a friend."

"Who happens to be a woman?"

"Yeah." Sam shoved his hands into his pockets.

"The same woman friend who you happened to have half-naked in your bed last weekend?"

Sam narrowed his eyes. "Goddamnit, you know it wasn't like that!"

"Could've fooled me," Max said, grinning wide. "Unless you're suddenly gay, I'm going to call bullshit."

"Think whatever you want," Sam said, waving his friend off. "You're going to anyway. But I'm telling you, there's nothing sexual going on."

"Whatever you say."

A knock on the door captured Sam's attention. "That's probably her. Keep your mouth shut. She's meeting me here because I'm helping her with something."

Max smirked. "I bet you are."

As he walked to the door, Sam rolled his eyes and said, "It has to do with her family, asshole."

Max held up his hands in mock surrender. "Whoa! Settle down. If you say nothing's going on with this chick, then fine, I believe you."

"About damn time." Sam opened the door.

Leah stood there smiling, wearing a low-cut black tank top and a pair of dark-wash jeans that clutched at her hips, her arms filled with a white bakery box, a man's red flannel shirt, and a notebook. She lifted the lid of the box and flashed him the half-dozen cupcakes she'd brought with her. "They're chocolate," she said with a big grin. "Your favorite, right?"

Sam blinked at her impressive display of cleavage and moved aside to allow her entrance. "Um...yeah."

"Oh, hello. Max, right?" Leah said, giving him a small wave. "I didn't know you would be here."

He nodded, obviously checking out her spectacular chest as well. "I was...er...just leaving."

"Sorry to hear that." She passed by him. "I'm just going to set these down in the kitchen. It was nice seeing you again, Max."

The moment Leah was out of hearing range, Max closed the space between him and Sam. "Nothing going on, huh? I saw the way you were eyeing her goods...and I'm not talking about the ones inside the box."

Sam shook his head in denial. "I'm not the only one who looked at her chest, asshole. And just because I'm not blind doesn't mean I'm sleeping with her. I already told you, we're just friends."

"Oh, by the way, Sam, you left your shirt at my place last night," Leah called out from the kitchen. "I washed it for you and brought it with me."

"Thanks," Sam yelled back, heaving out a hard breath. He gave Max a nonchalant shrug. "I must've forgot it."

"The woman walks in with your clothes, showing off her goodies, and handing out her sweets like it's Halloween, yet you're still going to pretend nothing's going on. Un-fucking-believable." Sam started to speak, but Max raised his hand to stop him. "Face it. You're in denial, buddy."

"Damn it, Max. It's not like that."

"Whatever you say." Max stepped out the door but turned and faced Sam. "Look, I wasn't going to say anything, but since you obviously are into this chick, there's something you need to know about last weekend. I sort of told Leah's friend that... well, I told her you had a small dick."

"You did what?" Sam blinked rapidly and shook his head, as if he hadn't heard him correctly. Then Max's words registered, and anger punched through Sam's gut like he'd been shot with a high-powered nail gun. "What the fuck do you mean you told Leah's friend I had a small dick? Why the hell would you do something stupid like that?"

Max started to grin but apparently decided it was wiser not to. Instead, his brows furrowed and caused deep grooves to form on his forehead. "Look, you'd ditched Leah to dance with that other chick so I thought you weren't interested. I was just trying to help her out."

"By telling her friend I had a small pecker?"

"Seemed like a good plan at the time." Max shrugged nonchalantly. "Sorry, man. I thought you and Leah were hitting it off, but then you left her sitting there all alone. She looked miserable, and... well, I felt bad for her. But since you claim you're not into her, then it shouldn't matter, right?" The grin he'd suppressed moments before finally surfaced.

Leah sauntered into the room, carrying a plate with two

cupcakes. "Sam, if you think I screwed you in all the right ways last night, you're going to love—" She stopped talking when she saw Max still standing there with his mouth open wide. Her face reddened. "Oh! I...uh, thought you'd left already."

"He did," Sam said, shutting the door in his friend's face.

Shifting her weight nervously, Leah stood there staring at the closed door. "I...I'm sorry. I didn't realize he was—"

"It's fine," Sam said, gruffly. He walked over and plopped down on the couch, leaning his elbows on his knees. "He's gone now. It doesn't matter."

Without a word, Leah set the plate in front of him on the coffee table and returned to the kitchen. She didn't run, but her fast walking pace led him to believe she'd considered it. Probably to get away from the embarrassment chasing her down the hallway.

Sam picked up the cupcake and stared, trying to find something wrong with it, but he couldn't. The black cake was springy to the touch and smelled decadent and rich. Dark brown frosting swirled into a beautiful peak, topped with pieces of shaved and curled chocolate. He set it back on the plate and sighed. The goddamn cupcake was perfect and exactly what he wanted.

Like Leah.

The thought had popped into his head faster than he could push it out. But he wasn't ready for another relationship. Sam needed to make that clear to Leah before he ended up hurting her. And he *would* hurt her if they didn't have this conversation before pretending to be a couple in front of her family.

Sam doubted he'd have any problems convincing her family he was Leah's fiancé. Hell, he couldn't even convince

Max that they weren't together, and they hadn't even started the ruse yet.

Then Sam remembered what Max had confessed to him. *Why do I give a shit if Leah thinks I have a small dick? It's not like I'm going to...Because I do care. Goddamnit.*

Leah came back into the room, carrying her notebook while licking icing from her fingers. First one, then another, sliding her tongue over each before inserting them into her mouth. Something tugged painfully in his groin as his cock pulsed and hardened against the inside seam of his jeans. She stopped next to him, tossed the notebook on the end table, and sucked another finger into her delicious mouth just as she realized he was watching. Her eyes sparkled with something that clearly looked like an invitation.

Christ. If she tastes anything like she looks and smells, I'd be in heaven.

Sam wanted to oblige her, wanted to slip those delicate fingers of hers into his mouth and suck the icing off, right before he pulled her into his lap and...*No, I can't.* The attraction between them was obvious, maybe plain for anyone to see, but he couldn't act on it.

His gaze lowered to the cupcake in front of him as his fingers rubbed at the back of his neck, easing the tension building inside him. He cursed under his breath. "I don't want this." He hadn't meant the words to come out so harsh.

"Okay," she said with a question looming in her voice. "I'll take it back then." She reached for the cupcake.

Sam's hand shot out, capturing hers. "You touch that cupcake, and I'll have to break your fingers."

For a second, an amused grin played on her mouth, but then it changed to a grim line. "I guess I don't understand what you mean then. What is it that you don't want?"

Sam sighed and gestured to the both of them. "I'm talking about *this* ... a relationship."

Disappointment colored her face. "Sure," she said, shrugging before turning away from him.

Ah, hell. He'd hurt her feelings. Again. "Leah, I don't want you to think that this has anything to do with you. It doesn't, I swear."

"It's okay, Sam. I get it."

"Do you?" he asked, hopeful she really understood what he was trying to tell her. It wasn't that he wasn't attracted to her. The problem was, he didn't want to be. "You sure?"

"Yes. And it's fine." She sat down, but her eyes wouldn't meet his. "We're friends, right?"

"Right. Just friends."

* * *

Leah knew exactly what Sam was trying to say.

It's not you; it's me. The same tired line she'd heard before. *Yeah, real original.*

"Have you had dinner yet?" he asked.

"No. I planned on grabbing something on the way home."

"Why don't I order a pizza then? My treat."

Oh, sure. Change the subject by feeding the fat girl. But she was kind of hungry. "Okay."

Sam stood and walked to the end table across the room, picking up his cell phone. "What do you like on yours?"

"Anything. Well, except mushrooms and anchovies. Oh, and black olives. Yuck."

Sam cracked a smile. "Got anything against sausage or bell peppers?"

"Nope." She glanced up at him, and even though it wasn't a very nice thing to do ... "By the way, can you ask them to

cut the meat into tiny pieces. I like my sausage *really* small."
She smirked.

The look on his face and the way he quickly turned away
from her as he dialed the numbers offered her a bit of satisfaction. But that quickly vanished when Sam accidentally
ordered sausage and bell "pecker" before cursing under his
breath and quickly correcting himself. Then a spasm of guilt
rippled through her. *Serves him right though, since he's the
one playing mind games.*

One minute he looked at her like she was a delectable
French pastry he'd willingly devour. The next, he was acting
weird and insulting her. *Whatever.* If he wanted to be just
friends, that was fine with her. She didn't want to be with
someone that didn't want her anyway. Mostly.

When Sam ended the call, he headed toward the kitchen.
"Want a beer?" he asked.

"Sure, why not?"

While he was out of the room, Leah glanced around,
noting the oversized furniture. A massive oak entertainment center. Large flat-screen TV. Even the oversized
leather recliner and matching couch were much bigger
than a normal person would have. *Overcompensating*, she
thought, remembering the remark she'd made about his little sausage.

"Is it too big?" Sam asked.

"Huh?" Leah said, quickly looking up at him.

He handed her an open beer and plopped back on the
couch. "The TV. Is it too much?"

"Oh. Um, no, I guess not."

"All the guys usually congregate at my house during football season. That's why I got the biggest one I could find. I
don't think women are as easily impressed with the size of a
man's toy though."

"That's not what you said the other night," she said bluntly. "Besides, have you seen the size of my mixer?"

"Who could miss it? I figured the next time I need to mix some concrete, I'd borrow it."

She grinned and swigged on her beer.

"While we're waiting on the pizza, why don't we go over some of the basics for our upcoming trip?"

"Such as?"

"Tell me about your first job."

"Okay, um...well, my grandparents used to live in a beach-front condominium, and I decided to stay with them over the summer. I got a job in housekeeping that I absolutely hated. It was disgusting. Every day, I was forced to clean makeup out of the white towels by soaking them in a huge tub and then scrubbing them with bars of soap."

"Doesn't sound too bad."

"I thought the same thing until I found out the bars of soap were leftover from the guests' rooms. The thought of touching something that probably ran up some old man's ass crack was enough to make me gag."

Sam laughed. "Should I ask how you cleaned stained sheets?"

"It varied, depending on the stain...and no, you don't want to know."

He chuckled again. "So what else?"

"Short list?" She waited for him to nod, then took a deep breath. "I can't whistle, I'm afraid of birds, and I always check behind the shower curtain before peeing."

"Seriously?" he asked with a huge grin on his face.

"Sam, if you make fun of me..."

He shook his head. "I won't, I promise. I'm just curious about one thing though. What do you expect to see behind the curtain when you check?"

She cringed. "A…um…murderer?" It sounded like a question.

Sam stared at her for a full ten seconds before he burst into laughter.

"Damn it, Sam," she said, throwing a couch pillow at him. "That's it. I'm not telling you anything else."

"Aw, come on," he said, still chuckling. "It's funny."

"No, it's not."

His laughter quieted. "Okay, I'm done. Keep going."

"Nope."

"You have to, otherwise we won't be able to convince anyone we're a couple. Go ahead. I promise I won't laugh."

She eyed him suspiciously, but continued. "Well, I don't like raw tomatoes. I don't care for spaghetti. I hate anything grape or cherry flavored."

"And mushrooms, anchovies, and olives."

"Right. Basically, there's an ongoing list of things that I don't eat or don't like. Almost makes you wonder why I look the way I do, huh?"

The corners of Sam's mouth turned down, and his face turned serious. "Why do you do that to yourself?"

"I'm not a sexy bombshell."

"Neither am I."

Leah sighed. "Stop it. You know what I mean."

"Not really. You're a beautiful girl. Smart. Funny. Any guy in his right mind would be banging down your door."

Yeah, right. You're not. "Look, Sam, I—" But before she could finish her sentence, the room went dark.

Chapter Eight

Sam and Leah both stood at the same time and collided in the dark, forcing him to grab her shoulders to steady her as she crashed into his chest. Slowly, his eyes adjusted to the moonlit shadows on her face. "Sorry about that. You okay?"

She looked up at him. "Yeah."

Even with only the dim light coming through the window, he could see how bright her green eyes were. Bright enough to light up the world.

"That damn breaker has been giving me problems for two days. I've been meaning to change it out, but I keep putting it off." He released her and said, "Stay here. I'll be right back." Moments later, he returned wielding a flashlight. "Mind giving me a hand by holding this while I fix the breaker?"

Leah followed him down the hallway and into the tiny laundry room, waiting patiently while he grabbed a screwdriver from a nearby drawer and opened the breaker box. "Okay, here. Point the flashlight right here while I check the breakers."

The moment he started flipping switches, Leah yelled, "Wait! Hold on a second." She ran out of the room, taking the flashlight with her.

What is she doing? "Leah?"

"I'm just getting something real quick," she called out from the other room. "Don't touch anything."

When she returned, she was carrying a pillow she must've retrieved from his bed. She set the flashlight down on top of the washing machine, pointed in the direction of the breaker box, and then held the pillow in a swinging position. "Okay, I'm ready. Go ahead."

Sam paused and shook his head. "Want to fill me in on what the hell you're doing?"

"I'm preparing myself in case you get electrocuted."

"What's the pillow for, Babe Ruth?"

She sighed heavily. "For knocking you off the electricity so I don't touch you and get shocked as well."

He nodded. "That's what I thought." Sam wanted to smile, but he forced himself to keep a straight face, which was hard to do with her standing there ready to clobber him with a pillow and looking so damn cute. "You do know I turned off the main breaker, right? There's no power running to this box."

"Oh. Well, you can never be too sure about these things." She continued to stand there with the pillow held up high.

"Um...good thinking." He cleared his throat and turned away from her before grinning. "Okay, here I go."

Sam lifted the screwdriver up and touched it to one of the breakers. The moment he did, he made a little *zzzzttt* noise with his mouth and shook, as if he were being electrocuted. He did it so quickly that he barely had time to turn back to her when the pillow crashed into the side of his face, stunning him and knocking him off balance.

He stumbled and fell, landing hard on his back on the tiled floor. The flashlight rolled across the washing machine, onto the dryer, and then off the end, clunking him in the head. "Ow!" Sam yelled.

Leah screamed his name and threw herself on top of him. "Oh God! Are you okay?" He let out a little moan. "I'm sorry. I didn't realize you were playing until it was too late. Sam?"

Wincing, he rubbed the nonexistent knot on his head that he was sure to have in a few minutes. "Sonofabitch. That hurt."

"Well, that's what you get for scaring the hell out of me. Don't you know better than to play with electricity?" Moisture pooled in her eyes, and her bottom lip trembled. She really had been scared for his safety.

"Hey," he said, brushing his hand across her soft cheek, "I'm sorry. It was a bad joke. I didn't mean to..."

Something about the way she looked at him took his breath away. Her eyes were wide, glazed with tears that hadn't yet fallen. Her breath came fast, a soft panting that landed on his face with every intoxicating sugar-scented exhale. He wanted to taste those full lips of hers once more, feel her body heat as his hands gripped her curvy waist.

Her fingers grasped at his shirt, and her breasts squished against his chest. He could feel the hardness of her tight nipples through their clothes. No doubt he could take her right here and now. Bend her over his washing machine, put it on spin cycle, and drive into her from behind as she came around his dick.

And God, he wanted that release. For her, as much as for himself. But just as he leaned up to gently touch his lips to hers, someone knocked on the front door.

Ah, hell.

* * *

Leah held the flashlight on the young delivery boy as Sam paid for the pizza and told him to keep the change. Then Sam kicked the door closed with his foot and carried the pizza over to the coffee table, tossing it down rather hard.

Hmm. Obviously irritated.

Leah wasn't quite sure why he was suddenly mad, though it apparently had something to do with what happened between them in the laundry room. But what *had* happened? She was still in the dark about that one, figuratively and literally.

If she hadn't known any better, she would've thought Sam had been about to kiss her. But that couldn't have been right. Could it? No. Probably just her wishful heart willing it to be true. After all, Sam had made it clear from the beginning: the only goods of hers he was interested in were the ones she made at the bakery.

Sam took the flashlight from her hand. "Have a seat while I grab some plates from the kitchen."

"But the lights…"

"We'll eat first, then worry about the lights." The tone of his voice wasn't angry but had an edge to it. He shoved his fingers through his hair and glanced around. "I think I may have a candle around here somewhere so we don't use up the batteries in the flashlight."

Leah plopped herself down on the couch as he headed to the kitchen, leaving her alone in the moonlit living room. While she waited patiently for his return, her fingers doodled over the cold skin of the leather couch as she listened to him clatter dishes around in the other room.

When he returned, he had his arms full, juggling two more beers, two plates, a roll of paper towels, and a lit candle. And his demeanor had seemingly shifted back to normal. "I found the candle in the cabinet over the stove," he said with quick grin.

She helped him set everything down and scooted over to give him a place to sit. Since he was closer to the pizza, he served them both up a slice on a plate and then sat back, tucking his beer upright between his legs.

"Okay, so while we're eating, why don't we go over the things I need to know about your family?"

"Actually, I brought a list," Leah said, motioning to the end table next to him before taking her first bite.

He set his plate down on the armrest and reached for the notebook she'd left there. After reading a little, he looked up. "This is just their names and general information about them. That's not quite what I had in mind."

She glanced over his arm at the page. "I thought I pretty much covered everything. Did I leave something specific out?"

The corner of his mouth lifted. "Yeah. All the dirt on your family."

"All the what?"

"You know, the juicy stuff. Things I can use to make them hate me."

Leah shrugged. "I don't know that there's anything I could tell you then. We're a close-knit group...even if we don't always show it."

His grin widened as he pointed at her. "*That* right there. That's the stuff I want to know. Tell me the things that annoy you about them."

"Oh. Um, all right." She thought for a moment. "Well, in my family, we don't ever say 'I'm sorry.' We just sort of wait for the storm to pass over and then pick up right where we left off, as if the incident never occurred."

Sam took a bite of his pizza but kept his eyes glued to her face. "What else?"

"I don't think there's much I can tell you about my grand-parents. When they both retired, they sold their condo-minium and bought a beach house."

"Come on, Leah. You can do better than this. Give me something good."

She thought for a minute. "Ethan, my younger brother, graduated high school last year and is color-blind."

"Color-blind? Really?"

"Yeah. I'm sure it's a hardship, but it's not the handicap he pretends it is. He still lives at home with my parents so my mom babies him a lot. He's sloppy and lazy, and we bicker a lot."

"Oh, now this is getting good," Sam said in between bites. "Keep going."

"My dad's name is Bill. He's ridiculously superstitious and constantly tells the same stories over and over again. He thinks they're funny, but trust me, they're not. Oh, and he's a tight wad. Hates to spend money if he can get out of it."

"And your mom...Nancy, right?"

"Yes, and she collects antiques. Which is weird, since she usually wants everything to be so...perfect, I guess." Inwardly, she cringed. If she didn't tell him the truth about her mom, he'd pick up on it himself the moment they arrived on Friday. So Leah sighed and said, "Including me."

"What do you mean?"

"My mom is a bit critical of me. My weight, specifically. She thinks my BFF is a burrito, and before you came into the picture, she thought the only chance I had at getting married was lost when Gavin dumped me. She hates that I'm not a size two and reminds me of it every chance she gets."

"Ouch. That's harsh."

"Not really. I'm used to it."

"Shitty thing to get used to."

Leah shrugged. "She constantly makes snide remarks, though she thinks of it more as 'sharing her wisdom.'"

Sam's lips formed a thin, tight line. "Sounds more like cruelty."

She shook her head. "I know it sounds bad, but I don't think she means it the way it comes across."

"Don't do that," he said, tossing his empty plate on top of the pizza box. "You don't have to defend her. It's wrong for her to belittle you, whether she means to or not. There's no excuse for anyone—especially family—to treat someone that way."

"I know, but it's just—"

"No buts, Leah."

She smiled halfheartedly at him, knowing he was right. "Okay, so it's my turn to ask you questions, right?"

"Nope. You don't need a turn."

Leah stared at him, feeling her face contort with confusion. "What do you mean? Of course I do. How else will I know what to tell them about you?"

"They're not going to ask you anything about me. I'll be there, remember? They're going to ask me directly."

"Well, what if one of them gets me alone and asks me something about you that I don't know the answer to?"

"They won't. You're old news. *I'm* the one auditioning to be their son-in-law. And like any new toy, they'll be glued to me, fighting over who gets to ask the next question. You probably won't have to talk at all. In fact, if you don't bother showing up, I doubt they'd even notice."

Leah laughed. "I don't know whether I should be offended or glad the attention won't be on me."

"Well, you're not out of the hot seat yet. I still have more questions. And this time, I need to ask you something really personal."

The smile faded from her lips. "You're not going to ask me how much I weigh, are you?"

Sam gave her a *yeah, right* look. "No. Not *that* kind of personal. Think of something a little more *intimate*."

There's nothing more intimate than asking a girl what she weighs, is there? I mean it's not like he's asking me…Oh, shit!

Heat rushed to her face, but she hoped he wouldn't notice her blushing in the dim lighting. "You're not talking about what I think you are, are you?"

A broad grin widened his face. "Bingo!"

Uh-uh. No freaking way am I talking about that with him. "Um, maybe we should draw the line right there."

"Oh, come on, Leah. We're both mature adults here. It's a natural act, one that most women tend to like. Besides, it's just a yes or no answer. Has a man ever—"

"No," she said, closing her eyes and taking a deep breath. "The answer is no." He was completely silent so she cracked one eye open and caught a glimpse of his dumbfounded expression. "Stop looking at me like that."

He shook his head and forced his jaw to snap closed. "Sorry. I guess I'm just surprised, that's all. It's not really the answer I expected." Then he continued to stare at her, apparently not knowing what else to say.

"See? This is why I didn't want to talk about it."

Sam took a swig of his beer and tapped his foot insistently, as if he were nervous or something. "It's not a crime to be a virgin, Leah."

"*Virgin?* I'm not a…" Leah realized she had misunderstood what Sam was asking her. She thunked her head on the back of his couch. "God, this just keeps getting worse."

He laughed. "Wait. So if you're not a virgin, then what the hell did you think we were talking about?"

"Um, I never had a guy..." She glanced at him to see if he was following her. "You know."

His eyes widened, as if he understood, but he grinned and played dumb by asking, "Do I know?" At least she thought he was playing.

"God, don't make me say it out loud. This is embarrassing enough already."

"No reason to be embarrassed, Leah. They're just words," he said evenly. "Just say it. You've never had a guy..." He waited for her to finish the sentence, but she didn't. "Aw, come on! There's like a hundred ways to say it. Just pick one: perform oral sex, go down on you, yodel in the canyon, eat your pu—"

"Okay, stop. Now you're just being crude." She shook her head at him and laughed. "*Yodel in the canyon?* Who makes up this shit?"

Sam chuckled. "No telling. But when you run a construction crew, you tend to pick up a few things."

"No kidding."

"Mind if I ask one more question?"

"I doubt it could be any more embarrassing than the last one so why not? Go for it."

He stared into her eyes, and his face turned serious. "Why?"

Okay, maybe I was wrong. "It's just...well, I didn't want them to."

He looked even more puzzled now.

"Look, Sam, I know you think my mother is being mean by making comments about my weight, but she's right about one thing. I'm not a size two. And the last thing I want is anyone in the male population to get an up-close view of my thunder thighs and realize that for himself."

A vein throbbed on the side of Sam's forehead as he scowled at her. "Sweetheart, I've seen you in your underwear and *any* guy would be lucky to have your bare thighs wrapped around his ears."

Though a familiar heat seared her cheeks, she couldn't help thinking the one thing he wasn't saying aloud. *Yeah, sure. Any guy except him.*

Chapter Nine

Leah flung open the doors of her closet and tore through it looking for something to wear. One by one, she whipped clothes off their hangers, tossing them onto the bed as possible choices and continued searching for something better.

"What are you looking for?" Valerie asked, watching her friend rush around the room like a maniac.

"My pants. I can't find my dark rinse Levi's. Those have a slenderizing effect."

"Didn't you already pack for your trip down to the coast?"

"Yes, but I haven't figured out what I'm wearing on the drive there. I need something that doesn't make me look fat. Well, fatter than I already am."

Val rolled her eyes. "What's wrong with the pair of pants hanging in front of you?"

Leah shook her head violently. "God, no! Those are skinny jeans. Too tight. Too tapered. I'll look like a chubby baby seal in those."

"Maybe you should've gone shopping for a new outfit like I suggested."

"No way! I hate trying on clothes. The dressing rooms are always hot, and nothing ever fits right. It's mentally and physically exhausting."

"Aw, sweetie, if you're this unhappy with your weight, why don't you just join a gym already?"

Leah shot her a searing look. "I told you why. I want to lose weight *before* I go to a gym."

Val groaned, reclined on the bed against the headboard, and stuffed another cheesy nacho chip into her mouth.

"You've been the same size for three years. How do you eat that crap without gaining more weight?"

"I work out."

Leah sighed. *Figures.*

Valerie laughed. "I only work out a couple of times a week for the health benefits. And so that I can eat crap like this without gaining weight." She stuffed another chip into her mouth and grinned. "But if some guy doesn't like me for who I am, or the size I am, then that's too bad. It's not my issue, it's *his*."

"Yeah, says the girl who actually goes out on dates and can get any guy she wants."

"Oh, please," Valerie said, shaking her head. "Leah, we're roughly the same size. The problem with you is that you worry too much about what other people think. You're beautiful. You just need to stop letting other people tell you how you should see yourself."

"I know . . . and I'll try."

"Promise?" The moment Leah nodded, Valerie grinned and held up the bag of chips. "Want some?"

Leah laughed. "No, that's okay. I apparently was so hungry earlier, I ate my lipstick off. Now I have to reapply it."

"Those are just your nerves. You really should learn to calm down."

Calm down? Ha! Easy for her to say. She isn't about to deliver the performance of a lifetime to her family with a guy whose sole purpose is to make them hate him. All because he feels sorry for me.

She snatched a random pair of pants off the hanger and punched her legs through them, one at a time. Then she jumped up and down as she yanked them up over her round hips. Sucking in her stomach, she buttoned and zipped them, but with such a tight waistband, her slight, yet unflattering muffin-top would clearly poke through any shirt she paired with these pants. A bummed sigh escaped her lips.

"Problem?" Valerie asked.

"You mean besides me feeling like sausage encased in entrails? Or how easily I can wind myself just by squeezing into a pair of pants?" Leah shook her head. "This isn't going to work. I don't have a shirt baggy enough to hide my mushy middle in these jeans."

"Hmm." Val cocked her head, then jumped off the bed and strolled to the closet. She sifted through the rack until she found what she was looking for. "Try this one on," she said, tossing Leah a black top. "It's the same one you wore under your apron on opening day."

Without arguing, Leah slid into the shirt and waited for her friend's assessment, though she'd already formed her own opinion. The ruching of stretchy fabric in the front of the shirt had a slimming effect on her tummy and was just loose enough to conceal any unsightly bulges. The fair amount of cleavage it displayed served as an added bonus, since it might be enough to keep a man's eyes from traveling farther south to notice the more unseemly curves of her pear-shaped figure. "Well?"

Val's face broke with a slow grin. "Perfect."

The rumble of a truck pulling up had them both racing to the bedroom window overlooking the front of the bakery. "Oh, shit!" Leah said as Sam stepped out of his red truck and shut the door behind him. "He's here early."

Sam's muscular, denim-clad legs stopped on the sidewalk while he adjusted the collar of his green button-down shirt and ran his fingers through his dark chestnut hair. His biceps bulged against his short sleeves, stretching the pressed shirt tighter across his broad chest and causing Leah's inner muscles to clench.

"And hellooo, totally delish!" Val exclaimed.

Leah nudged her with her elbow. "I don't know why you're acting surprised by that. You've already seen him before."

"Uh-uh. Not looking like *that*, I haven't. Holy hell. No wonder you're ignoring Max's warning about him being the anatomical equivalent of a Ken doll. A girl doesn't need a dick at all when the man can make you come just by looking at him."

Leah snorted and took another appreciative glance at Sam. Maybe Val had a point after all. Not that it mattered though. Sam was only doing all of this to soothe his conscience and get her out of the jam he put her in to begin with. He wasn't interested in anything more.

"Don't worry," Valerie said, double-timing it to the stairs leading down to the bakery. "I'll stall him. Just finish getting ready."

"Val..."

"It's okay. I'll be good, I promise." Valerie winked.

Well, Leah could use a few more minutes to get ready. If only a dab of lip gloss would make her look twenty pounds lighter. "All right, tell him I'll be down in a minute."

Valerie started down the stairs, then hesitated and glanced back at Leah. "Honey, are you sure this is just him doing you a favor?"

Leah nodded, confused as to why her friend was asking such a thing.

"Then do yourself a favor," she said, her eyes lowering as if she were deep in thought. "Don't get too attached to Sam this weekend. It will only lead to heartbreak—yours, not his." She offered Leah a sincere smile then disappeared from sight.

Of course, Valerie was right. Maybe if Leah reminded herself of that enough, she could keep from growing too fond of Sam. Though it was probably a little too late for that already. The only way she'd be able to protect herself was by not reading into anything that happened. Because pretending to be engaged to a guy she liked for an entire weekend wasn't going to be an issue. The problem was knowing he'd never reciprocate those feelings.

Leah sighed heavily and slipped on her favorite pair of sandals. She was lucky to find anything in her closet to wear but hated that she still felt like a frumpy louse. Surely, there was something more she could do.

According to every guy she'd ever dated, there were two things a man preferred bigger on a woman—her breasts and her lips. And since Leah had an overabundance of both, it was probably best she play up her strengths. Grabbing her pink makeup case, she rummaged through it until she found her lipstick and compact mirror. Then she carefully applied the bright red stain to her full lips, admiring her handiwork as she smacked them together.

There. All done.

Now maybe between the pouty red lips and the lack of clothing covering the boob zone, Sam would be too distracted to look elsewhere. Unfortunately, both still held a strong sexual implication she should be trying to avoid altogether, but it did make her wonder if he'd notice. *Guess it's time to find out.*

With her duffel bag in hand, Leah headed downstairs, rounded the corner, and stopped in her tracks. Valerie leaned lazily against the counter next to the cash register while Sam had his back turned to her, working diligently on an electrical outlet on the opposite wall. That particular outlet hadn't worked since Leah had acquired the place.

He already had the cover off and three wires—a black, a white, and a copper one—exposed, hanging loosely from the small square hole in the wall as he set down the broken outlet and picked up another. *Where in the hell did he get that?*

Sam grasped the white wire and wound it around the end of the screwdriver he held, making a loop, and connected it to the new outlet. Just as he began to tighten the screw to hold it in place, something dawned on Leah. All of the lights in the bakery were glowing as bright as ever, meaning only one thing. Unlike before, he'd forgotten to turn off the power running to the outlet. *Crap.*

"Sam, no!" Leah shouted, dropping her bag to the floor.

Startled by the sound, Sam jumped, and his hand grazed across the black wire. His fingers twitched, and his arm tightened before he jerked back, quickly freeing his hand of the live wire as he swore under his breath.

"Oh my God! Are you okay?" Leah raced to his side. "The wire shocked you, didn't it?"

Sam fisted his hand and then relaxed his fingers before letting them slowly stretch out once again. "Nope. I was just done looking at it." He glanced at her sideways and gave her a *yeah, right* look.

"Stop being such a guy and let me see," she said, grabbing his hand and flipping it back and forth to check for burns.

"It's fine," he said, wiggling his fingers in her palm. "See, everything still works."

Leah scowled at him. "What the hell are you doing changing out an outlet while the power is still on? Are you trying to kill yourself?"

"Of course not. Valerie said you were still upstairs getting ready, and I wasn't sure if you were using something that required electricity so I made do without turning off the main power. It was quicker than shutting off each individual breaker to figure out which one went to this outlet." He turned to the loose wires and got back to work. "And for your information, I would've been fine if you hadn't come in shrieking like you did."

She gasped. "So you're saying this was *my* fault?"

"Yep."

"Well, who the hell asked you to fix my broken outlet in the first place? Certainly not me." Her gaze shifted to Valerie.

Val was grinning her ass off at the verbal exchange as if it were her favorite TV show. "What?"

"You asked him to fix it, didn't you?"

When Valerie shrugged innocently, Sam spoke up. "She didn't have to," he said casually. "I noticed the scorch marks on the outside of the outlet and happened to have a new plug in the toolbox of my truck. I was just trying to keep your bakery from burning down. Because, after all, isn't that what a doting fiancé would do for his electrically ignorant bride-to-be?"

Val belted out a laugh, but Leah eyed him suspiciously. "You're looking to get another dessert out of this, aren't you?"

His mouth quirked in answer as he finished screwing the outlet cover back on. "Damn straight."

* * *

Leah gestured to the driveway up ahead. "Slow down. You're going to take a right here."

Sam tapped the brake lightly and turned onto a narrow driveway covered with loose, thick sand. His tires bogged down and slowed the truck to a crawl. He pressed the gas pedal harder, gunning the engine until the truck accelerated and glided over the soft drive with much less effort, then he followed the path up to a large yellow beach house that sat high off the ground on pilings. A white Avalon and a black BMW were parked beneath the home as if it were one giant carport so Sam guided his vehicle in next to them.

He glanced over at Leah, who plucked at the jeans on her thighs with her fingernails. She'd been fidgeting since they'd left the bakery two hours ago. "Nervous?"

"Aren't you?"

"Not particularly. Is there a reason I should be?"

"Well, since we're about to spend the weekend lying to my family about how much in love we are, and they're probably not going to buy it, I'd say that's a definite yes."

Sam didn't miss the panic that flashed in her eyes, and the urge to lessen her fears took over. He gently covered her hand with his and squeezed. "Leah, you worry too much."

Her shy smile sent a buzz through him that stopped short of his groin, and he had no doubt it would only travel farther south if he stayed in such close quarters with her. "Everything will be fine," Sam promised, removing his hand and climbing out of the truck. "Just play along with everything I say or do."

"Yeah, that's the part that has me worried." Leah sat there with her head down and limbs stiff, as if she were willing herself to move but was unable to do so.

Sam had a sinking feeling he might need both hands free to drag Leah upstairs to the front door of her grandparents' beach home so he ignored the overnight bags in the backseat. He strolled around to the passenger door, opened it, and offered Leah his hand.

"I just...need a minute."

"No, what you need is a tranquilizer. Look, the quicker we go inside, the quicker we get this weekend over with." When she didn't respond, he lifted her chin with his finger and gazed into her concerned eyes. "It'll be fun. I promise."

Sighing, Leah shook her head. "Easy for you to say. It isn't *your* family we're about to screw with."

"I know," he said, a grin spreading across his face. "That's the fun part." He grasped her hand, yanked her from the truck, and looped her arm through his as he led her toward the stairs.

"What about our bags?"

"We'll come back for them later. Let's just go up and say hello first so you can stop holding your breath. I don't want you passing out on me."

The old, dry wooden stairs creaked and bowed under their feet as they climbed each step, leading them to the large, sun-faded upper deck. From there, Sam spotted the ocean sparkling under the late afternoon sun. It was immeasurable, stretching out as far as his eyes could see. The warm breeze coming off the water wafted over his face, leaving behind a salty residue he could taste on his lips.

Leah stood there, staring at the front door of the beach house, then placed her hand on her stomach and shook her head. "Sam, I...I don't think I can do this."

"Too late to back out now. We're already here."

"We can leave. I'll call my mom from the road and tell her we couldn't make—"

The front door swung open, halting her words.

Leah's uptight mother appeared in the doorway wearing a navy blue pantsuit, gaudy overpriced baubles, and sporting enough high-grade silicone to caulk an entire bathroom. "Darling, you made it. And you brought Sam with you."

Leah looked confused. "Mom, you knew we were coming. You invited us, remember?"

"Yes, but after you left Gavin's wedding reception so quickly, I thought maybe there was a problem, and perhaps things wouldn't work out after all. It's not like it would be the first time you—"

"Nancy, it's so good to see you again," Sam said, purposely interrupting her. He wouldn't have minded putting a piece of duct tape over her mouth, but instead he grabbed her slender shoulders and pulled her to him, giving her a big, awkward hug. Then he punctuated his rudeness by releasing her and stepping through the doorway, not bothering to wait for an invitation. "You have anything to eat? I'm starving."

"Oh, um...well, I guess I can check on dinner and see how much longer," Nancy said, obviously flustered by his forwardness. "Come in, Leah. No need to linger in the doorway."

Sam glanced around the living room, turning his eyes onto the décor. Apparently, Leah's grandparents loved the beach so much that they'd brought it inside with them.

Palm trees adorned the fabric of the cushions on the white wicker furniture, branches of driftwood took up space on the entertainment center, various species of saltwater fish corpses were mounted around the room, and a glass bowl on the coffee table held a small collection of sand, colorful shells, and dried-out starfish—like some kind of ocean graveyard.

"Lots of dead shit in here," Sam noted.

An older gentleman entered the room, wearing a pair of khaki shorts, a white polo shirt, and a pleasant grin. His kind eyes—green, like Leah's—wrinkled with mirth as he crossed the room and offered his hand. "Hi, I'm Leah's father, William Martin, but you can call me Bill."

Sam shook the man's hand in an ironclad grip. "I'm Sam. Nice to meet you."

"Thanks for joining us this weekend. It'll give us some time to chat and get to know one another. And you, young lady," Bill said, glancing over at his daughter, who was nervously shifting her weight, "I thought I'd have to put you on a milk carton if we ever wanted to see your pretty face again."

Leah smiled and gave her dad a quick hug. "I'm sorry, Dad. I've been a bit busy lately."

"I'll say. You couldn't even give your old man a call to let him know you were dating someone, much less getting married? What kind of daughter are you?"

"Well, it all happened...rather suddenly," Leah told him. "Honestly, I barely had time to process it myself. Where're Grandma and Grandpa?"

"Grandma's in the kitchen cooking up dinner, and your grandfather is in the bathroom...uh, making room for dinner."

Leah and Sam laughed, but Nancy shook her head and curled her upper lip in disgust. "My goodness, Bill. Must you say things like that when we're about to sit down to a meal?" Nancy headed for the kitchen. "I'll just check on dinner and see how much longer it will be."

Unfazed, Bill swung his head in Sam's direction. "So, Sam, my wife told me you own a construction and remodeling business."

"That's right," he replied, nodding. "We do anything from small projects to building entire subdivisions. No job is too big or small for me."

"Maybe I could get you to do me a favor then. I've been wanting to replace my patio door, but I think I'll need to tear out part of the wall to accommodate the French doors I'd like to have installed. I wrote down the dimensions of both and brought a few photos with me, if you have a moment to take a quick look."

"Dad, it's Sam's weekend off," Leah argued. "He didn't come here so you could put him to work on one of your projects."

"That's okay, sweetheart. I don't mind looking at something for my future father-in-law. It's not a problem. Besides, you're the one who always say there's nothing sexier than a man who knows how to use his hands." He smacked her on the ass, and she let out a surprised yelp. "Lead the way, Bill."

Her dad walked into an office attached to the living room so Sam quickly followed. It was either that or stand there with a red-faced, pissed-off Leah glaring at him like she wanted to drive nails into every orifice in his body.

Bill pulled up the pictures on his cell phone and handed it to Sam. From what Sam could tell in the photos, the glass patio door connected to a large deck overlooking a flower garden. When Bill handed him a notepad with the measurements of both doors, Sam glanced over them and then flipped to a blank page to jot down some notes and figure out what it would take to remodel the door frame.

Leah joined them in the office a moment later and leaned

against the mahogany desk with her arms crossed. Apparently she still wasn't amused with the slap on the rear he had given her.

After a few minutes, Sam dropped the pen and handed the notepad to her father. "Here's my bid for the job. If you want it done sooner than next week though, I'll have to add in some overtime for my crew."

Bill blinked at him in surprise. "Wait. You're charging me to remodel the door?"

"Of course I am," Sam said with a firm nod. "It's not like I need the practice."

"But... but we're practically family."

Sam shrugged. "Family or not, I still get paid for the work I do. Well, except for the things I do for your daughter. But she pays me in other ways, if you know what I mean." He grinned, then waggled his brows suggestively. "Besides, Leah will vouch for me. I'm damn good at what I do, and satisfaction is *always* guaranteed." He glanced at Leah. "Isn't that right, baby?"

Her eyes widened, and she silently mouthed, "Oh. My. God." She ran a hand over her red face and shook her head in disbelief. The poor girl obviously hadn't been prepared for him to make sexual remarks about her, especially to her own father. And her dad didn't seem to know how to respond any more than she did.

Sam figured Bill would chastise him about the rude comment or possibly throw him out of the house on his ass. What he hadn't predicted was for the man to rub at his chin as if he were in deep thought and then smile. "You know, son, I appreciate a man who takes pride in his work and has confidence to spare. You seem like a bright, levelheaded businessman. Tell you what I'll do. Give me ten percent off on the labor, and I'll put in a good word for you with my neighbors who are looking for someone to remodel their pool house."

Fuck.

He hadn't expected Leah's father to counter his fake bid…even if it had been a fair one he'd drawn up. He'd never turned down work in his life, but he had no doubt Leah would kill him if he accepted the offer. *Oh, hell. She's probably going to kill me before the weekend's through anyway.*

Sam passed Bill one of his business cards and shook his hand. "You got a deal. Just give me a call when you're ready to get started on it."

Across the room, Leah cleared her throat in an obnoxious, unmistakable *what the hell do you think you're doing* kind of way. But he ignored it and refused to let his gaze meet hers.

"You okay, Leah?" her dad asked, concern tinging his voice.

"I, um…Yeah, I'm fine."

Sam snorted. "Oh, calm down, Bill. Of course she's okay. It's not like she's pregnant or anything."

Leah and her father both blinked rapidly but didn't say a word.

Gazing at Leah, Sam let his mouth drop open. "Wait. You *are* on the pill, aren't you?"

Her hands clenched at her sides. "Um, Sam," Leah said, her voice strained with irritation. "Maybe we should get our bags out of the truck. Like *now*." Then she marched out of the room.

Shit.

Chapter Ten

Leah shook her head. She had to have heard him wrong.

My God. Why would he say something like that in front of her father? She closed her eyes and took a deep breath as she waited out on the deck for him to join her. This was not at all how she had expected this weekend to begin.

She was still trying to figure out how he'd convinced her father to pay almost full price for his services. That man was frugal, to say the least, and never paid for anything he couldn't get for half off the regular price.

But that hadn't even been the worst of it. Him asking her about birth control in front of her dad definitely took some balls. Big ones that, at the moment, she would love to crush under her heel. *He's acting like such a douche.*

Okay, so obviously that was the point. Sam was normally an extremely likable guy. How the hell else was he supposed to make her family hate him? But did he have to do it in such a way that it embarrassed *her?*

He finally appeared at her side. "Ready to get our bags, love muffin?"

"Sam."

"What?" he asked innocently. He dropped an arm over her shoulders and pressed his face into her hair, as if he were nuzzling her neck. His voice lowered. "Your father is watching us from the window."

"Oh." Sighing, Leah moved quickly toward the stairs. Once they made it to the bottom, where the truck was parked in the shade under the beach house, she opened the door and reached inside for her bag.

"I've got it," Sam said, nudging her out of the way and grabbing both of their duffel bags from the backseat. Then he turned to face her and glanced around, as if making sure no one else was around to hear him. "We probably should've talked about this sooner, but about these sleeping arrangements..."

"What about them?"

"I'm just wondering if I need to sleep with one eye open."

Leah smirked. "After the things you said in front of my father, I'd say you might want to at least lock the door so he doesn't castrate you in your sleep."

"Actually, I was more worried about *you*."

"Me?"

"Well, yeah. If we're going to be sleeping together..."

Leah blinked at him as warmth pooled in her stomach. "W-what are you talking about? Why would we be sleeping together?"

Confusion warped his features. "When your mom mentioned hooking you up with Chad Howard during the reception, she said you would have a roommate. I guess I just assumed she meant—"

"You thought my mom was going to have me bunking with the building inspector?" A giggle escaped her lips. "No, of course not. My mom was referring to my brother, Ethan."

"You're going to sleep with your brother? I can't say that's any better."

"We normally have our own rooms when we come to visit, but since we have an extra guest, we'll have to change it up. You can take my room, and I'll sleep in Ethan's room. There's bunk beds in there."

Sam heaved out a quick breath, and his mouth softened with something that looked very much like relief. "I have no problem rooming with your brother and letting you keep your own bed."

"Oh, so now *you* want to sleep with my brother?" She grinned and then measured him with her eyes. "Sam, you're at least a foot longer than I am. You won't fit in a twin bed."

"It's fine. I'll take the bunk bed."

"Don't be silly. I'm sharing the room with my little brother. It's my family so it's my call. End of discussion."

He hesitated but nodded in acknowledgment. "Okay, fine. I guess I'm safe then."

"For now."

Sam chuckled and let his gaze wander over the surrounding area, then his eyes stopped on the trail that snaked between the sand dunes. A long boardwalk covered in sun-bleached wood planks led straight onto her grandparents' property. "So this is where your grandparents live year-round, huh?"

Leah started back up the stairs with Sam trailing behind her, bags in hand. "Yep. When I was younger, they owned a condominium—the one I told you about—and I would sometimes stay with them during the summer. They hated sharing the beach with all the tourists though so they sold it and bought this instead. They like their privacy. There are still people around, but not as many tourists come this far down the beach."

"It's nice," Sam said, glancing at the ocean as they reached the upper deck. "The water seems awfully close to the house though. I bet their hurricane insurance premium is a bitch."

Leah laughed. Only a building contractor would take in this gorgeous ocean view and think about insurance claims. "No doubt."

The front door opened, and her dad poked his head out. "Leah, your grandma is asking how much longer you two are going to be out here. She said she wants to meet your fiancé before she dies of old age." Then he winked at them.

"William Martin, I did not say any such thing!" a woman squawked from behind him.

Leah giggled and started for the door. "We're coming, Grandma."

As they entered, Leah noted her grandparents standing in the living room together, waiting patiently to meet Sam. Her grandma wore cream-colored linen pants and a burgundy blouse, and her white hair had been styled into a pretty bob. Her grandpa was dressed in dark polyester pants and a blue button-down shirt with a white cap on his head bearing a fishing logo. They were both smiling.

She gave them both a hug and turned to Sam as he set their bags down by the front door. "Sam," she said, motioning to the elderly couple next to her, "these are my grandparents, Jack and Penny Martin."

Sam stepped forward and shook Penny's hand first. "Nice to meet you, Penny. Heard a lot about you."

Leah bit her bottom lip. *Not really, but he must've thought it sounded good.*

"We're so happy you're joining us this weekend," her grandma told Sam, her voice as sweet and sincere as always. "Please feel free to make yourself at home. If you need anything, all you have to do is ask."

"Thanks," Sam said, nodding.

Leah's grandfather held out his hand to Sam. "Glad to meet you."

Sam gazed at the outstretched hand, but didn't accept it. "Jack, did you wash that hand before you came out of the bathroom?" he asked seriously.

The room fell silent. After a few seconds, her grandpa barked out a laugh and squeezed Sam's shoulder. "Good one, son."

Sam grinned and gestured to his surroundings. "Great place you have here. When Leah told me we were staying at her grandparents' beach house, I pictured a small bungalow on the water. But this place is a lot bigger and a bit fancier than I imagined." He wrapped his hand around Leah's waist and yanked her to his side. "Guess I hit the jackpot by choosing to marry this one."

Leah gritted her teeth. "Oh, stop it," she said, swatting at him playfully. Then she turned her attention back to her family. "Don't mind him. Sam's just kidding. He does that a lot."

"A good sense of humor is never a bad thing," her dad said, observing from the sidelines. "Shows that the man has some character and keeps things interesting. Does wonders for a long marriage." The quick glance he gave his wife didn't go unnoticed. By Leah or her mother.

What the heck is that all about? But Leah didn't have time to focus on that right now. She had too many other things to worry about at the moment. And most of that had to do with whatever the hell would come out of Sam's mouth next.

"Why don't I help you get settled in?" Leah's grandma said, motioning to the two overnight bags he'd set on the floor. "If you two will grab those and follow me, I'll show you where you'll be sleeping. And I hope you brought your appetite with you, Sam. Dinner will be ready soon, though you have plenty of time to freshen up if you'd like."

"Sounds good," Sam replied.

Leah stepped toward the bags, but Sam snatched both of them up from the floor before she could grab hers. They started to follow her grandma to the hallway, but Leah's grandfather put a firm hand on Sam's shoulder to stop his motion. "Sam, have you ever had crabs before?"

Sam grinned. "Well, Jack, I guess that depends on what kind of crabs we're talking about," he said, giving him a vulgar wink.

Leah felt the air back up into her lungs as she waited for her grandpa's response. Sam was obviously trying to shock the old man into having a reaction, but he didn't get the one he was probably shooting for. Nor one she expected.

Her grandpa chuckled and offered Sam a friendly slap on the back. "Yep, you'll do. Welcome to the family, son."

Still smiling, Sam continued toward the hallway where her grandmother waited for them. Leah walked fast and caught up with them just as her grandma swung open the bedroom doors to the room Leah had always used.

She loved sleeping in there.

Not only was there a connecting bathroom to the right of the entrance, but the décor was much more Leah's style.

There were some simple touches of beach nostalgia, but the room had more of a homey feel than any other bedroom in the house. Probably had something to do with the antique poster bed and the matching mule chest standing proudly in the corner. Her grandmother had owned both of them for as long as Leah could remember.

Her grandmother smiled. "Here you go, Sam. I put fresh sheets on the bed, and there are plenty of clean towels in the bathroom."

"Thanks. I appreciate it." Sam stepped inside and let his gaze wander aimlessly around the room, but then his eyes seemed to snag on something. He set their bags down on the old-fashioned quilt covering the bed and ran his hand along the smooth, polished surface of the wood's grain. His eyes widened. "Holy shit! Is this tiger maple?"

"It is," Leah's grandma said, her face brightening. "Why, how did you know?"

"My own grandmother used to have a bookshelf made out of this very wood. She wouldn't let us anywhere near it though. Said it was really old and expensive."

"Well, that's because it is. But this bed has been in my family for generations, and it was meant to be slept in. Especially by the handsome young man who is marrying my granddaughter. And who knows? If I get a great-grandchild out of you two sometime before I die of old age, I might even gift it to you in my will," she said with a wink.

Leah's head snapped to her. "Grandma! You can't rush us into having kids by bribing my fiancé with old bedroom furniture."

"I can if it works."

Leah laughed, but Sam didn't look amused. If anything, he looked uncomfortable as hell. She walked over and lifted her bag from the bed. "Um, I guess I'll just take my stuff to Ethan's room and get settled in."

"Oh, no." Penny shook her head adamantly. "I wouldn't dream of separating you from your fiancé. Leah, you'll be staying in here with Sam."

Leah's heart pounded against her rib cage so hard that her teeth chattered. "B-but...but..."

"No buts about it. Your grandfather and I are not so old-fashioned that we'd separate a couple who are in love and about to be married. Besides, this way, you won't have to sneak into Sam's room later tonight. I know how wild and crazy two young lovers can be."

Sam's brows gathered over his eyes as he glanced back at the full-size bed. Leah cringed, knowing what he must be thinking. *The bed suddenly seems a lot smaller than it had a few seconds before.*

The moment her grandmother left the room and shut the door behind her, Leah cleared her throat. "Um, I had no clue she would do that. I'm sorry. I can just sleep on the floor or something."

Sam gave her a withering look and pulled her bag from her hand, setting it back on the bed. "You're *not* sleeping on the floor. If either of us were to do that, then it would be me. But we're both adults here. There's no reason why we can't just share the bed. It will look more legitimate if any-one comes in while we're sleeping anyway."

"Are you sure? I mean, I tend to take up a lot of room. I'm...bulky." She grinned to show him she was teasing.

"I really wish you'd stop saying shit like that about your-self. I'm bigger than you and going to take up way more room than you ever would. Chances are, you're going to feel like we're sleeping in bunk beds...with you on top."

Liquid heat trickled down her spine and swirled in her

abdomen. "Well, I was just trying to make the whole situation less awkward for you." And for her. Because no way was she going to get much sleep with Sam lying next to her for two nights.

He shook his head. "I don't know why you think sharing a bed with you would make me uncomfortable. It's fine. Doesn't bother me at all."

Of course it doesn't. *Because he isn't the least bit attracted to me.* She sighed inwardly and tried to keep her tone even. "Okay then. Do you want to freshen up before dinner? If so, the bathroom is right through that door."

"No, that's all right. I only worked a few hours this morning to finish up a job, but since I had sawdust all over me, I took a shower before I picked you up. I'm good."

"Well, then I guess it's time to go back out and face the firing squad."

* * *

Sam and Leah left their bags behind, and he followed her down the hall toward the living room, where he spotted her grandfather sitting alone on the couch.

Leah glanced out the window at the sprawling deck. "Where are the others, Grandpa?"

The man never looked up from the television, where audience members clapped wildly in the background. "They're downstairs layering the picnic table with butcher paper. As soon as they're done with it, we'll go down and eat. If you two want to give them a hand, we can eat sooner."

"Oh, hell no," Sam said, plopping down on the sofa next to Leah's grandfather. "I'm on vacation. The only thing I'm doing this weekend is relaxing."

Sam's crass tone had Leah cringing, but he ignored it and

stretched out his long legs, kicking one booted foot over the other. He was just warming up for the show he planned to put on for her family.

"Well, don't get too comfortable," Jack said, smiling. "Otherwise, I'll never get rid of you."

Sam chuckled. "What are you watching? Some kind of trivia game show?"

The old man stared at him for a moment before replying cynically, "About the only thing the government doesn't try to stop me from doing nowadays."

The well-dressed announcer on the television straightened his tie and began the next question. "What was the name of Roy Rogers' horse? Was it Warrior, Trigger, or Hercules?"

"Hercules," Jack stated, sounding sure of himself.

Sam shook his head. "No. Actually, it was Trigger."

Grandpa's brows hunched over his eyes as he shot Sam a perturbed look. "Yep, that's exactly what I said."

Puzzled, Sam glanced to Leah and slanted his brows in question. She grinned and bit her lip, as if she were trying to swallow a giggle but said nothing.

A contestant hit the buzzer and answered, "Trigger."

The announcer nodded. "Correct!"

Grandpa's fist pumped the air, as if the old man had answered the question correctly, and Sam let out a hearty laugh. Apparently, Leah's grandfather had some issues with his memory. Or maybe he just didn't like to be wrong.

Bill entered through the front door, followed by Nancy and Penny. "Dinner's ready." He looked straight at Jack. "Dad, why don't you give me a hand carrying down the pot?"

Jack shook his head. "I'm on vacation."

Nancy stopped in her tracks. "Jack."

"Ah, hell. All right." Jack rose to his feet and glanced at Sam. "I don't know how that shit works for you. You'll have to tell me your trick."

Sam shrugged. "A magician never gives away his secrets."

"Asshole," Jack said playfully, then grinned as he headed for the kitchen.

Moments later, Jack and Bill passed through the living room again, an oven mitt on each hand and wielding an oversized pot billowing with steam. Leah's dad said, "Sam, if you're not downstairs in the next five minutes, you'll starve to death."

Penny followed behind them, carrying a tray of condiments, rolls of paper towels, and various other items. She swatted her son's arm, then glanced at Sam. "Don't listen to him. There's plenty to go around. I wouldn't dream of letting you go hungry." She smiled at him before waltzing out the door and shutting it behind her.

Sam grinned. He sort of liked the idea that the women in Leah's family wanted to keep him well fed. Nothing to complain about there.

He couldn't help but like both of Leah's grandparents. They seemed like great folks. Not only welcoming, but they were funny and made him laugh, which immediately put him at ease. But guilt loitered in his stomach, knowing that over the weekend he would probably be doing and saying things they weren't going to approve of.

And Penny's earlier comment still stuck in his craw. This whole thing was supposed to be a harmless hoax. He'd never set out to trick a nice old woman into believing she'd have great-grandchildren on the way someday soon. Having kids with anyone was the last thing on his mind.

Nancy came out of the kitchen carrying a glass of wine. "Leah, can you bring down the basket of bread on the counter? Also, would you be a dear and ask your brother to join us for dinner, please?"

"Sure. Where is he?"

"He's been holed up in his room playing games on that phone of his all afternoon. I swear he hardly ever puts it down anymore."

Leah walked over to the hallway and shouted, "*Ethan, dinner!*"

Her mother was almost to the front door when she paused mid-stride. "My goodness, Leah, I could have done that. Would it have killed you to walk down the hallway to get him? It's not like a little exercise would've hurt you any." Then she shook her head and continued outside.

Leah glanced over at Sam, obviously checking to see if he'd overheard her mother's shitty remark. Not only had he heard it, but he hadn't liked it one bit. He couldn't stop the irritation from bubbling up inside him and twisting his features into a scowl.

No doubt Leah recognized it for what it was because she wasted no time in heading to the kitchen. Sam rose and followed her. But just as he opened his mouth to speak, Leah's teenage brother barreled around the corner. His hair was gelled and combed to the side, and he wore a pair of khaki shorts and a tucked-in red polo shirt.

"Long time no visit, sis," the kid said sarcastically, grabbing a handful of grapes from the fridge and popping one into his mouth. "You're still short, I see."

"And you're still a dipshit," Leah said, making Sam grin. Her brother may have passed her in the height department, but she apparently wasn't about to let him forget the pecking order in which they were born.

Sam held out his hand to her brother. "Hi, I'm Sam, the fiancé."

Ethan shook his hand, then gestured over to his sister, while chuckling. "Hope you know what you're getting into with this one. I've seen her diary. Practically fell asleep while reading it."

"Yeah, like you know how to read?" she said, flicking his ear. "Besides, this comes from the nineteen-year-old who still wears what his mommy picks out."

Ethan glared at her. "Hey, I told Mom I didn't want to wear this stupid shirt."

"Nothing wrong with the shirt," Sam said casually. "If you like pink."

"Pink?" Ethan's brows lowered over his eyes, and his face grew serious. "My mom said this shirt was red when we bought it."

Leah gave Sam a strange look, as if she wasn't sure what he was talking about either. Because the shirt was definitely red. But Sam wasn't about to tell her brother that. He winked at Leah, and her eyes widened before she clamped her teeth down on her bottom lip to keep from laughing. Apparently, she found it humorous that he was trying to trick her color-blind brother into believing he was wearing pink.

"Hmm. Well, that's the lightest shade of red I've ever seen," Sam told him, shrugging. "But don't worry about it, kid. You look good in pastels."

"Uh-uh. No freakin' way," Ethan said, storming toward the hallway. "I'm changing my clothes. There's no way in hell I'm wearing a pink shirt. Ever."

Once Ethan left the room, neither of them could hold back the laughter.

"Oh my God. I can't believe you just did that to my little brother. You've probably just scarred him for life."

"Well, if you loved that, wait until you see what else I have in store for the rest of your family," Sam said with a chuckle.

She stopped laughing, and her face turned serious. "Sam, about that..."

The front door swung open, and Bill's voice rang out, "Hey, lovebirds, you two coming down or what? It's time to eat."

Leah picked up the bread basket and sighed. "We're coming, Dad."

Chapter Eleven

Leah motioned for Sam to follow her and led him downstairs to the large picnic table in the backyard, where her father and her grandpa unceremoniously dumped the contents of the pot onto the white butcher paper. A mound of piping hot crab, whole shrimp, spicy sausage, small red potatoes, and half ears of corn tumbled out, all adorned with the special Cajun seasoning her Grandma used. The smell hit her nostrils, and Leah's mouth watered.

Friday night dinner at her grandparents' place was easily one of her favorite things about their annual trip. Not only was it a great tradition and the food delicious, but it was the only time she ever got to witness her mother eating with her bare hands...and actually enjoying herself. She set the bread basket on the end of the table.

Sam stood beside her, looking a little confused.

"I take it you've never had the pleasure of a backyard crab boil before?" Leah asked, eyeing his face.

He shook his head. "No, but there's a first time for everything, I guess."

Ethan barreled down the stairs wearing a blue shirt as everyone took their seats. Dad asked Sam to reach into the red chest next to him and pass out the beers he'd already iced down. Sam did, handing them out across the table, one by one. When her brother held his hand out, Sam shoved a can of soda into his palm. "Sorry, kid. You've still got a few years to go before I pass you a beer."

Ethan groaned and rolled his eyes.

Her dad grinned admiringly at Sam, the man he thought of as his future son-in-law, and sadness tugged at Leah's heart. Not only because her father wasn't aware that Sam would never be her husband, or his son-in-law, but because she had no doubt Sam would have made a damn good one. On both counts.

Grandma placed a bucket of mini wooden mallets on the other end of the table and then passed out small serving dishes with lemon wedges and a trio of dipping sauces—melted butter, horse radish, and cocktail sauce—to each person. She even had ketchup for Ethan…because he was weird like that.

"Okay, since I don't see any plates or silverware," Sam said, confusion tainting his voice, "you're going to have to tell me the secret. How do we eat this?"

Leah held up both hands and wiggled her fingers. "You already have most of the utensils you need. The wooden hammers are for breaking open the crab shells."

"So basically I have to work for my dinner?" A grin stretched across his face, as if he were a child and the idea of playing with his food delighted him. "Or is this one of those 'fight to your death to see who gets the last crab' sort of things?"

"Bingo," Leah said, making the others laugh. "But I should probably warn you. I *always* get the last crab."

"Oh yeah? We'll see about that. You must have forgotten who swings a hammer for a living," he said, his eyes gleaming with a competitive streak. Sam grabbed a wooden utensil and began digging in.

"Oh, um, Sam. My grandma likes to say grace before we eat."

"Grace," Sam said loudly, then continued to eat. The shit-eating grin he wore wasn't lost on her though. He knew damn well what he was doing.

Leah leaned over to him and jabbed her elbow into his ribs, though she tried to pass it off as an accident. "Oops, sorry," she said as he winced and set down the wooden mallet. Then she turned to her family and smiled sweetly. "Go ahead, Grandma."

After the moment of prayer and bowed heads passed, her dad cleared his throat. "So, Sam, how did you get into the construction business?"

"My father, actually. He was a general contractor so I guess you can say it's in my blood. I started in his company when I was eighteen and worked my way up from flunky to crew leader to job foreman. He taught me everything I know. Then when he retired a few years ago, I took over the business."

"Ah, I see. Another Bank of Dad situation, huh?" Her dad winked playfully at his daughter.

Sam's brows furrowed in confusion, and Leah giggled. "I only had half the money to put down on the bakery," she explained, then took a sip of her beer. "My dad loaned me the other half. His zero percent interest rate is much better than the bank's, which makes him my favorite loan shark. He lets me keep my knee caps and everything."

His lips twitched, threatening to erupt into a smile.

"Actually, sir," Sam said, addressing her father, "after my parents retired, I moved here from Dallas and took over my dad's business only in name. He didn't bankroll my company. I'm the sole owner, but I wanted to carry on the name of his company...in his honor."

"Ah, I see. I'm sure that made him very proud," her dad said, nodding his approval. "Do your parents still live in the Dallas area?"

"No, sir. They moved to Crystal River, Florida, where my mom spends her days volunteering at a children's hospital and my old man spends most of his time teaching free wood-shop classes at a local college."

What the fuck? Leah elbowed him in the ribs. Hard.

Sam coughed and wheezed out, "Actually, I think my dad, uh...charges for those classes. He's a...selfish bastard like that."

"No, no. Not at all," her dad said, shaking his head. "Your old man should get paid for teaching a valuable skill. I think what they're doing is wonderful. They sound like great folks. Too bad they don't live a little closer. I'd love to meet them one day."

Her mother cut in. "Oh! Before the wedding perhaps?"

"Sure," Sam said confidently, then everyone went back to quietly eating their meal.

Whew! Okay, that wasn't so bad. Leah relaxed her posture and folded her hands in her lap.

Her mother smiled at them. "What are your parents' names, Sam?"

"David and Sharon Cooper. What do you want next—their social security numbers and blood types?"

"Oh, goodness no. I was just thinking I should probably get your mother's phone number from you and give her a call. With a wedding to plan, we have a lot of things to discuss."

Sam didn't hesitate with his answer. "Sorry, Nancy. That's not going to happen."

Leah's right hand shot out and latched on to his leg under the picnic table. *What the hell is he doing?* "Actually, Mom, what he means is—"

"What I mean is..." His warm hand closed over Leah's, squeezing and rubbing lightly, though his gaze never left her mom's face. "I haven't yet shared the news of our pending nuptials with my family. I would hate for you to ruin the surprise before I have a chance to tell them."

Her mother nodded. "Oh, I see. Well, we definitely wouldn't want that." She smiled at him. "When do you think you'll be able to let them in on the good news?"

Sam glanced at Leah and grinned mischievously. "Oh, I'd say in about two weeks."

"Two weeks? That's a long time to wait before you share your engagement news. They must be really busy if you don't speak to them very often."

Sam winced, as if he hadn't thought of that particular angle. "I, uh...well, I wanted to tell them in person. I'm hoping to make a surprise visit in...two weeks."

"That's sweet," Grandma said. "Leah, will you be going with him?"

Leah glanced at Sam. "Um, no. I have to work that weekend since I took this weekend off. I guess I don't know when I'll get to meet them."

"Oh, that's too bad," her mother said, then turned her attention back to Sam. "Well, please let me know when you tell them. I'd like to give your mother a call afterward. I'm sure your mother will be as excited as we—" She lowered her gaze and gasped. "Leah! Oh, my goodness, why aren't you wearing an engagement ring? Did you lose it?"

Leah tensed and glanced to the ring finger on her left

hand. "Um, no. It…didn't fit," she said quickly, panicking that they'd forgotten something as important as a ring. Of course her mother would notice something like that. "I…er, *we* had to send it off to get it resized. I should have it back in…about two weeks."

That's the best I could come up with? Jeez. I'm as bad as him.

"Oh, dear. That's too bad. I would love to have seen it on your hand. You know, if you lost a little weight, it would probably fit."

Leah cringed and swallowed the lump forming in her throat.

"Actually, it was all my fault," Sam said, shaking his head. "For a guy who measures shit for a living, you'd think I wouldn't have screwed that part up."

Her father gave Sam a firm pat on the shoulder. "Aw, hell, don't worry about it, son. An engagement ring isn't nearly as important as the person who's wearing it."

"You got that right, Bill." He grabbed Leah's hand, which was sitting on top of the table this time, and squeezed it again. "And I think the world of your daughter. She's an amazing girl with a great personality."

If that wasn't the worst compliment a guy could give a fat girl, then Leah didn't know what was. Next he'd be telling her parents how he met her in the bar.

"So how did the two of you meet, Sam?" her mother asked.

Damn. Leah tried to intervene. "We met at a—"

"Honey, don't interrupt. It's rude. I was talking to Sam."

Crap.

He must've seen the worry flash across Leah's face because he slid his arm around her shoulders and shook her a little. "It's okay, sweetheart. Believe it or not, I *do* remember how we first met." Then he smiled wide, and she knew exactly what he was about to say.

Abort! Abort!

"I met my bride-to-be at a bar," Sam said proudly. "Rusty's Bucket actually."

Well, shit.

A muted sigh came from the end of the picnic table where her mother sat glaring at her. "Leah, I really wish you wouldn't go into that horrid place. I've told you it's filled with hooligans. Just recently, I heard a man started a fight in there and knocked another guy out cold."

"Guilty as charged," Sam said, chuckling at her mother's dismay. "But in my defense, the bastard deserved it after the things he said to your—um, my woman."

Her grandfather beamed and slapped Sam on the back, as if he were pinning him with a badge of honor. "If you were defending my granddaughter, then I say there's no better reason to get into a pissing match with another man. Good for you, son."

Sam took a swig of his beer, then set it down. "Well, I wasn't about to let that guy run us out of there. We like to go down to Rusty's Bucket once in a while since that's where I pick up most of my women. Didn't Leah tell you we planned to have an open marriage?"

So many things happened at once.

Ethan choked on a shrimp. Her grandparents' eyes widened in distress. Leah swayed in stunned silence as the crab fell out of her hands and thudded onto the table in front of her. Mom's slim hand flew to her heaving chest, gasping in shock. Her mouth dropped open, and her painted lips formed a perfect O as air wheezed in and out of her, as if she couldn't breathe.

Jesus. She's hyperventilating. Leah jumped up and

furiously fanned her mother with a paper towel. "Mom? Mom, are you okay?"

Slack-jawed and unable to speak, her dad stayed in his seat, scowling at a grinning Sam as if he were about to maim him or kill him...or possibly both. But after a moment passed, a huge grin spread on her dad's face, and he burst into hysterics. "You sonofagun! For a second there, you almost had me." Then he chuckled some more until tears of laughter welled up in his eyes.

Sam glanced at Leah, then back to her father. "Well, Bill, I tried to keep a straight face, but you were much quicker than I gave you credit for."

Her mom recovered a little, but still panted heavily. "You mean, it was a...a joke?"

"Of course it was, Nancy," Sam replied, fake-chuckling. "I wouldn't have taken it so far though, if I had known you were going to turn into a fainting goat with cocksucker's cramp."

Oh, fuck me. Leah groaned and shook her head. This whole situation was getting way out of hand. "Okay, that's it. This has gone far enough."

Sam's head snapped to her. "Leah..."

But she couldn't bear it any longer. "Mom, Dad, I have something I need to tell you."

*   *   *

Sam couldn't let her do it.

Leah was going to tell her family the truth about their fake engagement and would then suffer through the consequences just to put an end to it all. Uh-uh. No fucking way. He got her into this mess, and he was damn sure going to get her out of it without causing her any more embarrassment... at least the kind that came with admitting they'd faked the entire engagement thing.

He shot out of his seat and snatched her up by the arm, dragging her away from the table before she could say another word. "We'll be right back," he called over his shoulder. "I need a minute alone with my fiancée."

Leah tried to dig her heels in, but Sam overpowered her. She stumbled behind him as he yanked her upstairs and into the house. He didn't stop moving until they reached their bedroom, where he quickly slammed the door behind them. Only then did he allow her to shake his hand off her wrist. "No, damn it. Don't do it."

She heaved out a large breath. "I have to, Sam."

"Why? Because you feel guilty?"

"Of course I do. Don't you?"

He shrugged and a grin tugged at his mouth. "Not particularly."

She glared at him. "Bullshit. If that's true, then why did you back down from the open marriage bit you fed them? You could have let them keep on believing it, rather than telling my dad you were joking, but you didn't."

"That wasn't my fault. I would have let them keep believing it, but your mother practically died on me out there. I couldn't keep it going after that, not without a defibrillator handy. So when your father assumed I was kidding, I just went with it. Sonofabitch, Leah, I only meant to shock the woman, not kill her."

"Jesus. This whole thing has gotten ridiculous. We need to call it off!"

He shook his head. "Look, I know you feel bad about tricking them, but you don't have to tell them the truth. It's only two weeks."

"Damn it, Sam. I can't do this anymore. I thought I could,

but I was wrong." Leah paced the room in small circles. "We shouldn't be doing this anyway. It isn't fair."

"Oh, give me a break. They'll be fine. They won't ever know the truth."

Leah stopped pacing and gazed up at him. "I wasn't talking about them. Yes, I feel bad that I'm lying to my family, but that's not what I meant."

"Is it because I told them the truth about my parents?"

"What? No. I mean, it would have been better if you had told them your mom was a drugged-out whore and your father was doing hard time for murder. But that's not what I'm talking about." She ran a shaky hand through her hair, then gazed up at him with glassy eyes. "This isn't at all fair to *you*. They're going to think you're this horrible person, all because you're…h-helping me." Her voice cracked under the stress of the situation.

"Hey, don't cry," he said softly. When she covered her face with her hands, he gathered her into his arms and pulled her into his chest. "It's all going to be okay, I promise. This was all my fault. I shouldn't have put you in this position to begin with."

She sniffled as her hands traveled up his back, wrapping around his shoulders. "I don't want to lie to them anymore." Her strained voice warbled. "I…I can't deceive them like this for two weeks. I just can't."

Leah shivered against him, and his stomach twisted into a knot. *Damn it.* He hated that she was so distraught and wanted to relieve her of the burden he'd placed on her.

He held her tightly against him for a moment longer, then pulled back just enough until he could see her puffy face. "Leah, if you want me to go back out there and call my mother a whore, I will."

Though her eyes were still red and watery, the corners of

her mouth lifted slightly in amusement. "I don't think that will be necessary."

"Thank God," he replied, breathing a huge sigh of relief. "Pretend or not, I don't think I could have actually done it. My mother is a great lady. You'll love her. I mean, you would...if you were meeting her...which you aren't." *Christ. Could I sound like more of a insensitive dumbass?*

As if he'd made her uncomfortable, Leah pulled out of his arms and moved away. "What are we going to do, Sam?"

He thought for a moment. "Okay, I have an idea. How about we end the engagement this weekend?"

Her brows drew together in confusion. "What do you mean?"

"We were almost home free anyway. If you hadn't said anything, your dad probably would have already been throwing me out on my ass for talking to your mother the way I did. So why don't we up the timeline?" A smiled played on his lips. "Instead of two weeks, give me until the end of the weekend. By then, your family will be begging you to dump me."

Fear flashed in her eyes. "W-what are you going to do?" she asking, wringing her trembling hands together.

"Let me worry about that. All I need you to do is to go back out there with a smile on your face."

She shifted nervously and chewed on her bottom lip. "Sam, I don't think I can."

A knock sounded on the door, and Leah squeaked. Sam placed his finger against her lips to silence her.

"You kids okay in there?" her father asked, his voice gruff.

"We're busy, Bill. Give us a minute, would ya?" Sam's impatient tone proved effective because, seconds later, he heard the sound of her dad's retreating footsteps. He dropped his hand from Leah's mouth.

"Oh, man. That was so rude," Leah whispered, holding her palm against her stomach, as if she were suddenly feeling ill. "Do you think they know something is up?"

"No, they don't know anything. And yes, my comment was rude...because they aren't supposed to like me, remember? Isn't that the goal here?"

"I know, but...God, I hate this." She fidgeted with the hem of her top and sighed. "We're going to hell. You know that, right?"

"Well, at least we'll have each other when we get there." Sam smiled to let her know he was teasing and then motioned to the door. "As soon as you're ready to face your parents again, we'll go back out."

Leah took a deep breath, wiped her fingers beneath her damp lashes, and then straightened her posture. "How's this?"

He admired her willingness, especially since he knew she was still upset, but there was no way she could walk out there in her current state. Her face was pale, her hands shook uncontrollably, and her eyes were swollen. She definitely looked like she'd been crying...which she had. "You can't go out there yet. They're going to know something is wrong."

Leah covered her face. "Oh God. I'm ruining everything, aren't I?"

"Relax. It's fine," he told her, though nothing he said seemed to help.

She shook her head furiously. "Jesus. They're going to see right through me when I go back out there. They're going to realize something is wrong, then we're going to have to come clean anyway, aren't we? This can't be happening. What do we do, Sam?"

Well, for starters, he needed her to calm down right-the-fuck now, but she only continued working herself up more. He didn't even have time to answer her questions before she started flipping her lid again.

"Christ, why did I say anything? They're probably going to ask me what I wanted to tell them. Damn it. Why did I have to open my big, fat, stupid—"

His hand shot out and whipped her around so fast that her eyes widened. She nearly lost her balance, but he yanked her against his chest to steady her. Then, hoping to snap her out of her panic-induced state, he did the only thing he could think of. He pressed his lips firmly against hers and kissed the shit out of her.

She stiffened instantly, and her hands clutched at his shoulders. But as his mouth moved against hers, inviting her to participate, she relaxed her grip and allowed the tension in her body to melt away. Unfortunately, he couldn't say the same for himself.

With anyone else, a distraction like that might have been a good idea. But with Leah, he hadn't considered the side effect she would have on him in return. And it damn sure wasn't a small one.

The moment her tongue touched his, desire blazed through him, and a guttural moan sounded in his throat. The woman tasted as sweet as sugar, and just like any other decadent dessert that had ever passed his lips, he couldn't get enough of her.

His arms banded tighter around her, pulling her closer, as he fed his craving. He licked every inch of her sexy mouth, tasting her erotic saccharine flavor. The warmth of her hot body permeated his clothes, seared his skin, and heated his blood. A pleasurable ache hit him low and deep, and his rapidly hardening length collided against the seam of his jeans like a battering ram.

Whoa! What the hell are you doing, Sam?

But he ignored the nagging voice inside his head. He wanted Leah. Badly. Probably more than anything he'd ever wanted in his life. And he wasn't about to put a stop to anything involving her lips on his.

Quit kissing her, dipshit. You're only making things worse.

Persistent little fucker. "Shut up," he whispered to the irritating voice.

Leah pulled back and stared at him. "W-what did you say?"

"Nothing," he said, quickly pulling her mouth back to his.

Once again, Leah went limp in his arms, allowing the renewed tension to evaporate and surrendering to the sensations swirling between them. He could take her right here, right now—and probably would have—if they weren't . . . standing in a guestroom . . . inside her grandparents' home.

Yep, that's what I was trying to tell you, idiot.

Fuck.

After one final sampling of her lips, Sam relented to his subconscious and tore his mouth from hers. It took a hell of a lot more willpower than he thought it would. His heart beat wildly in his chest, but he sucked in a ragged breath to slow his pulse rate.

Leah stumbled back and gazed up at him with confusion flickering in her glazed green eyes. "W-why did you kiss me just now? There wasn't anyone here to see it."

"I needed you to calm down."

"Oh." Her cheeks glowed a vibrant shade of red. She lowered her head and turned away from him. "Right. I understand."

Sonofabitch. He'd given her the primary motive for the kiss, which was the truth. But what he hadn't told her was that he'd *wanted* to kiss her. Hell, even now, he could still taste her sweetness on his lips, which only made him want to do it again. Because no matter the original reason for the kiss, locking lips with her was definitely not a hardship.

"Leah..."

"We should get back before my dad comes looking for us again." She waltzed past him, opened the door, and walked out, not bothering to wait for him.

Chapter Twelve

God, Leah felt like a moron.

From day one, Sam had made it perfectly clear he wasn't the least bit attracted to her. Not only that, but he'd even warned her not to read into anything that might happen during their weekend vacation with her family. So why the hell had she done something so stupid as to ask him about the kiss? She should have known it had meant nothing to him...even if it had felt like something to her.

His lips on hers had catapulted her into a Zen-like state all right. But it had also sent shock waves of electrifying pleasure zinging through her central nervous system at rapid speed. Guess that just proved what a great actor he really was. *If you ask me, the man went into the wrong career.*

The kiss had been nothing more than his way of calming her down—a distraction, which also doubled as a figurative slap in the face. But the way her cheeks stung with heat, he might as well have slapped her for real.

It was embarrassing enough to know he wasn't into her. She didn't need or want him to explain why or make excuses. Nothing he could say would make her feel better anyway. She just wanted to get through this weekend as quickly as possible.

Leah made it back downstairs just as Sam caught up to her. Her family sat at the table, all of them looking a little put out at having to wait for them to return. "Everything okay, honey?" her dad asked her, eyeing Sam warily as he took his seat.

"Sure," she said nonchalantly, sliding in next to Sam. She gave her dad a sincere smile to placate him. "Let's eat."

Everyone relaxed as they resumed their meal. Enough so that her dad started making some light conversation. "So what kind of cake are you making for your birthday, Leah?"

"I haven't decided yet," she said, wiping her mouth. "I don't know. Maybe chocolate this year."

"How about a lovely carrot cake?" her mother asked. "That sounds delicious, doesn't it, dear?"

"Sure, um, I guess so."

Sam set down his fork and wiped his mouth. "Hold on a minute. You make your own cake for your birthday?"

"Well, yeah. I've done it every year since I was eight."

The corner of his lips turned downward. "But it's *your* birthday," he argued, his eyes narrowing slightly.

She waved him off, not wanting to make a big deal out of it. "Don't be silly, Sam. It's still my birthday, no matter who makes the cake. I always make everyone's cake, including my own. I am the baker in the family, you know." Then she added, "Besides, it's no different than when I've made desserts for you in the past."

His jaw clenched, and a muscle ticked in his cheek, but

he didn't say anything else about it. Apparently, he didn't appreciate her comment or the way her family did things, which wasn't all that surprising. But since he'd be out of her life after this weekend, it didn't really matter what he agreed with.

A half hour later, the banging of crab mallets came to an abrupt end. The only sounds lingering were the occasional background chatter and the appreciative sighs that occurred due to full bellies.

"Damn it. You ate the last crab, didn't you?" Sam asked, his face serious.

Her face broke with a smile. "I told you it was mine."

"Yeah, but only because your dad helped you cheat. The moment you told him I loved football, he used that knowledge to distract me and slow me down."

"Who, me?" Dad asked, feigning innocence.

Sam chuckled. "Okay, okay. Fine. I get it. Family sticks together. But after I marry your daughter, there won't be any more of this favoritism bullshit."

Laughter sounded around the table, which drowned out the sharp intake of Leah's breath. Well, mostly. Sam was sitting right next to her, and his body stiffened. He closed his eyes and sighed, as if he hadn't realized what he'd said until that moment, then glanced back at her with an apology looming in his eyes.

Her throat tightened, but she managed to speak. "Why don't we help clean up this mess and then we'll go for a stroll down the jetty before the sun sets?"

He stood, seemingly eager to get away from the others. "Yeah, I think that sounds good."

Grandma raised a hand to stop him. "Don't worry about the dinner. There's plenty of us to get this cleaned up. It's going to be dark soon. You kids go have some fun."

"Are you sure?" Leah asked. "I mean, we don't mind helping—"

Grandma shooed them away from the table. "Scoot, you love birds."

* * *

They strolled down the boardwalk in silence, and Sam noted a lone jack rabbit nibbling on a cactus pear in the weeds a few dozen yards ahead of them. As they approached, the clatter of Leah's shoes against the wooden walkway alerted the hare to their presence, and the rabbit lit out over the sand dunes like its tail was on fire.

Sam understood that feeling well.

The night he'd met her, Sam had been perfectly content, relaxing in the backyard of his new single life, when Leah had encroached onto his territory too. Not that it was all her fault or anything. He'd left the damn gate wide open. But that knowledge didn't make him any less skittish about her being on his property.

"So what did you think of dinner?" Leah asked.

"Overall, I would say it was pretty good. Especially considering the price and the quality of the food. And the staff. Man, they were great."

She laughed and played along. "Yeah, the place was pretty chill. They had a real laid-back atmosphere. Almost felt like I was in my grandma's backyard."

He chuckled. "It did, didn't it?"

Smiling, Leah bumped her shoulder into his. "Come on, I'm serious. Did you really like it?"

"Are you kidding? Fresh seafood and beer. I could marry you." He grinned back at her, knowing damn well that conversation was bound to come up again anyway.

"Well, technically you already are. Or so they all believe. You really sold them with that last comment."

"Yeah, I'm sorry about that," Sam said, giving her an uncomfortable grin. "I don't know why I said anything to your family about when we get married. I guess I got caught up in all the role-playing. I wasn't thinking, and it sort of popped out before I could stop it."

"It's okay. It's not like I thought you meant it or anything." She gave a noncommittal shrug and pushed a loose strand of hair behind her ear. "Besides, it actually worked out in our favor. None of them have a clue that we aren't really engaged. God, I wouldn't be able to face any of them if they ever found out. I'd look like such a loser."

His jaw tightened, and a muscle twitched in his neck. "No, actually you wouldn't. But it doesn't matter because they won't ever find out. I promise I'll take the secret to my grave with me."

She smiled shyly but didn't look at him. "Thanks. I appreciate that."

"I still need to make them hate me though. I'm just not sure how to do that without causing your mother to go into cardiac arrest. I damn near killed her and don't want to have a repeat performance of that episode."

Leah giggled. "It's okay. You don't have to do anything else tonight. Save your energy. We'll have all day tomorrow to come up with something. I'm sure an opportunity will present itself."

"And what if one doesn't?"

"Sam, we have to spend the entire day with my crazy-ass family. If you didn't get enough of them today, trust me, you will be looking for a reason to have them send you packing for sure by tomorrow."

The corners of his mouth lifted, but his heart just wasn't

in it. After spending time with her family at this evening's dinner, he didn't think they were all that bad. No, actually, he'd gotten a kick out of them.

Sure, there were some minor issues her family needed to work on, but what family doesn't have problems? The members of Leah's family weren't nearly as horrible as he had originally believed. Dysfunctional, perhaps. But not bad people.

At dinner, Leah's grandparents had needled each other relentlessly, but it was obvious that the years Jack and Penny had spent together were the best years of their lives. And Bill, Leah's father, had spent most of the meal making Sam laugh with his constant antics, while Ethan hadn't been the pain in the ass she'd described. Even her mother, Nancy, had been on her best behavior, making it through the rest of dinner without a single shitty remark about her daughter's weight. Maybe there was hope for the woman after all.

As Sam and Leah approached the sandy trail that snaked through the dunes, their steps grew softer. Large mounds of sand blocked the view of the ocean ahead of them, but the dull roar of the distant waves rolling onto the unseen shore registered in Sam's ears. His mind painted a serene image of gentle, blue-green tides washing up on undisturbed shores. But when the boardwalk ended and they stepped out of the protection of the dunes, he realized how wrong he had been.

The murky ocean was nothing short of violence and turmoil. Gray barrels of saltwater rose high in the air before somersaulting forward as the choppy swells and wicked whitecaps raced toward the shoreline. A line of white pelicans swam against the fast-moving currents, though they made little progress. Sandpipers foraged along the water's edge, dodging the inflated man-o'-wars and ugly brown patches of seaweed littering the beach.

A fierce wind kicked sand up in its wake, the grit scratching Sam's eyes and temporarily blinding him. He managed to wipe it away in time to see Leah's hair whip wildly around her head, then violate her face with no remorse.

"Damn," Sam said. "I didn't realize the wind would be so bad out here closer to the water."

But this apparently wasn't Leah's first rodeo. She pulled an elastic hair band from her front pocket and tied her dark locks into a quick, uneven ponytail. "I think we're supposed to have a few storms come in over the weekend. It's usually windy, but not always this bad."

With the ferocious wind at their backs, they continued on their way. Only minutes from the beach house, they neared a huge wooden fishing pier. It rose at least fifteen feet above the ground with DANGER and KEEP OUT signs posted above the barricaded entrance.

Leah started to walk under it, but Sam grasped her arm to stop her, eyeing the structure for hazards. "Should we be walking beneath it?"

She grinned, as if he was being silly worrying about her safety. "This section is okay to walk under. They closed the entrance because the storm that swept through about eight years ago damaged the end where most people fished." She pointed out into the ocean.

Sam's gaze followed the pier out over the water until it reached the end. Sure enough, a huge section with sagging boards and missing poles had sunk into the sea below it. "Did you ever fish on that thing?"

They started walking beneath the pier together. "Once or twice, but my grandpa used to fish from it all the time. Ever since they closed it, he fishes from the jetty or occasionally from the shore on calmer days."

"Does he ever catch anything decent?"

"Sure. Lots of flounder, drum, and even a few sharks."

"Sharks, huh? Big ones or little ones?" he asked as they exited out from the other side of the pier.

"Does it really matter?" She continued walking beside him but stared blankly at him. "A shark is a freaking shark, if you ask me."

Sam chuckled at her high-pitched tone. "So I guess that's your way of saying we aren't going skinny-dipping while we're here on vacation."

She cringed, as if the thought horrified her. "Are you kidding me?"

"Oh, come on. I wouldn't let a shark get you."

"Who's worried about that? There's no way I'd get naked in public. Nosiree. Not happening."

"Ya know, it's not like anyone would be around to see you after dark. Besides, the water would hide everything you don't want seen."

"Oh, sure. Let's go at feeding time so a shark can kill me and drag me out into open water. Then my naked remains can get caught in a shrimper's net and be hoisted on board by the time the sun comes up. Jesus. You're nuts. I'd die of embarrassment."

His eyebrow rose a fraction of an inch.

Leah grinned. "Okay, so it wouldn't really matter since I would already be dead. But still..."

Sam didn't push the issue. Obviously, she wasn't comfortable with the idea of being naked in front of him, and he had no doubt she would have made him promise not to look. And he would have, but hell, it would have been a lie. Because if Leah ever planned to take off her clothes and strip down to nothing, he damn sure wanted a front row seat.

Probably good that wasn't going to happen. The last thing

he needed was the two of them naked together in an intimate setting without some kind of barrier—distance, clothing, or even her family—separating them. Unfortunately, the only kind of barrier he wanted between them was a condom.

Get your mind out of the gutter, dumbass.

They wandered down the beach in silence, avoiding the seagulls circling overhead. A pod of porpoises amused themselves in the distance, gliding along the surface of the ocean and then darting through the intermittent barrels produced by the forceful waves.

Within minutes, Sam and Leah arrived at the jetty. The manmade formation consisted of slabs of marbled rock, uniformly placed in a straight line that extended from the shoreline out into the ocean. As they carefully made their way over the damp, jagged rocks, breakers crashed against the outside boulders, spraying a fine, salty mist into the air around them.

When they made it to the end of the jetty, Leah climbed onto a boulder, kicked a clump of seaweed aside, and sat on top of the large rock with her legs crossed. "Maybe one of us should start an argument."

Sam plopped down next to her and dangled his legs over the edge. Though the tide surged beneath the block structure, his feet were high enough to keep from getting wet. "You want to argue with me?" he asked with a grin.

"I mean, in front of my family."

Oh yeah. That. He shrugged lightly. "Might work."

"Well, I was thinking that, if they witnessed the whole breakup themselves, then I wouldn't have anything I'd have to explain later. I know that's me being a coward, but I really hate the thought of having a conversation where I have to tell them you dumped me. Basically, I'd rather feel like a coward than a loser."

He rubbed a frustrated hand over his face. "Look, if it makes it any easier, you can break up with me. Even in front of them, if you want. I don't mind."

Leah sat there quietly, as if she were contemplating the idea.

The ocean gushed between the rocks, washing over the sea anemones, urchins, and barnacles clinging to the base. A school of minnows swam freely in the shallow pools left behind as the flooding withdrew.

Finally, she said, "I don't think it's going to matter who breaks up with whom. In the end, no matter what happens, my mom will still figure out a way of somehow blaming me for screwing up the relationship. She did the same thing when Gavin broke it off with me."

Sam's jaw tightened, and he gritted his teeth. "You should really tell her to back the hell off. What your mom is doing doesn't even qualify as overstepping her boundaries. She's just flat out ignoring them."

"Yeah, but she *is* my mother."

"So?"

"So I can't tell her to stop."

"Sure you can," he said, nodding. "You just say, 'Mom, knock it the fuck off.' "

Though he said it playfully in hopes she would laugh and he would get his point across, Leah scowled and shook her head. "Sam, I can't tell her that without hurting her feelings and . . . well, I don't really want to do that."

His eyes widened in disbelief. "Yet she doesn't seem to mind hurting *your* feelings."

"I . . . I know she doesn't mean to."

He rolled his eyes. "That's the excuse you've told yourself for so long that you've actually come to accept it as the truth. But it's not good enough, Leah. No one should hurt someone they care about...for any reason. Whether they mean to or not."

Leah shifted uncomfortably, then rose to her feet. "We should probably head back now. It's going to be dark soon, and there aren't any lights on the jetty."

Sam climbed to his feet, noting the sun resting on the horizon while casting an orange reflection over the water. "Okay, fine. But at least think about what I said, okay?"

She nodded.

"Ladies first," he said, sweeping his arm out from his side.

Leah treaded lightly as Sam followed closely behind her. With the sunlight fading rapidly behind them, the wet surface of the moss-covered boulders became more slippery, more treacherous. They didn't even make it halfway down the jetty when Leah's foot slipped off a ledge, and Sam reached for her. Although he managed to grasp her in time to keep her from falling and becoming wedged in between the sharp rocks, her sandal didn't have the same luck.

She cursed under her breath and started to climb down in between the slabs to get it, but Sam grasped her arm and stopped her. "No. You stay there and let me get it." But before he was able to get down far enough to reach it, the tide rushed in and washed the floating shoe out to sea. "Um, actually, never mind. The shoe is gone and will probably wind up as shark bait."

"Damn it. That was my favorite one."

Sam gave her a strange look. "Your right shoe was your favorite?"

She chuckled and pulled off her left sandal. "No, I mean the pair. They were the most comfortable shoes I own. I bought them on sale last summer, but I doubt I'll be able to find another pair just like them." She glanced out to sea and gazed at the sun dipping into the ocean as the light faded even more. "Just great. We need to hurry and get off these rocks before we're stranded out here after dark. Unfortunately, this is going to slow me down a lot. Maybe you should go on ahead of me."

"You're kidding, right?" When she didn't answer him, he glared at her, pissed that she planned to walk across the rocks with no shoes on her feet. "I hate to tell you this, but you aren't walking barefoot. If the sharp-ass rocks don't cut your feet, the rusty fishing hooks or broken glass will. And who knows what kind of bacteria you could pick up."

She put her hands on her hips. "Well, it's not like I can stay out here all damn night."

"I'll carry you."

Leah rolled her eyes. "You're *not* carrying me."

"Why?"

"Because I'm too heavy."

Sam pinched the bridge of his nose and breathed out hard. "You know, you really piss me off when you say things like that about yourself. You're not too fucking heavy. I should know. This isn't the first time I've carried you, remember?" He turned to face away from her and knelt down. "Now hop on my back, and I'll piggyback you the rest of the way."

Leah put her hands on his shoulders but hesitated to jump on. "Maybe you could just let me borrow your shoes, and I'll give you a piggyback ride instead."

He glared at her over his shoulder.

She grinned. "Okay, fine. But when you can't walk tomorrow because I broke your spine, don't come crying to me."

Sam was starting to lose his patience. "Would you just get the hell on already?"

Leah leaned onto his back and wrapped her arms around

his neck. As he rose, he grasped both of her legs behind her knees and pulled them up around his waist, locking them in place at his hips. Wiggling against him, she got into a more comfortable position and squished her breasts more firmly into him.

His dick hardened. The hell of it was that he'd imagined this scenario many times before, but in all those visions, he hadn't been facing away from her. Nor had either of them been wearing clothes.

"All good?" he asked.

"Yep."

Sam started down the jetty, mindfully treading over the uneven rocks and being careful not to misjudge the landing of each of his steps. He wasn't all that worried about himself, but if he tripped while carrying Leah, she was bound to get hurt, and there was no way in hell he'd let that happen.

Once they'd made it safely to the beach, Sam released her legs and let her slide down his backside until her feet hit the soft sand. "Thanks," she said.

He nodded. "No problem."

"Your back okay?"

Ignoring her irritating question, Sam ground his teeth together and started walking. They strolled down the beach with Leah dangling one lonely shoe from her fingertips. Daylight was nearly gone, but the security lights on the old pier still worked. Like a beacon, the yellow lights guided them back to her grandparents' boardwalk with ease as the sounds of her family's laughter wafted to their ears.

Without thinking, Sam reached down and coiled his fingers around Leah's free hand. She jumped a little at first then relaxed as her family came into view. The group had moved over to the lounge chairs surrounded by bamboo torches, and the faint scent of citronella infused the air. The group all greeted Leah and Sam with good-natured smiles.

"Did you two have a nice walk?" her dad asked.

"Yep, it was great," Leah replied. "Well, except for the mishap I had with my shoe." She held up the sole survivor and wiggled it in the air. "Unfortunately, it was the only pair I brought with me on this trip, and the other one has been lost at sea. Chances are, it will probably end up on a deserted island being worn by a stranded man whose only friend is named Wilson."

Warm and encompassing laughter filled the air around them.

Her mom waved her hand at Leah. "Don't worry about it. We wear the same size. I have an extra pair I brought that you can have. I'll pull them out of my suitcase when I go upstairs. In the meantime, why don't you two join us?"

Leah glanced at Sam, then bit her lip. "Ah, not tonight, Mom. I got up at four o'clock this morning to prep for my shift at the bakery. I'm tired. I think I'll just go up, take a quick shower, and then hit the sack early."

"What about you, Sam?" her father asked. "You want to sit with us for a while?"

"Thanks, Bill, but I think Leah has the right idea. I was up pretty early this morning myself." He smirked and dropped an arm across her shoulders. "Probably better for me to go to bed with your daughter now instead of waking her up later." Sam leaned in closer to Leah. "Right, baby?"

She stiffened at the sexual connotation and gazed back at him with incredulous, *I'm going to kill you* eyes, while the awkward silence of her family members forced her to respond. "What Sam means is...he, um...has a bad back."

His eyes narrowed, but he didn't speak. He had a feeling where she was going with this, and he didn't like it one bit.

Leah continued. "When I lost my shoe, Sam had to pig-gyback me off the jetty, and his back started acting up again. I told him I would rub it for him before bed so he could fall asleep pain-free. It's the least I can do since it's my fault anyway."

White-hot flames of anger swept through him, but he doused them to keep from saying something he would regret and giving away their ruse. "Oh yeah. Right. That's what I meant." He grinned sinfully though, because there was no way he'd let her get off scot-free for making that remark about her size. "And I believe that wasn't the only thing you promised me," he said, rubbing his thumb across her bottom lip as her mouth fell open.

"Good night, everyone," Leah said to the others, steadily shoving Sam toward the stairs.

Her face had turned several shades of red by the time she guided him into the house and straight into the bedroom, where she slammed the door behind them. Her head snapped to him, and judging by the way she glared at him, he wasn't going to stay "pain-free" much longer if he kept saying shit like that in front of her family. But he couldn't help himself. It was fun to see all of their reactions. Especially hers.

"Jesus, Sam. You just made them think I was going to...to..."

He wore a shit-eating grin. "To what?"

She didn't speak.

"Oh, come on. Don't tell me you can't say that one out loud either," he said, shaking his head at her. "Just say it already. I made them think that you were going to give me head. Or you can use: blow job, playing the skin flute, smoking a pole, or sucking a dick."

"Why can't I just call it oral sex?"

"Because you aren't a doctor," he said with a chuckle.

"And if you think for one second that they bought that bad-back bullshit, you're wrong. Right about now, they're all wondering if we're going to screw like bunnies in your grandparents' house."

She stared at him wide-eyed, then sighed heavily. "God, why did I ever let you talk me into agreeing to this stupid plan?"

"Hey, just be glad I didn't stay down there with them. You never know what might have come out of my mouth without you around to shut me up."

"Yeah, no kidding." Leah reached for her overnight bag, then eyed him suspiciously. "I'm going to take my shower now. But if you dare to make a single sexual noise or even so much as squeak the bed while I'm in there, I'm going to throw my shampoo bottle out the door at you." When he sat down in the chair and folded his hands innocently in his lap, she smiled. "By the way, you could have stayed downstairs with them if you wanted to. You didn't have to come up just because I did."

Sam shook his head. He wouldn't have minded hanging out downstairs with her family for a little while longer, which was exactly why he chose not to. "It's okay. I'm really tired anyway. It's been a long day." As Leah rooted through her bag and pulled out some clothes, a thought burned through him. "Did Gavin ever stay down there...with your family, I mean?"

Leah glanced up, twisting her head toward him, seemingly surprised by his unexpected question. "Actually, Gavin's never been here before. I invited him once, but he said he didn't want to spend his weekend sitting around with a bunch of old people so he didn't come."

"God, your ex is a fucking jerk."

"Tell me about it. My weight has always fluctuated by

about twenty pounds, and one time Gavin thought it would be a lovely gesture to tell me I looked better when I was on the lower end. He's a peach, isn't he?"

Damn. He really wanted to kick the shit out of that jackass now. "That's a dick thing to say. Leah, as nice as you are, I can't figure out why the hell you were with someone like him. You deserve way better than that."

She lowered her head, not allowing her gaze to meet his. "Yeah, well, being with a jerk is sometimes better than being alone."

With her silky dark hair, emerald eyes, and those killer feminine curves that would drive any man wild, she should never have been made to feel that way about herself. And he knew exactly who to blame. *She can thank that prick Gavin and her nitpicking mother.*

Sam's hands fisted on his knees. "That's a crock. You have this screwed-up mentality, all because of his fucked-up perception of women. Gavin wouldn't know a damn thing about a real women. He obviously was trying to form you into the Barbie doll type I saw on his arm at the reception. Because what he said about you...it's not true."

"Thanks," she said, heading to the bathroom with a bundle of clothes under her arm. "I appreciate you saying that, but you can't know for sure."

Outrage sloshed in his veins. He glared at her back as she set her clothes down on the bathroom counter and turned back to close the door. "Wait a minute," he said, his frustration straining his voice. "You won't take what I say at face value, but you'll listen to what your dumbass ex tells you?"

"Yes," she said as she started pushing the door closed. "Because Gavin has seen me naked."

Lucky bastard.

Chapter Thirteen

Damn, she just wanted to get it over with.

Frustrated, Leah heaved out a breath, flipped over onto her back, and slammed her head back against the pillow as if it were a brick wall. It was bad enough she was going to be sharing a bed all night long with the guy she liked. But did he have to make it worse by staying in the bathroom so long and drawing out the inevitable weirdness that was sure to rear its ugly head the moment he crawled under the covers?

What the hell was he doing in there—avoiding her until she fell asleep?

Actually, she'd considered the idea herself except, in her version, she had planned to be in a deep sleep before he came out. Unfortunately, she hadn't been able to manage it. Her anxious nerves twitched beneath her skin, electrifying her body and her mind.

She apparently wouldn't be able to nod off until they got the initial awkwardness over with and out of the way. Once that was no longer an issue, then she would get down to the business of sleeping…if that was even possible with Sam's sexy body lying next to her.

She sat up and listened for any sounds of movement coming from the bathroom. Beyond the shower water running for twenty minutes straight, Sam had been completely silent the entire time. As if he had hit his head and was lying unconscious on the bathroom floor while bleeding to death. Or what if he'd fallen asleep in there and drowned?

God. Maybe she should check on him. "Sam, are you okay in there?"

He gave a guttural and very male, "Yeah."

Okay, so he wasn't dead. That was a good thing.

"Well, are you almost done? I…uh, need to brush my teeth." *Again.* Leah cringed at the lie. She had already brushed her teeth once, but maybe one more time wouldn't hurt. They *were* going to be sleeping in close quarters after all.

"I'll just be a minute. I've still got to wash my hair and bathe."

Leah squinted at the door in confusion. Wash his hair and bathe? Then what the fuck had he been doing in there for the last twenty minutes—shaving his legs?

She dragged herself out of the bed and inspected herself in the full-length mirror on a wooden stand that sat in the corner of the room. The navy blue cotton shorts she wore weren't nearly long enough to hide the slightly dimpled skin on her upper thighs. And the thin white tank top hugged tight across her chest, the flimsy fabric showcasing an unsightly underarm bulge and her enormous-looking puckered nipples.

Damn. Why hadn't she brought something else to sleep in? *Like a sweater. Or possibly a jogging suit. Maybe even a tarp.*

Leah paced the room restlessly, waiting for him to finish. When he finally opened the door, steam billowed out into the bedroom. A shirtless Sam appeared through the fog, wearing only a black pair of athletic shorts. His hard, well-muscled chest held a smattering of dark hair, while the hair on his head dripped water onto his broad shoulders, leaving droplets dotting his smooth, tanned skin.

Her mouth went dry.

Sam with a shirt was hot. Sam without a shirt was fucking orgasmic. But she couldn't stand around there staring at him all day so she rushed into the bathroom and tried to clear her mind of anything involving orgasms. Especially where he was concerned.

It was never going to happen. She knew that.

Leah brushed her teeth—*for the second time*—and hoped he was in bed with the lights off before she returned.

No such luck.

Sam stood at the foot of the bed with his arms crossed against his magnificent chest, waiting for her return. "Since you messed up the covers on both sides of the bed, I wasn't sure which one was yours."

"Doesn't matter to me."

"Okay, then just pick one. I don't care either way."

Leah choose the side closest to the bathroom and quickly slipped beneath the covers. Then she lay there staring up at the ceiling while her heart hammered relentlessly against her rib cage. Sam flipped off the light switch and slid in next to her, the scent of his soap loitering on his warm skin and clinging to the air around him.

She closed her eyes and inhaled the scent, reveling in its richness and admiring the citrus undertones. Both of them lay there quietly with only the awkward sounds of their synchronized breathing filling the room.

If she had thought the bed looked small before, it now seemed more like a twin bed with Sam lying next to her. He wasn't touching her, but that didn't matter. He was still way too close for comfort—hers specifically.

"Um, Leah?"

"Yeah?"

"Is this as uncomfortable for you as it is for me?"

Okay, so apparently she wasn't the only one thinking about it. "A little," she whispered. "I'm sorry. If you want, I can go sleep in Ethan's room or on the couch. I'll just make something up and tell them we got into an argument."

Sam lifted his head off his pillow and looked at her, though she couldn't see his expression in the darkened room. "I think you totally missed the boat on that one. I just meant I've never slept in the same bed with someone before without touching them. I feel like I'm sleeping with my brother or something."

Oh. Well, okay. "I didn't even know you had a brother."

"I don't. I'm an only child. But if I did have a brother and I slept in the same bed with him, I'm pretty sure this is what it would feel like."

Lovely. So sleeping with me reminds him of sleeping with a brother he doesn't even have. That's comforting to know. "Do you want to talk about something? Would that help?"

"Couldn't hurt, I guess. You don't sound like my nonexistent brother," he said, chuckling. "What do you want to talk about?"

She hesitated for a moment but decided to go for it. "Well, since I've already told you personal things about my relationship with my ex, why don't you tell me about the last girl you dated?"

"You don't want to hear about that disaster."

"Oh, come on. You know all about my past with Gavin,

but I don't know anything about your dating history. Fair is fair. Tell me."

"All right, fine. Just remember you asked to hear this stupid bedtime story." He paused to clear his throat. "Once upon a time, I decided it was time to settle down and get serious about finding someone I wanted to spend the rest of my life with. Then I met Sylvia and changed my mind. We didn't live happily ever after. The end."

Leah laughed, which made her body relax and feel a little more at ease. "Okay, back up. What made you change your mind about her?"

"We had been dating for only a month when I found out she planned to marry me."

Leah blinked rapidly in the dark, then asked, "But wasn't that what you just said you had wanted at the time—someone to spend the rest of your life with?"

"Fuck, I knew better than to open my big mouth. All of this makes me sound like a prick, doesn't it?"

"No, no, it's not that. I guess I just don't understand the situation. I mean, if you both wanted to get married...I don't know. It just doesn't make any sense. I don't see what the big deal is."

"The big deal is that I figured I'd *eventually* get married. Not after only a month of dating someone. It's a little quick, don't ya think?"

Ah, so that's his problem. "So, in other words, you got cold feet about getting married?"

"Hell no. There was never any 'getting married' to it. I barely knew the woman, and she decided on her own that we were getting hitched. It's not like I proposed to her or something."

"Okay, so she fell for you hard and fast. Doesn't sound like such a bad thing. People tend to do that when they're in love."

"That's the thing though." Sam repositioned himself, which shook the bed. "Sylvia didn't love me any more than I loved her. She just wanted to keep her stupid timeline on track."

Giggling, Leah squinted at him in the dark and crinkled her nose. "Is that something like a biological clock?"

"No, I mean this crazy-ass woman had an actual timeline for everything—dating, marriage, kids, buying a house. We hadn't even had sex, but she had already picked out our children's names. Apparently, we had two—a boy and a girl. Derek and Jasmine. Derek had my dark eyes, and Jasmine had Sylvia's blond hair. They were both honor roll students, and Sylvia wanted to start college funds for them already. I'm telling you, the woman was as fruity as they come."

Leah stifled a laugh. "So you broke up with her?"

"Hell yeah, I broke up with her. Best thing I ever did. But you want to know the really odd thing? She didn't care that I dumped her. She was just pissed that I fucked up her timeline." He breathed out a sigh. "That's when I decided I should probably back up a little and figure out exactly what I want in a life partner before trying to find her. I'm not always known for thinking ahead. I tend to act in the moment."

"Oh, you mean like when you announced that you're engaged to a woman you barely knew?"

Sam nudged her with his elbow. "Yeah, like that, smart-ass."

Leah giggled. "So basically you're afraid of ending up with another Sylvia on your hands? Is that it?"

"Pretty much."

"But isn't that the whole point of dating—meeting a few wrong ones so you'll know what the right one looks like when you meet her? I mean, how else will you know what to look for in a partner?"

Sam paused thoughtfully. "I have no idea. But I do know what I *don't* want. My first wife taught me that lesson well."

"I didn't know you had been married before." Leah couldn't stop the surprise in her high-pitched voice. "When was this?"

"Years ago," Sam said on another sigh.

"What happened?"

"Back when I was twenty-one, the girl I was dating at the time ended up pregnant. We hadn't known each other very long, and it wasn't planned. Just a careless mistake on our parts. I couldn't even say I loved her, but she still wanted to get married."

"And you didn't, I take it?"

"Well, not exactly. I didn't think it was a smart idea because we hardly knew each other. She kept pressing the issue though. I was trying to be a stand-up guy and do the right thing by her and the baby so I eventually agreed to marry her. It was a stupid mistake, and I'll always regret that decision."

"Why's that?"

He blew out a long, slow breath. "She lost the baby a few weeks after we got married and was having a hard time coping with the loss. Hell, we both were. I had planned to stick it out with her and try to make the marriage work, but... well, I didn't."

"Oh. I'm sorry to hear about the baby. I can only imagine how much of a strain that probably put on your relationship."

"It did, but that wasn't why I left. I had put aside all of my own sorrow about the baby in order to help her through her grief. But when I came home from work early one day and caught her with another man in my bed, that put an end to putting her needs before my own. I packed my shit and left, then filed for a divorce soon after. We haven't spoken since."

"I'm sorry to hear that."

"Don't be. We didn't belong together. If I hadn't been such an idiot for letting her talk me into marrying her so fast in the first place, I could have saved both of us the trouble of going through an ugly, senseless divorce. After all that, I figured out real quick that rushing into a relationship wasn't a smart idea on any level."

"What about Sylvia? Did you explain all of that to her? Surely, after hearing that, she would understand your reluctance to jump into marriage."

"Yeah, I tried, but she still wouldn't stop going on and on about how I messed up her big life plans." He lifted his head off the pillow again. "I'm telling you, Leah, that was the strangest fucking relationship I've ever been in."

She smiled. "Says the guy who's lying in a bed with his fake fiancée."

Sam let out a boisterous laugh. "Yep, true. But sadly enough, this is probably one of the most normal, stable relationships I've ever been in."

Nonrelationship, Leah mentally corrected. "Okay, so I get why you don't want to rush into anything, but why aren't you at least dating anyone now?"

"Because I think a person should make themselves the best version of themselves—a stronger, better person—before trying to find the person they are meant to be with. Don't you agree?"

Leah rolled her eyes. It was obvious what he was trying to do. "You're trying to turn this around on me, aren't you?"

"Nope. Not at all. Just offering a friendly suggestion."

"Keep it."

Sam chuckled. "You know, the kind of advice we don't like sometimes turns out to be exactly what we need to hear in that moment."

"True. But you might want to remember that yourself. Especially since you're the guy who says he wants to settle down but then breaks up with a girl who wants to marry him, only to turn around and announce that he's fake-engaged to another woman."

* * *

The next morning, someone knocked on the outside of the bedroom door, catapulting Leah out of her unconscious state. Her eyes flicked open, and surprisingly, her gaze landed on a close-up view of Sam's face. He was lying next to her, staring at her with a wide-eyed, openmouthed expression. She had no doubt about what he was thinking in that moment, but neither of them seemed capable of movement.

The rap on the door happened again, only harder this time. "This isn't a Holiday Inn," her father teased, chuckling on the other side of the door. "Rise and shine, lovebirds. We're leaving in an hour." Then the sound of her father's footsteps slowly faded down the hallway.

The moment her dad left, Sam rolled away from her, sliding his large, firm hand off her left breast. "I, uh... sorry. It was an accident."

"It's okay," Leah said quickly, trying to make the situation less awkward than it already was. "Your hand was... warm." She cringed. *Oh God. What the hell did I just say?*

He glanced back at her, his eyes glimmering with intensity as his jaw tightened. "I could put it back, you know?"

They stared at each other in silence, as if they were measuring each other's comfort level. She didn't know how to respond to what he'd said, and he seemed content to let the words sit out in the open, dangling from his tongue. His eyes darkened, smoldering with heat, and then he grinned.

Oh, calm down, Leah. It's only a freakin' joke. She inhaled a deep breath, reminding herself that Sam was just teasing her. She'd witnessed the panic that had crossed his face the moment they both realized where his hand had been. He obviously hadn't meant anything by the accidental groping. *But still... Why does everything he say sound like he's making an offer?*

Again, someone knocked on the door, and Leah groaned. "Jeez. We're coming, Dad."

"Breakfast is already on the table," he told them, using an annoyingly cheerful morning voice. "Last call. If you don't hurry, you're not going to have time to eat before we leave."

She threw the covers off and climbed to her feet, straightening her clothes, which had twisted in her sleep. Grabbing her bag, she lugged it to the bathroom and got dressed in there while Sam used the bedroom to change his clothes. After brushing her teeth and hair, then slapping on a minimal amount of makeup, she reentered the bedroom in a pair of jeans and a green T-shirt emblazoned with the Sweets n' Treats logo.

Sam had already pulled on a pair of Levi's and a white T-shirt that hugged his biceps in the most delicious way. "Where are we going today?"

"Every year we have the same routine. We go to the aquarium, and then we eat lunch in the Water Gardens."

"Is that a restaurant or something?"

"No, it's more of a... well, you'll see." She nodded to the door. "Ready?"

"After you."

They headed to the kitchen, where they joined the rest of the family for a quick fruit and bagel breakfast. They barely had time to finish their orange juice before her father rushed the entire group out the door.

Downstairs, her grandpa leaned over to Sam and said, "Since you aren't familiar with the area, why don't you and Leah ride with us?"

"Sure," Sam agreed with no hesitation.

"No, that's okay," Leah said, trying to quickly intervene. "There's no need. I know my way there. We'll just take Sam's truck."

Confusion warped his face as he cocked his head and studied her curiously. "Why take three vehicles though? I'm okay riding with your grandparents."

Well, I'm not.

But she couldn't dare say that with her grandpa staring her down. So against her better judgment, she said, "Okay, fine. I guess we'll ride with them."

By the time they arrived at the aquarium twenty minutes later, Sam's face had paled, and he looked like he'd just ridden the largest, fastest roller coaster ever built. He stumbled out of the backseat of the Avalon and held on to the door, as if his legs were too wobbly to hold him upright.

"You guys go ahead and get the tickets," Leah said to the others. "We'll catch up with you at the main entrance." She waited for her family to drift out of earshot before turning to Sam. "I'm so sorry," she muttered softly.

"For what? Not mentioning your grandfather drives like someone's hands are over his eyes? Christ. The fucker almost killed us four times."

"Oh, come on. It wasn't *that* bad."

He glared down at her. "How would you know? You were huddled in a fetal position on the floorboard babbling to yourself."

"I wasn't babbling. I was . . . praying."

Sam grinned. "Yeah? Well, since when is *Please don't let us fucking die!* a prayer?"

"I did *not* say that."

"Close enough," he said, straightening his posture. He shut the car door and staggered toward the main entrance with Leah walking next to him. "By the way, we're riding home with your parents."

"We can't do that, Sam. My grandpa will probably wonder why we didn't want to ride with them anymore."

"Then I would tell him the truth: I don't feel like dying today."

She sighed. "You can't do that. I don't want to hurt his feelings. What if I promised to make you something extra special in exchange for us riding home with my grandparents?"

"Hell, no. Leah, there isn't a dessert in this world that would bribe me to get back into that wrecking ball your grandpa drives."

"Really? Well, that's too bad. I was thinking about making some chocolate mousse after tonight's dinner. But...oh well. Now I guess I don't have to." She shrugged lightly, as if it didn't matter to her in the least.

"Damn you," he growled, his face puckering. "You don't fight fair."

Leah couldn't contain her grin. "I don't know what you mean."

"Okay, fine. I'll ride in the death machine one more time. But if I die before I get the chocolate mousse, I'm coming back from the dead to haunt your ass."

Leah laughed and pointed out her family, who were waiting patiently near the roped-off entrance. They joined the group, and all of them walked inside the aquarium together.

The viewing room hosted an array of aquariums built into

the wall, though a few large round tanks sat out in the middle of the floor. They moved together, weaving around the room and visiting each individual exhibit to learn about the different specimens.

It was an hour later when they finally started for the next section of the building, and Leah's pace increased drastically. The colorful saltwater fish, moon jellies, and octopus were fun to watch, but there was a different species of marine animal she looked forward to the most every year. And it was in the upcoming exhibit.

Moments later, she stood off to the side of a massive 12,000-gallon tank surrounded by children. The touch pool always drew a large crowd because it was the only exhibit where the waist-high walls allowed visitors to reach over the side and get a hands-on experience with the marine animals. Over the children's heads, she could see what looked like at least thirty stingrays gliding effortlessly through the shallow water in different directions.

She hadn't even realized she'd left the others in her group behind until Sam stepped up beside her and huffed out a breath like he'd been running to catch up with her. "Got a little excited, did ya?"

"Huh?"

"For a second there, I thought you were bolting on me and leaving me to fend for myself with your family," he teased, offering her a quick grin.

"Oh, I'm sorry. This exhibit has always been my favorite one. I could watch the cownose rays all day long. They're just so graceful and mesmerizing and...cute."

Sam chuckled again. "I'm pretty sure that is the first and last time I will ever hear anyone call a stingray cute."

She smiled. "Well, they are."

His head nodded to an aquarium employee who was

selling small boats of shrimp to feed to the stingrays. "Have you ever fed one?"

Leah glanced back at the huge tank, noting all the children still circling it, then gazed back at Sam. "Actually, I think that's something they probably do more for the kids than the adults. I'd look silly being the only grown person up there."

"What? No way. Besides, you wouldn't be the only adult up there. I'll go with you."

"Sam, I don't think—"

But it was too late. He gestured to the employee, pulled out his wallet, and bought two boats of shrimp before Leah could stop him. They stood there watching the worker as she used her hand to demonstrate the proper way to hold the shrimp in order to feed the rays. It was obviously a spiel she'd repeated many times over. Then she moved on to the next paying customer.

"Come on," Sam said, although Leah just stood there. He grinned. "Would you stop worrying about what other people think and just have some fun already?"

She hated the idea of looking stupid up there among all the children, but she really, really, really wanted to feed a cownose stingray at least once in her life. And if Sam was willing to go up there and look dumb with her...well, then screw it.

Leah trailed behind him as they squeezed into an opening at the side of the tank where the salty scent in the air grew stronger and clung to her nose. They each grasped a dead shrimp from the paper boat, curled their fingers around it like the employee had showed them, and then lowered their hands into the cool water. A chill ran up her arm as they waited for a ray to head their way.

Within seconds, several brown rays with white underbellies made a beeline for their outstretched hands. Upon their arrival, one of the creatures bumped gently into Leah's knuckles and felt around with its mouth until it found the hole on the side of her fist and suctioned the shrimp she cradled from her fingers.

She squealed in delight. "Oh my God! That was the weirdest sensation ever. I have to do it again."

Sam fed the ray in front of him and grinned. "It *is* a strange feeling."

A young boy who couldn't have been more than four years old stood on the other side of Sam and caught their attention when he turned back to a woman sitting on a bench five foot behind him and shouted, "Mommy, I'm not tall enough. I can't reach the stingrays."

Sighing, the woman rubbed a hand over her very pregnant belly, as if the thought of lifting her young son was as painful as her swollen abdomen looked. "Okay, Billy. I'm coming."

But before she managed to struggle to her feet, Sam spoke up. "Ma'am, if it's all right with you, I'm happy to give your son a boost."

Relief washed over her face, and she settled back into her place on the bench. "Thank you. I'd really appreciate that."

He knelt down beside the child. "Hi, Billy. I'm Sam. You like stingrays?"

"Yeah," the kid said shyly. "They're cute."

Sam glanced back at Leah with a *you got to be kidding me* face, and she grinned wide. Then he turned his attention back to little Billy. "That's funny. My fiancée said the same thing."

Thousands of butterflies took flight in her stomach. It was one thing to hear Sam call her his fiancée in front of her family, but it was a whole different thing for him to say it so casually to someone else. Even if the kid wasn't old enough to know what it actually meant.

Sam pointed to the tank. "Billy, how would you like to feed a stingray?"

The child's face lit up with glee. "Really? Cool!"

"All right, but you have to hold the shrimp like this," Sam said, demonstrating the proper way to curl his fingers to keep them from getting nibbled on. "Think you can do that?"

"Yes, sir."

Leah smiled. Not only was Sam good with kids, but their whole exchange was absolutely adorable. Warmth radiated through her, and a strong sensation hit her low and deep. If she didn't know better, she would almost swear she'd just ovulated.

"Okay, I'm going to pick you up and lean you over the wall so you can reach. Ready?" Sam asked, waiting for Billy to nod. "Okay, here we go."

He lifted the small boy into his arms with ease and leaned carefully over the side of the tank until the child's hand reached into the water. Seconds later, an overzealous ray approached, slapping its wings on the surface of the water as it impatiently demanded its meal, then sucked the shrimp from Billy's hand.

"He got it!" the little boy shrieked. Sam set the kid down, and he ran to his mother, excitement blazing in his eyes. "Mommy, did you see that? I fed a stingray!"

"You did? That's awesome!" She gave her young son a big hug and mouthed a silent thank-you to Sam, who offered her a nod in return.

Leah shifted closer to Sam. "That was really sweet of you."

"I love kids."

"I can tell." It was too bad that his ex-wife had lost their child. Sam would have been a great hands-on father.

As they tossed their empty paper boats into a nearby garbage can and headed for the on-site sanitizing station so they could wash their hands, they passed by the bench where Billy sat recounting his memorable experience to his mother. "I can't wait 'til Daddy gets home from work tonight. I get to tell him all about the strange man who picked me up and held me like he does."

Sam's eyebrow rose slightly, but he kept moving toward the wash station and whispered, "I'm pretty sure Billy's mom is going to have some explaining to do later when Daddy gets home."

"Ya think?" Leah said, laughing.

Chapter Fourteen

S am couldn't believe he'd let Leah talk him into getting into her grandfather's vehicle once again, especially for chocolate mousse of all things. But after another short, death-defying ride in Jack's unofficial stunt car, they arrived at the Water Gardens in one piece. Barely.

Fuck, someone should really teach that old man how to drive.

As everyone piled out, Sam took a good look around. He didn't see any water, but he could damn well hear it. And it was loud. "It sounds like a waterfall coming from the other side of that wall."

"Yep, it is. Actually, it's lots of them," Leah replied as her grandma popped open the trunk of their car and grunted as she hefted out a large wicker basket. "Wait, Grandma, I'll get that for you."

"No, let me have it," Sam said, taking the handles of the basket before Leah could grab it. "I'll carry it. Just tell me where you want it."

"Thank you, Sam," both women said simultaneously while smiling sweetly at him. He returned the favor, but something dawned on him, and the grin he wore melted.

Shit. What the hell was he doing?

He was supposed to be putting a bad taste in all of their mouths when it came to his relationship with Leah. Yet here he was trying to be a gentleman by offering to carry heavy things for his fiancée's grandmother.

Fake fiancée, he mentally corrected. Christ, why couldn't he seem to remember that? If this plan to make them all hate him was going to work, he would have to stop being himself in front of the others. And that included doing nice shit.

He glanced over at Leah's father, who gave Sam a slight nod of approval, and a sharp pang of guilt stabbed straight through him. He liked the man. Hell, he liked all of them, though he couldn't figure out why.

"This way," Leah said, guiding him down the walkway as the sounds of rushing water grew louder and louder. She motioned to a set of cement stairs ahead. "Watch your step. We have to take these stairs down to the field."

She started down first, and Sam followed close behind her.

Halfway down, he caught his first glimpse of the gardens. A huge, grassy meadow sat in the middle of an oval concrete stadium. Like a sports arena, except instead of bleachers, there was a solid rock wall surrounding the field. Clear water spouted from the top of the concrete structure, gushed down the jagged rock wall, and landed in the bubbling fountains below.

Picnic tables by the dozen adorned the field, situated under shade trees and surrounded by an array of flower beds and hedges. Leah chose the closest unoccupied wooden table, and he set the basket down on the tabletop as they waited for the others to catch up to them.

When they arrived moments later, Leah's grandmother motioned to the water fountains surrounding the field. "So what do you think, Sam? Isn't this a relaxing place to have lunch?"

"Sure," he said, taking in the sights around him, then shrugging. "If you don't mind eating in a giant toilet bowl."

Before, Sam would have thought it was funny the way everyone's lips curled in disgust. But the moment he saw the disappointed look her grandma wore, he cringed on the inside. His intentions were never to make any of them feel bad about themselves.

God, they really are going to think I'm an asshole after this weekend.

To avoid Penny's eyes, Sam glanced out over the field and let his gaze wander to the other visitors in the park. They strolled back and forth, checking out the water features and tossing coins into the fountains. Some even sat on blankets in the grass, breathing in the fresh air and admiring the beauty of the fountains from afar. Because although the sun was high in the Texas sky, it really wasn't all that hot. Not with the warm breeze blowing over the water and the fine mist cooling the air. It was like Mother Nature's own personal air-conditioning.

Penny apparently had quickly shaken off Sam's comment about the toilet bowl because she lifted the lid on the wicker basket and began unpacking it. "I brought us all some turkey sandwiches, chips, fruit salad, and apple fritters. There's bottles of water in here too. If you don't want that, there's a soda machine at the top of the stairs."

Without a word, Leah's brother took off at a dead run, making Sam grin. By the time Ethan returned, everyone had sat down, ready to eat. The group made light conversation as they took turns chatting in between bites. Almost immediately, Sam noticed Leah wasn't saying much of anything. Actually, she'd barely said two words since they'd left the aquarium.

His gaze shifted onto her, but she didn't seem to notice. At first, he thought it was because she was people watching or marveling at the water fountains, but when she continued to stare off into space then grimaced, he knew something was wrong.

"Everything okay, sweetheart?"

She must've been deep in thought because it took her a moment to realize he'd spoken to her. "Um, what?"

"You all right? You seem a little out of it."

"Oh, I'm fine. Just thinking, that's all." She paused for a moment, then changed the subject. "If everyone is finished, we can wander around and check out the other fountains inside the park."

"I'm done," Sam told her, sliding his legs out from under the picnic table and the others followed suit.

After throwing away their trash and tossing the empty bottles and cans in the recycle bins, Ethan ran his grandma's basket to the car while the rest of them waited for him near the top of the stairs. When he returned, they strolled leisurely through the park until they happened upon a dancing water feature.

Rows of small fountains spouted water in sequence to classical music emitted from mounted speakers. The soothing arrangement started slow and graceful, then escalated to a faster, dynamic tune, while the rhythmic water hypnotized them. Toward the end, the well-choreographed show delighted its audience with a surprisingly high spurt of jet-streamed water.

"That was pretty cool," Sam told Leah.

She gazed up at him with her bright green eyes. "You

should see it at night. They turn on the color-changing lights, which really make it spectacular. Next time we come back—" Her words cut off, and a fleeting look of disappointment flashed in her eyes. "I mean, if we had more time here together, I would show you, but...I know we don't."

The finality of her words sank in, and his smile dissipated. Tomorrow was Sunday, and they would be heading home. Not only that, but he was supposed to make her family hate him, and at this point, he wasn't even sure if he wanted to anymore.

When he'd first suggested the idea to Leah, they had all been strangers to him, Leah included. Sure, he'd been attracted to her, but he still hadn't considered any real longevity to their liaison—romantic or not. It was supposed to be a temporary relationship...a fake one at that. And although he hated to think it, if he hadn't gotten her into a jam with her family to begin with, he would have already parted ways with her.

But since then, he'd spent so much time with her and had gotten to know her better. They'd become fast friends, and he'd started to imagine—*for some stupid reason*—that they'd remain that way even after the charade came to an end.

That couldn't happen though. Not realistically.

Once he upset her family enough to want him out of her life for good, Leah would dump him, and they would be forced to go their separate ways to keep her family from becoming suspicious. Because it wouldn't make sense for Leah to break up with her fiancé one day and then hang out with him the next like nothing had happened.

His chest tightened at the thought of not talking to her again. "Leah, I need to talk to you," he said, unable to tone down the urgency in his voice. His eyes flickered to her family members, who were still watching the dancing fountains, then landed back on hers. "Alone."

Her brows drew together. "Okay. Um, Mom, we're going to walk ahead. You guys catch up when you're done here."

"Okay, sweetheart. See you in a few minutes."

As Sam put his hand on Leah's back and guided her away from her family, his mind reeled. Sure, he and Leah would probably see each other around town once in a while. Maybe even stop to say hello. But that wasn't the same as spending time together and making each other laugh. And Sam really liked that she made him laugh.

They followed the sidewalk near a jogging path while he tried to think of a way for him to still see her. After they broke up, they would have to cool it for a while. No question about that.

Maybe after a few months though…

Yeah, that might work.

But damn, even a few months seemed like an awfully long time to wait before seeing or talking to her again. As it was, the more time he'd spent with her, the less time he wanted to be away from her. Not just because she was pretty to look at or made him desserts though. No one made him smile or laugh as much as she did. Not even his friend Max. And although he'd only known Leah for a short time and they would soon be parting company, the thought of not seeing her again made Sam feel like…he was losing his best friend. His heart rate kicked up, and his skin crawled at the thought. *Shit. No. There's got to be another way.*

Once they were completely out of her parents' sight, Leah stopped abruptly and turned to face him with genuine concern flashing in her eyes. "What's wrong?"

She was warm, genuine, kind, and an all-around decent human being. Her easy charm, laid-back personality, and remarkable sense of humor were some of his favorite things about her. Leah always went out of her way to keep from hurting other people's feelings, even if that meant taking a lot of flak in the process.

He admired her ambition in opening her own business and respected how hard she worked to achieve her dream of running a successful bakery. Even for a girl who had self-esteem issues when it came to her body, Leah was completely confident in the desserts she created in her kitchen. And rightly so.

Sam recalled what she'd said the night before about how being with a jerk was sometimes better than being alone, and it still pissed him off. Royally. Because no woman should ever feel that way. Especially one as sweet as Leah. She deserved better than that.

Sonofabitch. He liked her. A hell of a lot more than he should.

"Sam?"

"We need to figure something else out."

"About what?"

He ran a nervous hand through his hair. "I mean, we need to come up with another way out of this engagement. Something that doesn't require your family to hate me."

She blinked rapidly. "What? Why?"

Shit. Good question. If only he could answer it without getting her hopes up that they were anything more than just friends. He wished he could tell her how beautiful she was, how amazing he thought she was. But doing so would only complicate things between them. It was unfortunate, but his physical attraction to her was going to get him into deep shit if he wasn't careful. "Because." *Jesus. That's all I could come up with?*

"*Because?* What the hell kind of answer is that?" She

gazed at him for a moment, and then her eyes narrowed and her nostrils flared. "Damn it, Sam. Don't tell me you're backing out on me. You promised to help me get out of this mess." When he didn't respond right away, she threw her hands in the air. "Oh, that's just great. So this is why you've been on your best behavior today? You changed your mind about helping me and didn't want to tell me?"

"No, no, that's not it. I'm not backing out on you. I'm just...wanting to amend our previous agreement."

"How come? What changed?"

"I guess I did."

She crossed her arms and glared at him.

He sighed. "Look, I know you're upset. I'm sorry. I don't really want your family to hate me, okay? They're good people, and...well, I like them."

Most of them anyway.

Leah closed her eyes and rubbed at her pulsing temples. "God, I can't believe you're doing this to me. You're putting me in a position where I have no choice but to tell my family the truth."

"No. You won't have to do that. I'll help you figure out a different way for us to end the engagement. That way we can do so amicably and no one has to get thrown under a bus."

Her eyes shot open. "Are you nuts? That'll never work. Who the hell breaks up with their fiancé on good terms?"

"Leah, it'll be fine. We'll make it work, I promise. Just give me a little more time to figure out—"

"Bullshit!" Her whole face reddened as if liquid fire ran through her veins, flaring her anger. "This was your idea. You told me it would work, and it didn't. I'm not going along with any more of your half-baked schemes."

"Damn it, Leah. It would have worked...had I actually

given your family a good enough reason to hate me. But I didn't. I couldn't, all right?"

Leah crossed her arms and shifted her eyes away from him, breathing heavily. She was pissed, and he couldn't blame her one bit. Her gaze hovered over his right shoulder momentarily then flickered back to his. "Well, that's just too damn bad because *I* can." She put her hands on her hips, and her face bent with rage. "You cheating prick!"

His head snapped to her, along with some other nearby heads who overheard her remark. "Huh?"

"Who is she?" she said, raising her voice even louder. "Who's the whore you've been sleeping with behind my back?"

Sam squinted at her and shook his head. "What the hell are you talking about?"

"Oh, don't play innocent with me. I knew you were a player when I met you, but I didn't think you would keep seeing other girls on the side. God, I'm such an idiot. I should've known better than to get mixed up with someone like you."

A throat cleared behind Sam. "Is everything okay, Leah?"

Fuck. Sam recognized that voice. He twisted his neck to see her father standing ten feet away. The rest of her family was there too, and all of them were witnessing Leah's ridiculous, uncalled-for temper tantrum with wide eyes. *Just fucking great.*

"Oh, everything's perfect, Dad," Leah said with sarcastic flair. "Only Sam is apparently cheating on me." She covered her face with her hands and fake-sobbed into them.

Goddamnit. That shit looks believable too.

Sam turned back to her family and held up both of his hands in surrender. "I'm not cheating on her, I swear," he said before spinning back to Leah. He lowered his voice to keep the others from hearing. "Leah, stop this. What the hell are you doing?"

She kept her hands over her face but whispered back in a clear, determined voice, "I'm ending this...with or without your help." Then she fake-cried into her hands some more, jerking her shoulders up and down as if she were expelling brokenhearted tears.

Christ, he wanted to throttle her. And he probably would have if she hadn't drawn such a large crowd of onlookers. Her family members weren't the only voyeurs who had stopped to watch the one-woman show starring Leah while glaring at Sam like he was something they'd scraped off the bottoms of their shoes. Damn her. He was a lot of things, but a cheater sure the fuck had never been one of them.

Sheepishly, Sam held up one finger to her family, silently asking them to give him a minute alone with her, and then steered Leah away from the growing crowd. He pulled her around a corner, where a long line of bushes blocked them from view. Once he was sure they were far enough away that her family couldn't overhear anything, he stopped and wheeled around on Leah. "Okay, stop this shit right now."

Her face straightened instantly, and she glared back at him. "Nope. If you don't want to help me anymore, then that's fine. But you aren't leaving me a choice. I'm tired of lying to them, and I want this over with...today."

He shook his head adamantly. "Not like this."

"Why? What do you care if they hate you? I mean, it's not like you'll ever see them again anyway. *I'm* the one who has to face them for years to come, not you."

"I know, but..."

"But what? Jesus, Sam. Do you plan on becoming my dad's bowling partner or something?"

He shrugged lightly. He *did* like to bowl on occasion, but

he didn't think now would be a good time to bring that up. Especially since she was insistently tapping her foot, waiting for an answer to her question.

When he didn't give her one, she huffed out an irritated breath and threw her arms in the air. "Perfect. So now you have nothing to say?"

Actually, he had plenty to say, but the words clung to his tongue for dear life.

After another moment of silence passed between them, Leah said, "Damn it, Sam. Say something already. What the hell is your problem?"

Without thinking, Sam replied, "You are, damn it. At the moment, *you're* my fucking problem."

Stunned, Leah's mouth fell open, lip quivering, and her incredulous gaze fixed on him. She may have faked the whole crying bit with her family, but there was nothing pretend about the moisture now glistening in her glassy eyes. Her gaze lowered, and she bit into her bottom lip as if she were contemplating what she'd done to upset him.

But she hadn't done anything. Not really. Unless acting like her adorable self was something. She looked so worried though, as if she was concerned that he really was mad at her. And he was. Because he hated that she didn't know how beautiful she really was. Even when she was completely fucking clueless.

"I...I don't understand. Why do you care if my family hates you or not? Are you mental or something? You can't possibly enjoy being fake-engaged to a woman you aren't even attracted to."

He reached out and snagged her arm, pulling her closer. "You seriously don't know, do you?"

"Know what?"

Unable to stop himself, Sam slid his hands up her neck,

threaded his fingers into her hair, and pressed his mouth to hers. Her breath hitched at the unexpected gesture, but she didn't protest or push him away. Good. He liked knowing that he affected her the same way she did him.

His lips continued to move against hers, seeking more of the response he so desperately needed, until she tangled her fingers into the front of his shirt and leaned against him as if her legs were unable to hold her upright.

Desire flooded over him, attempting to wash away any senses he had left. But he didn't care. He angled her head, slid his tongue past her lips, and deepened the kiss. Every part of her mouth tasted like warm molasses. Sweet. Decadent. Intoxicating. Enough to drive a man entirely out of his mind. And the vanilla scent perfuming her fevered skin only worsened his craving.

Which was exactly why he broke the kiss and tore himself away from her. They were in a public park where there were children around, and he was practically dry-humping her leg. *Jesus.*

Leah licked her plump, swollen lip as if she was still trying to taste him there, but confusion filled her eyes. "W-what...was that for?" she whispered, sounding unsure of what the hell had come over him.

Sam's gaze darted briefly over her head and then back to her. He breathed out an expletive. "It was for me," he said, knowing damn well that, in about three seconds, she'd never believe a word of what he just said.

When a thoat was cleared behind her and Leah wheeled around to see her family standing there, her body tensed. She stared at their smiling faces for only a moment before turning back to gaze at him with a scowl plastered on her face.

He knew exactly how it looked. Although he'd spotted her relatives standing behind her *after* he'd kissed her, she undoubtedly believed he'd done so for their benefit to make them think the two of them had made up.

And as much as he wanted to correct her assumption, he wouldn't get a chance until he got her alone.

* * *

Leah's heart sank.

The moment she caught sight of her family, she quickly realized what a fool she had been. She lowered her eyes and felt the heat of embarrassment rush into her cheeks. She had thought he kissed her because he wanted to, not because he had to. Damn it. Why did she keep doing this to herself?

He'd told her not to read into anything when it came to the two of them pretending to be a couple, yet she couldn't seem to help herself. Each time he kissed her, touched her, or made some offhand remark about their nonexistent future together, she had been dumb enough to let herself hope that, somewhere deep down inside him, he'd meant every bit of it.

But he hadn't. Not once. There was nothing between them, and if that hadn't been perfectly clear before, it sure as hell was now.

Disappointed, she focused on the pavement beneath their feet, blinked away the unshed tears burning her eyes, and swallowed the lump forming in her throat. Her lips pinched tightly together.

I can't do this to myself anymore.

Even just being friends seemed like an unlikely feat for the two of them after everything that had happened. Relationships—including friendships—were already complicated enough without the added stress of one person having feelings that the other didn't return.

Maybe that didn't matter to Sam since he was the one who wasn't returning the sentiment, but it sure as hell mattered to her. Unfortunately.

From this point forward, she couldn't allow herself to keep hoping he'd come around or change his mind. Not only because it made her feel worse about herself, but... well, it hurt too damn much.

"Is everything okay over there?" her father asked, the sound of his husky voice wavering among neutral bystander, overprotective father, and fierce executioner.

Leah glanced at him and, without answering, turned her attention back to Sam.

His laser-beam gaze seared into her. "Leah?"

No way would she let him see how much he'd hurt her. Even if it had been unintentional, which she was sure it was. Sam would feel terrible if he knew he had hurt her, and then he would probably try to comfort her by telling her what a great person she was. Because that was what nice guys like Sam did.

But she didn't need his pity. Or want him to feel bad.

Leah planted a fake smile on her face. "Everything's fine. If you guys are ready to go home, we can head back to the beach house now." She spun on her heel and stalked toward her family, not bothering to check to see if Sam followed.

Her dad raised a suspicious brow, as if he still wasn't certain what to believe. "You sure you two are okay?"

"Yep, let's go," Leah said, then headed down the sidewalk toward the parking lot.

The car ride back to the beach house was excruciatingly painful. Though her grandpa's driving hadn't improved any since that morning, Sam and Leah sat stiffly in the backseat listening to the oldies radio station playing quietly in the background while her grandma prattled on about the thunderstorms expected to make an appearance later in the evening.

Sam's somber expression told Leah that he wasn't happy about something, but she was damn tired of trying to decipher his thoughts and actions. Besides, she almost always got it wrong anyway. Like here she was hoping he was upset because he realized he'd somehow hurt her, but deep down, the man was probably just disgruntled by the injustice of having a small penis.

The errant thought passed through her mind so quickly that she couldn't help the unexpected giggle that accidentally slipped past her lips. She covered her mouth and glanced over at Sam to see if he'd heard it.

"Something funny?" Sam asked, shifting his eyes onto her, though there was no amusement in them.

Oops. "Um, no. Nothing." She smirked as she turned her head to look out her passenger window. Okay, so it was a low blow... even if it was supposedly true.

Sure, the information Valerie had shared with her about the size of Sam's package had come from Max, and he *was* one of Sam's closest friends. But that didn't mean he had knowledge of how big his buddy's dick was. Friends or not, that kind of intimate detail probably wasn't shared often among men. And even if Max had seen it for himself, Leah doubted Sam would have been fully erect at the time. *Otherwise, I have way more to worry about than the size of Sam's dick.*

What constituted big or small anyway? The average penis was only around five or six inches in length, though most guys probably thought that was tiny in comparison to a porn star's equipment. Not to mention the different elements that factored into it all: length, girth, and even swelling.

Maybe Sam was just a grower.

She started to glance over at his crotch, but a twinge of remorse settled inside her. *Oh God. Stop it, Leah. Quit thinking about the man's junk already. He's not even into you.* Releasing a plaintive sigh, she went back to staring out her passenger window and watching the palm trees blur past.

By the time her grandfather pulled into the driveway, the late afternoon sun had already begun its descent toward the horizon, and the heat had started to dissipate. The others stood below the beach house chatting while Leah politely excused herself and headed upstairs to busy herself in the kitchen.

She'd promised she would make chocolate mousse for dessert, and if she was good at anything, it was at keeping her word. Unlike Sam. If she had known he was going to pull this crap and back out on her at the last minute, then she would never have let the fake engagement ruse continue.

In such a short period of time, everything had become so muddled. Now she needed to figure out what she was going to do before she and Sam got in any deeper with her family. Basically, before her mother started planning the wedding of the century that neither of them would be attending. Sheesh.

Twenty minutes later, the front door creaked open. Leah figured it was her grandmother coming up to grab the hamburgers they were supposed to toss on the grill for dinner. But just as she spooned the last of the mousse into the glassware she'd lined up on a tray, a man's voice said, "Can I help with anything?"

Leah's head shot up to see Sam standing in the kitchen doorway with his hands shoved deep into his pockets like a little boy who had been scolded for something he'd done wrong. "I think you've done enough," she said, setting the empty mousse bowl aside and reaching for the plastic wrap.

Warily, he entered the kitchen but stayed near the door

as if he expected he might need a quick getaway if kitchen utensils started flying toward him. "Look, we need to talk."

"I don't want to talk to you right now. I'm still mad at you for the crap you pulled earlier."

"Leah, just let me just explain."

"What is there to explain? You want to change our agreement and come up with a new plan. But there's no time. I can't keep lying to my family. The old plan was fine."

"Not if we were going to remain friends, it wasn't."

Leah eyes met his. He wanted to be friends with her. Just friends. And the thought made her want to bawl her eyes out. Because what she wanted was something completely different. Something he wasn't willing or able to give to her.

Wordlessly, she covered the entire tray with a sheet of plastic wrap before carrying it over to the fridge. She moved a few things around to make room for it, then set it down inside and closed the refrigerator door to find Sam standing on the other side. She tried to maneuver around him, but he blocked her path.

His piercing eyes held hers, not allowing her to look away. "We are friends, aren't we?"

Yeah. Friends. Leah stuffed all of her unwanted feelings for him into an emotional storage compartment and shoved it into the attic of her mind, hoping it would grow dusty and moldy and she'd forget all about it. "Sure," she muttered, shrugging a nonchalant shoulder. "Of course we are." *Damn it.*

His stance immediately relaxed, and she moved away from him. "Then how do you feel about being friends with benefits?"

Leah froze with her back to him. *What did he say?*

"Leah."

She turned to face him. "I...don't think I know what you mean."

He grinned. "Oh, I have a pretty good feeling you do."

As he eased toward her slowly, Leah backed away until her ass bumped into the counter behind her. He couldn't possibly mean...

Sam placed his hands on the counter, caging her between his arms. "Well?"

"Well, what?" she asked breathlessly.

He chuckled. "Come on, Leah. You can't possibly be this surprised to find out I'm attracted to you."

Wanna bet?

She shook her head in denial. "Are you kidding?"

His heated eyes glanced down her body and back up to her face. "Do I look like I'm at all joking?"

No. Actually, he looked like he wanted to eat her up. But she still couldn't wrap her brain around this new development. Sam was attracted to her? Since when? And why? "I...I don't know what to say."

"You don't have to say anything. I don't want to push you into doing anything you're uncomfortable with. Just think about it, okay? You know how I feel about relationships. I may not be looking for a serious one, but that doesn't stop me from being your friend...or from wanting to fuck you."

Holy shit! Heat pooled in her abdomen, blazed up her neck, and landed in her cheeks. She tried to remain calm, but her vagina wouldn't stop yelling *Yes! Yes! Yes!* from beneath her clothing. "I'll...um, think about it," she said coolly.

"Okay, good," he said, dropping his arms and taking a step back to give her room. "No matter the answer, it's not going to affect our friendship any. Just let me know what you decide."

She nodded and let out a slow breath. "Where are the

others?" she asked, changing the subject as quickly as possible. "We need to get the hamburgers on if we want to eat dinner sometime tonight."

"They're still downstairs. Your dad set fire to the grill."

Leah looked at him funny. "You mean he lit the grill?"

"No, I mean he set fire to it. It looks like a goddamn bonfire down there," he said seriously. "I was on my way upstairs when your grandma asked me to get the hot dogs because our hamburger cookout has now turned into a weenie roast. She also asked me to get you out of the house before your dad burned it down and accidentally killed his only daughter."

Leah smiled. "So you came to play white knight and save me, huh? And here I was thinking you were just hoping to get a sample of tonight's dessert."

"Who, me?" His eyes widened, feigning innocence. "I would never resort to putting your life in danger just so I could get my chocolate fix," he said while eyeing the empty mixing bowl she had used for the mousse.

"Oh really? Well, I was going to ask you if you wanted to lick the bowl, but since we *are* in danger of burning alive..." She placed the bowl in the sink and turned the water faucet on high, rinsing the leftover chocolate away.

Sam shook his head. "Damn it, woman. What the hell are you doing? We could've spared a few extra minutes."

"Ha! I knew it."

He grinned at her. "You are an evil woman."

"Says the man willing to let me die for the sake of chocolate."

Sam belted out a deep, rich laugh. "Actually, I was hoping you would run screaming from the house and leave me in here alone with the dessert. But I guess you probably figured that tactic out already."

"So you lied about the weenie roast, huh?"

"Nope, not at all. That part was true. Except the grill is in the middle of the backyard now rather than under the house, and the only danger you were in was me eating everyone's dessert."

"It wouldn't be any good right now. It has to chill for at least half an hour so it will set up properly. Otherwise the mousse will be runny."

"Well, we can't have that, now can we?" He nodded toward the door. "So are you coming downstairs with me or what? I wouldn't want your grandma to get onto me if I don't get her granddaughter to safety."

"Yeah, I guess so. But only for a little while." The corners of her mouth lifted. "I probably shouldn't leave the dessert unguarded for too long."

Sam winked at her and nodded. "Smart girl."

After loading their arms down with all the fixings for hot dogs, they headed down to join the others. Sam really hadn't lied about the bonfire. The flames on the charcoal grill were so high that Leah was surprised the fire department hadn't been called out.

"There you are, Leah," her mother said, sitting at the picnic table with the others. "Your grandmother and I were just discussing some ideas for the wedding."

Leah grimaced. "Mom, we don't have to do that right now. There's plenty of time to do that later." *Like when I am engaged to a man who is actually going to marry me rather than one who just wants to sleep with me.*

God. She still couldn't believe what Sam had proposed upstairs. The thought of sleeping with him sent a shiver up her spine.

"Sweetheart, we have to start talking about these things now. Do you know how much thought goes into a wedding?"

It must have been a rhetorical question because her mother barely took a breath before the next question flew out of her mouth. "What do you think about having canapés served at the reception rather than a full-course meal? It would be much more sophisticated, I think."

Sam plopped down at the far end of the table, cleared his throat, and fiddled with the collar of his shirt, seemingly uncomfortable with the entire conversation. After everything he'd told Leah about his past with women, the last thing he obviously wanted to do was plan a wedding. Even a fake one.

Of course he should have thought about that before he bailed out on their plan and then let her family believe they had made up at the park. If he had just left things alone, the engagement would already be called off, and he wouldn't have to endure the torture of listening to her mother go on and on about a stupid wedding that would never take place.

Leah rubbed her temples. "Mom, we haven't even set a date yet."

"Well, that's easy enough. I've been thinking about where we should have your wedding, and I had a great idea. It should be at the Water Gardens. It's a wonderful location, and the fountains would make a beautiful backdrop for the wedding photos."

Leah shifted her weight and bit her lip. "Um, I don't know, Mom."

"Well, why not? It would be perfect. You always said you wanted to be married here, but it would be a much more suitable location than what you had in mind."

Leah glanced over at Sam, and her right eye twitched nervously. She thought he would still be slinking away from any talk of marriage or wedding plans, but his gaze was glued to her, as if he were waiting to hear her response as well.

"Mom, let's not talk about this right now. There's plenty of time for that late—"

"What other location?" Sam asked, injecting himself into the conversation and effectively cutting Leah off. When she didn't answer him right away, he shifted his eyes onto her mother. "What other place, Nancy?"

Her mom waved her slim hand through the air dismissively, as if she couldn't even bother considering the idea. "Oh, Leah had this crazy plan about having a wedding on the beach. But I told her it isn't a smart choice for formal wear."

"And I told you that I don't want a formal wedding," Leah corrected, crossing her arms.

"Sure you do, dear. Every girl wants to look beautiful for her wedding. Besides, squeezing into a fancy gown on your special day would give you a good incentive to lose a few pounds."

Leah swallowed the gasp that tried to vacate her mouth and scowled at her mother. My God, did she have to say that right in front of Sam of all people? It's like the woman purposely tried to embarrass her at times.

"That's enough," Sam said, his eyes focused firmly on Leah's mother. "I don't want to hear those kind of insulting remarks about my fiancée."

Leah cringed. *Oh, no.*

Her mother blinked in apparent shock. "Insulting? I…I'm not insulting her." Then she pushed her hair away from her face as she regained her composure. "I'm just trying to give my daughter some good advice. Lord knows she never listens to it anyway."

"Nancy," he said, lowering his voice in warning. "I asked you nicely to stop nagging Leah, but now I'm telling you, drop it already."

"Oh, Sam, don't be ridiculous. I'm just trying to point out—"

Sam slapped his hand down on the picnic table so hard the entire table shook, and her mother startled. "Damn it, Nancy! What part of this do you not understand? I've let this go on far too long, and I'm ashamed of that, but I'm not going to do it anymore. I won't stand by while you embarrass your daughter—or yourself—any more than you already have."

Her mother huffed out an exasperated breath. "I'm not embarrassing her. There's nothing shameful about Leah wanting to improve herself."

Sam's eyes narrowed as he shook his head. "I agree. But the only person here who wants to improve Leah is *you*."

Chapter Fifteen

S am bit his tongue so hard that he swore he tasted blood.

He'd had enough of Nancy's bullshit, and if he had kept his mouth shut any longer, that would have made him just as bad as the rest of them.

Without a word, Nancy rose from her seat and went upstairs without so much as an apology. *There goes her Mother of the Year award.*

Not that she would have ever received one from Sam. What kind of mother needles her only daughter nonstop about her weight? It was as if she was oblivious to how she snuffed out the light in her daughter's eyes every time she publicly humiliated her.

The tension hovering in the air was so thick that Sam had to clear his throat to keep from choking on it. Thankfully, Leah's grandmother took control of the situation and turned everyone's attention to the food.

As each of them took turns burning their wieners in the blaze, Sam noticed how quiet everyone had grown. The silence had settled over them like a warm, comfortable blanket. Soon after everyone had finished eating, Jack and Penny retired for the evening, reminding Bill to make sure the fire was completely out before he left it unattended.

While Bill stood in the middle of the yard dousing the fire, Sam glanced over at Leah. "You okay?"

"Sure. Everything is fine," she said, trying to sound cheery, though her low, remote tone gave her away. Not allowing her gaze to meet his, Leah moved to a nearby lounge chair and sat on the end of it. With her shoulders slumped and her chin down, she twisted her fingers together over and over again, growing more and more distant by the second.

Sam sat behind her on the same lawn chair, his weight making her rise a little as he positioned himself and scooted closer to her. He leaned forward until his chest was almost touching her back. "You don't have to pretend with me," he whispered.

"I—I'm not." Before he had a chance to say anything else, she rose from her chair. "I think I'm going to turn in too." Then she started for the house.

Sam couldn't let her walk away without telling her one thing though. "Leah?"

She stopped in her tracks and spun toward him. "Yeah, Sam?"

"A beach wedding sounds perfect to me."

An appreciative smile spread across her face, then she continued on the path to the stairs and disappeared from sight.

Bill came over and plopped down in a plastic lawn chair that was adjacent to Sam's. "Do you mind if I have a few words with you, Sam?"

Sam nodded. "Sure. What's on your mind?"

Leah's father glanced over at his teenage son, who was

sitting at the picnic table playing a game on his phone. "Ethan, why don't you do me a favor and go grab us a couple of beers from the fridge upstairs? I'd like to talk to Sam alone."

Uh-oh. This can't be good.

"Okay, Dad." Ethan headed toward the stairs but stopped halfway there. "By the way, when you say a couple of beers…"

"A couple…meaning two. One for me and one for Sam. If you're thirsty, your grandma has some juice in the fridge for you."

Ethan rolled his eyes and continued on his mission.

Bill shook his head. "That boy loves to push his luck, doesn't he?"

"I'm betting he gets it honestly," Sam said.

"Ah, yes. Well, that he does. And that's exactly what I wanted to talk to you about." Leah's dad clasped his hands and threaded his thick fingers together in front of him. "Nancy really doesn't mean any harm. I know that the things she says sound terrible coming out of her mouth, but they are coming from a place of love. She just doesn't know how to communicate them in a way that doesn't sound like she's…"

"Insulting your daughter with every breath?"

"Exactly. I'm not trying to make any excuses for her. Nancy's own mother—God rest her soul—was much the same way. Worse in some ways. Because in that woman's eyes, Nancy had to be perfect. And nothing she ever did measured up. Every family has their burdens, and this one is ours. But I don't want that to scare you off."

Sam shook his head. "Nothing your wife says about Leah would ever make me change my opinion of your daughter. It's more of a reflection on Nancy's insecurities than it is on Leah's."

"I absolutely agree. That's why I'm going to ask Nancy to see a therapist when we get back home. This has gone on long enough. I'm sure Nancy doesn't want to revisit her past, but she has some issues she needs to work out about her deceased mother. That woman was harsh and never had a kind word for my wife. It may take some time, but I'm hoping she'll make an appointment. Leah's birthday party is coming up soon, and I can't imagine a better present than that."

"Party?" Sam asked, raising a brow. He knew Leah had a birthday coming up sometime in the near future, but this was the first he'd heard about an actual party. Seemed odd, given that he was supposed to be her fiancé. "Is it a surprise party or something? This is the first time I've even heard anything about it."

Bill looked at him strangely then shook his head. "No, Leah knows all about it. I'm surprised she hadn't mentioned it. It's nothing fancy. We just sit around eating cake while we watch Leah open her gifts. It'll be at our house two Saturdays from now at six o'clock. You're welcome to come, of course."

Ah, okay. So that was why Leah hadn't mentioned it. It would be past the two-week mark, and they were supposed to be broken up by then. "I'll see what I can do, but I may have to work that weekend," Sam lied.

Bill nodded. "Well, that's another reason I wanted to talk to you. I'd like to set up a date for you to install those French doors. I was thinking we could do it..." He halted his words at his son's arrival.

"Here you go, Dad," Ethan said, handing his father a beer. Then he passed Sam a can of soda and clasped him on the shoulder. "You know what they say about payback, right?"

Sam threw back his head and let out a hearty laugh. "You're all right, kid."

Ethan gave him a fist bump and then went back to the picnic table, where he settled in to play on his phone once again. Sam held the soda away from him as he popped the top, making sure the little shithead hadn't shaken it up before handing it over. When it didn't explode out of the can, he settled back on the lounge chair and took a sip.

"That boy and his phone, I swear," Bill said, shaking his head. "He hardly ever puts it down." A tender smile slid onto Bill's face. "I guess he will eventually . . . when the right girl comes along and gives him something better to stare at."

Sam nodded. "Happens to the best of us."

An hour and two beers later, Sam said good night and went upstairs to turn in. Entering the room, he noted Leah lying on her side of the bed facing toward the bathroom. He couldn't see her face and didn't know whether she was awake or not, but he tried not to disturb her as he grabbed his bag and locked himself in the bathroom.

Still on edge from the talk he'd had with her father, Sam cursed under his breath and stripped down to nothing. He twisted the shower handles, making the water as hot as he could stand, then stepped under the spray. He felt like a dirtball—a scumbag, really—for the way he kept tricking her family into believing he was going to be Leah's future husband, which would make him a part of their lives for the long haul.

As if that wasn't bad enough, then he'd gone and asked Leah to have sex with him. Friends with benefits. Jesus. Her dad was right about one thing. Leah *did* deserve better. Better than Gavin and better than him, if he were being honest.

She needed a guy who would take a chance on her because she was worth it. Not some chickenshit like Sam who was afraid to get into another relationship because none of his earlier ones had worked out.

But the mere thought of her being with someone that wasn't him really pissed him off. God, he was an ass. *I don't want you, but no one else can have you.* How was that for a fucked-up way of thinking?

And it wasn't actually true. He *did* want her. He just didn't *want* to want her. He'd love nothing more than to slide into that bed, pull her panties off, and crawl up in between those amazing legs of hers.

But he couldn't do it. He'd told her he would give her time to think about it and wasn't willing to push her for an answer. Maybe he shouldn't go down that road with her at all, but if her answer was yes, he had no doubt he would pay the toll. He hadn't meant for all of this to happen, but now that it had, he needed to figure out a way to get her out of his system. And fast.

In the meantime, he would resort to other measures.

Sam's gaze fell onto his chest and followed the trail of running water down to his dick. His brow furrowed at the sight. God, he was pathetic. But he needed to do something to take the edge off. He blew out a slow breath and let his hand follow the same path.

Twenty minutes passed before Sam emerged from the bathroom. He was a little more relaxed than he had been before but still felt like shit. The mere idea that he might be fucking with Leah's head by asking her to sleep with him did a number on his conscience. He didn't want to hurt Leah, which was exactly what could happen if he didn't put a stop to all of this now.

He tossed his bag onto the chair in the corner, then made his way over to the bed in the darkened room. Pulling back the covers, he slid beneath them only to come into direct contact with a warm, soft body. While he was in the shower, Leah had apparently rolled over in her sleep and was now lying in the middle of the bed, sprawled out on her back. Not wanting to wake her, Sam squeezed himself into the eighteen inches of bed she had left for him and positioned his left arm under her pillow.

The motion jostled her a little, and she startled, moaned, and then rolled toward him, curling into his chest. He considered waking her and getting her to scoot over, or even getting out of bed and walking around to the other side to sleep, but something happened that held him firmly in place.

She murmured his name.

Without a word, he pulled against his chest and kissed her.

Leah startled awake as his lips brushed firmly against hers, massaging them in a slow, sensual motion. "Sam?" she whispered.

"Yeah, it's me." Then he kissed her again. This time, his tongue dipped inside, making a shallow sweep of her mouth. When her tongue met his head on, he groaned and pulled her tighter against him. What started out as a simple kiss quickly changed into a passionate tangling of tongues.

His pulse raced as his heart pounded against his lungs, beating the breath right out of them. He only probed deeper though, and Leah moaned.

Sam stiffened, then tore himself away from her. Damn it. He'd promised not to push her into anything. "Leah, I—" He cut himself off and lay there staring at her, not knowing what to say.

The plea in her confused eyes gutted him. Then she tried to maneuver away from him to the other side of the bed.

"Leah, wait..." Sam pushed her onto her back as he rolled on top of her, pinning her body beneath his. "Look, I know I said I wouldn't push you but..."

She panted softly and shook her head, as if she didn't understand. "What the hell do you want from me, Sam?"

"I want my mouth on you."

Her brows knitted together. "Yeah, well, you had your mouth on me."

Sam grinned sadistically. "That's not exactly what I had in mind." Then he leaned forward and grazed his lips over the shell of her ear. "You have about three seconds to stop me before this gets out of hand."

She blinked at him in stunned silence as the seconds ticked by.

When he was sure she was willing to partake in whatever the hell this was, he said, "I'll take that as a yes."

He rose to his knees, shoved the covers off the bed, and wedged himself between her legs. The room was dark, which he hoped helped to soothe her frazzled nerves about her body. He grasped her calves, massaging and kneading them, acclimating her to his basic touch. Slowly, his hands worked their way up her legs until his fingers landed on her bare thighs.

She trembled, and her posture stiffened.

Okay, apparently not.

Sensing her hesitation, his roving hands stopped immediately. "You sure you're okay with this?" he asked softly, searching her face for an answer.

Leah shook her head.

"Then maybe we should start with something else first."

She paused, then smiled shyly at him. Her eyes lit up with pure determination as her hands moved down to peel the tank top off her body. He hadn't expected that, but he stilled her hands with his and shook his head. "Okay, now you're just taking away all of my fun. Do you unwrap other people's presents on their birthdays too?"

Leah gave him a meek smile. "Sorry. I was just... trying to get it over with quickly."

He snaked his arms around her, pulled her to a sitting position, and whisked the tank top over her head with dizzying speed before dropping it to the floor. "Fast enough for you?"

"Yep." A giggle slid from her lips, but she stifled it the moment his gaze lowered to her full, round breasts.

His breath caught in his throat. He hadn't meant to blatantly stare, but he couldn't seem to stop himself from doing so. "Jesus. You don't know how beautiful you are."

She shook her head in disbelief. "You don't have to say that."

His glaring eyes shifted to hers, and his voice roughened. "I didn't say it because I had to. I said it because I meant it."

"But it's just that—"

Sam kissed her again, taking his frustration out on her mouth. He wanted her to feel the bold caress of his tongue and the way his lips burned against hers to make her breathtakingly aware of the brutal strength of his attraction. Whether she wanted to believe it or not.

"Before this is over, Leah, I'm going to make damn sure you see yourself the way I see you."

Before she had a chance to speak, his firm mouth closed over one hardened nipple, making her body jolt. He sucked strongly, and she arched her back, thrusting out her chest even more, which only provided him with a better angle.

His free hand cupped her other breast, stroking and fondling, until his thumb strummed over her tight bud. She closed her eyes and breathed deeply, as if she enjoyed the feeling of him touching her. Then a low moan rose from her throat, and her fingers threaded through his hair, encouraging him to continue. After several more minutes of lavishing attention to both breasts by switching between his mouth and his hands, Sam sat upright.

He smoothed his hands over her bent knees at his sides

and began slowly working his way up the outside of her thighs. He tugged her shorts down her legs and off her feet before tossing them to the floor. His dick hardened instantly at the sight of Leah lying there in nothing but a pair of black panties. As he reached for them, his fingers whispered over the silky material, then slipped beneath the stretchy waistband. Taking his sweet time and enjoying the hell out of it, he eased them down her legs until they joined the other garments on the carpeted floor.

His hands traveled slowly back up to her knees, which were now locked tightly together. He glanced up and grinned. "Spread your legs, sweetheart."

She trembled as she took a deep breath and reluctantly obeyed the command.

Sam's mouth watered with the need to taste her. So much so that he didn't even hesitate, didn't give her time to prepare. He just leaned forward and flicked his tongue over her clit to capture her flavor. Leah practically shot off the bed like a bottle rocket, but he managed to grip her hips to keep her in place. Then he lowered his mouth to her once again. Buried in the apex of her thighs, Sam flattened his tongue against her and gave her another long, drawn-out lick.

Fuck, that's good.

He firmed the pressure on her sensitive bundle of nerves and lapped at her insistently as he reveled in the vibrations coming from her throat. He grinned when she whimpered and opened her legs wider to provide him better access. He knew that he was the first man she'd ever let get this intimate with her, and he was determined to show her what the hell she'd been missing out on.

* * *

With each feathery stroke of Sam's tongue, a fierce yearning coiled in Leah's belly, and her eyes slid shut in ecstasy. A gripping sensation built inside her, threatening to rip her apart at the seams. Her body quivered at the thought.

"Oh God," she moaned. "Sam...please..."

She didn't know what the hell she was begging him for, but the urgent, breathless plea seemed to fuel his greedy mouth to work faster, licking and sucking, while coaxing the orgasm from deep within her. And she was close. So damn close.

When she finally reached her peak, a strangled, incoherent sound tore from her throat, and she involuntarily bucked her hips against his face. Sam's mouth molded to her as systematic waves of pleasure took over her body, and she cried out again from the delicious torture.

Heaven. She'd died and gone to heaven.

Actually, she probably looked like a dead person lying there with her limp body melting into the bed like an overheated ice cream cone. She felt fragmented. Shattered. Her bones disintegrated, her body lethargic.

He gave her a gentle nip on the inside of her thigh, then rose to his feet with a proud grin on his face. "You okay to continue?"

When she only gave him a sluggish nod, he chuckled. "Okay, so round two it is," he said, still smiling as he moved to the door. "But you're going to have to hold on a second while I go downstairs and get a condom out of my truck. I stashed a couple in the console at the last minute."

Leah twisted her neck sideways to look at him and blinked rapidly.

Sam grinned. "Yeah, so I brought condoms on our trip," he said with a shrug. "I'm a guy. Sue me."

She smiled back at him, then gestured lazily across the dimly lit room.

"What?"

Leah panted softly but couldn't seem to speak. She motioned again.

His brow rose. "You have a condom...in here?"

Leah smiled.

He glanced in the direction she pointed then back at her. "In a drawer?"

She shook her head, though it wasn't a very coordinated effort.

"Is it in the bathroom?"

She shook her head again.

"You know it would be easier if you just spoke already, rather than playing a game of charades."

"My bag," she managed to whisper, though it took a lot of effort. Then she gestured to the chair where she'd left it.

He unzipped the duffel bag and rummaged through it, using his hands to feel around the inside until he found what he was looking for. As he pulled out the foil packet, he said, "Guess I'm not the only one who took condoms on our trip, huh?"

Normally a comment like that would have sent her into an embarrassed state, but she couldn't seem to muster up the energy to be mortified. Besides, he'd already admitted to doing the same thing.

Condom in hand, Sam sauntered back over to the bed and stopped at the end. She watched as he pulled his shirt off and added it to the pile of clothes on the floor, then reached for the button on his shorts.

Unfortunately, she couldn't see what he was doing from the waist down, but the rasp of his zipper sounded in her ears. Although she was curious and wanted to take a quick peek at what she had signed up for, she fought the urge to lean up onto her elbows.

Not only was she completely spent from the magnificent orgasm he'd bestowed upon her, but breaking her neck to catch a glimpse of his dick would look a little conspicuous. The last thing she wanted to do was make him feel self-conscious about his size. She knew how it felt to wear that badge of shame and wouldn't wish that kind of neurosis on anyone.

Besides, not every guy with a big one was good in the sack, and there was no way every guy with a small one sucked in bed. That just wasn't possible. Or reasonable. The saying about the boat and ocean probably held a lot of truth. So even if she didn't have any expectations about the size of Sam's...boat, that didn't mean she couldn't hope for some rough seas and decent swells.

Either way though, it didn't really matter to her how much heat he was packing. This was Sam, after all. Her Sam. The man she'd fallen head over heels for.

The man she...loved.

Leah smiled, realizing the truth. She did love him. More than she'd ever loved anyone before. And she didn't give a shit if he had a matchstick in his pants, as long as it was *her* matchstick, and she was the only one getting to blow it.

Not that he'd asked her to reciprocate or anything. *Wait. Why hadn't he asked me to return the favor?*

In her experience, most men liked it when a woman went down on them. Then again, none of the guys she'd ever dated in the past had mentioned having an issue with the size of their dick. They weren't hung or anything. Just average-sized, which they seemed comfortable enough with.

But damn, if Sam's package was as small as Max had told

Valerie, then the poor guy must have been too embarrassed to say anything.

Leah sighed inwardly. *Damn it. Why didn't I pick up on that sooner?*

When she heard the crinkling of foil, guilt coursed through her, leaving behind a selfish residue. God, he probably thought she was a jerk for not offering the same oral pleasure he'd given to her.

"By the way," Sam said, his knuckles brushing against her sex as he positioned himself. "I'm going to try to be quiet as I can, but you might want to hold on to the headboard for this."

Cute, Sam. But after what Valerie told me, we'll probably be lucky if the condom doesn't fall off.

Sam shoved into her with a deliberate thrust, and Leah gasped, her body tensing as she grated her nails across the wood in search of the headboard. *Oh, sweet Jesus.*

He held himself still, as if he were waiting for her to get her bearings. Thank God. Because she needed a moment to adjust to the overwhelming sensation of fullness and the heavy pressure against her cervix. All of which meant only one thing.

Max had fucking lied. Big time.

Chapter Sixteen

Sam groaned.

God, she was tight. His cock ached to move inside her, but not yet. He knew she hadn't expected him to be as large as he was, and he wanted to wait for her to give him the go-ahead before he continued. He couldn't help the smile spreading across his face though. "You okay, sweetheart?"

Leah said something unintelligible, which only made him grin more. Then she wrapped her fingers around the edge of the wooden headboard and added, "Mmm-hmm."

Digging his fingers into her hips, he withdrew until he was almost all the way out, then slid home again. Her body trembled as he filled her, and she moaned. Warm and pliant, her wet heat squeezed around him, clamping down on him, which made breathing almost unbearable, but her insistent pleas ignited a primal urge to do it again.

Hot and hard inside her, he continued to pump into her over and over with a fast-paced rhythm that was barely sustainable. It had been a while since he'd been with a woman, and the searing need to climax was already burning through him with every plunge.

Sam's breathing grew more ragged. His entire body vibrated with the need to satisfy his craving for her once and for all, and he didn't think he could hold off much longer. "Christ, Leah, if we don't slow this down, I'm gonna—"

"Oh God! Come," she demanded quietly, arching her back off the bed. Her inner muscles squeezed tighter, gripping him relentlessly, as she climaxed around his length.

Thank God.

The antique bed shook back and forth with the force of his thrusts as Sam drove into her even harder, pounding with a fast-paced rhythm until the pressure exploded from within. His dick throbbed inside her as hot blood coursed through his veins. When his knees threatened to buckle, he leaned forward and palmed the headboard to hold himself upright.

Splayed out in front of him, Leah's curvy body purred with a sigh of satisfaction. She wore a dazed expression with glassy, unconcerned eyes, as if the last thing on her mind was that she was still naked while Sam's hot gaze enjoyed the view. Progress, if you asked him.

Once their labored breathing began to slow, Sam gently separated from her and wiped a bead of sweat from his brow. "You okay?"

In that moment, Leah's nerves must've come rushing back in full swing. Not letting her eyes meet his, she sat up quickly, awkwardly covering her breasts with her crossed arms. "I...um, yes."

Sam pretended not to notice but wanted to give her a second to collect herself without his presence making things worse for her. "I'll be right back," he said, heading into the bathroom.

He shut the door behind him and quickly disposed of the spent condom. Then he washed his hands while he berated himself for being such a fucking idiot. He had told her he wouldn't push her about the friends-with-benefits thing, yet the moment he got her alone and in bed, he did just that. Fuck.

Leaning on the sink, he huffed out a hard breath. Did she regret it? Had he just made things awkward between them because he'd seen her naked? Was it possible that he'd screwed everything up by giving in to his impulses to have her under him?

God. Of course I did. What could he do about it now though?

There was no way they could go back to being friends who had never had sex before. Shit just didn't work that way. A guy couldn't stick his dick in a woman and then tell her he'd made a mistake. Especially when it hadn't felt like a mistake at the time. But now she wouldn't even so much as look at him.

Fucking great.

See? This was exactly what he hadn't wanted. To mess up the one thing they had going for them—their friendship— all because he didn't know how to keep his fucking hands to himself and his dick in his pants. Now he had to go back out there and tell her he didn't want things to change between them...a dick move on any guy's part after he'd already slept with the girl. *Sonofabitch.*

He would just explain it all to her. Tell her that, while he really liked her, he didn't want their relationship to change. They would have to keep things casual between them from this point on. Nothing heavy. Definitely not anything that would signify a relationship...like sex. That would only end up complicating things even more than they already were.

No more sex though? Really?

After knowing how good she had felt, he hated the idea of not having her again. Or that some other guy might have her. But no, he had to be fair to her. No matter what, he couldn't risk their friendship more than he had already. So no sex. Ever.

Okay, ever again.

Sam sighed, then returned to the bedroom to find a fully clothed Leah standing by the window. "I take it you found your clothes."

Her gaze lifted to his. "I, uh...sorry. I wanted to get dressed before you came back." She ran a nervous hand through her mussed hair, then looked away from him.

Damn it. She was already retreating back inside herself, which had him gritting his teeth. "I'm actually glad you did," he said, thinking of what he might have done if he'd returned to find her still naked.

Sam strolled over to her, determined to say what was on his mind. But his thoughts lingered on how good her gorgeous, curvaceous body felt in his arms, how she writhed beneath him as he drove into her over and over again. And he couldn't do it. He couldn't say words he didn't mean. So instead he said, "This just means I get to undress you all over again."

* * *

The next morning, Leah yawned sleepily.

Warm and relaxed, she hated the idea of getting out of bed since it was her last chance to sleep in before her work-week began. She even tried to drift back into unconsciousness, but before she counted her last sheep, her sensible side kicked into gear. It was Sunday, which meant they would be leaving for home this afternoon, and if she was going to make it down to the beach before high tide rolled in, then she had to wake up now.

Damn it. *Sometimes it really sucked to be an adult.*

Groaning, she rolled onto her back and stretched her arms out to the side, only for one of them to come into contact with a solid form. That was the moment she remembered she was naked...and not alone. *Sam. Shit!*

She pulled her arm back quickly and flickered her eyes open, blinking them a few times to clear her vision. The muted glow of blue morning light filtered through the cream-colored curtains, illuminating the bedroom. Sam was lying on his side, facing her, with the sheet covering both of them from the waist down. And he was close. Too close.

Had she actually been lying against his chest and hadn't realized it?

She barely finished the thought when Sam shifted his position, molding his hard, masculine body intimately against her side. Still asleep, he threw one of his legs over hers and dropped a heavy arm over her waist. Then his fingers moved toward her lower abdomen, stopping just inches away from her lady bits.

"Mmm," he moaned, nuzzling his face into her hair as his rapidly hardening length dug into her hipbone.

Holy fuck. She tensed, and her thighs trembled.

His slow, even breaths convinced her that he was still asleep and completely unaware of where his roaming hand had wandered off to. But his twitching fingers were so close to where she wanted them most, and the sensation sent electric shock waves radiating through her nerve endings.

The insatiable man had taken her three times last night, and each session had lasted longer than the previous one. And knowing him, if he woke up now, he would probably have his way with her again. Clearly, the man was trying to kill her. Death by...desire? That was a thing, right?

Then Leah cringed at the thought of him waking up next to her while she was nude. It was anxiety-inducing enough to let Sam strip her bare in a darkened room. But it was a whole different kind of embarrassment for him to see her naked in broad daylight. One she wasn't ready for.

Leah inched away from him until his hand fell off her waist and she was able to slide out of the bed without him detecting her absence. If you asked her, she'd already had enough awkward or embarrassing moments with this man to last her a lifetime. Her mother had made certain of that.

Sam too, if she were being honest. *Friends with benefits. Jeez.* She still couldn't believe he'd propositioned her with that.

If someone had asked her a week ago if she wanted to have sex with Sam, the answer would have been a resounding and undeniable yes. But once he'd actually asked her to take their friendship to the next level, she hadn't known if she could go through with it. Last night she'd thought long and hard about it and still hadn't come to a decision. She'd actually considered telling him no. Until she awoke with his mouth on hers.

She still wasn't sure what had happened last night to make him kiss her that way. It wasn't like they'd had any kind of real conversation about what they were doing in the heat of the moment. And damn, there had been lots of heat. More than she'd ever thought possible.

But today, things were different. There were feelings to consider. Well, hers anyway. Sam had made it clear that the only things he was interested in were friendship and benefits. Anything beyond that hadn't been agreed upon between them.

Probably for the best anyway.

After today, the whole engagement charade would be over. Sam hadn't made her family hate him so Leah had no choice but to take matters into her own hands. He didn't know it yet, but after they returned home, she planned to avoid any contact with her family for a few days, then drop by to tell them that he had broken off their supposed engagement.

Undoubtedly, she would be a hot mess when she delivered the news that she and Sam were over. Even now, just the thought of never seeing him again had tears lodging in her tight throat. She wasn't even sure what excuse she would give them yet, but this was the only logical and most reasonable option she had. Never in a million years would anyone in her family believe that she'd actually broken up with him. None of them were that stupid.

It was obvious that she cared about him. Probably too much really. It was really ridiculous when she thought about it. She was dreading the loss of a fiancé that she never really had to begin with. But why?

Because I'm a damn fool, that's why.

A stupid, sentimental fool who had made the biggest mistake of her life. She'd fallen for a guy who wanted to have sex with her but had no interest in being in a relationship. *Smart move, Leah.*

There was always a chance that Sam would change his mind about having his cake and eating it too. Hell, who knew? Maybe he already had. Or even worse. What if while he was sleeping with Leah, he actually met the woman of his dreams?

She swayed dizzily. *Oh God.* Just the idea of that happening was like an icy hand plunging into her chest and gripping her heart with brutal force.

Unfortunately, her time as Sam's fiancée had finally run its course. And although he still had an offer on the proverbial table, Leah knew that, if she didn't start putting some distance between her and Sam, she would be the one ripping her own heart out when the time came to say good-bye.

With her nerves stretched taut, she glanced at him once more, then sighed heavily. For her own sake, she had to let him go.

Chapter Seventeen

Sam flopped over on his stomach and groaned. God, he was such a fucking coward. After Leah had gotten dressed in the bathroom, she'd tiptoed out the bedroom door, closing it quietly behind her. The moment he heard the door snick shut behind her, he regretted not saying anything. Why hadn't he just told her he was awake and stopped her from leaving?

Because I didn't want her to think I'm some kind of damn pervert who feels women up in their sleep, that's why.

He'd never been accused of groping women in his sleep before, but it was as if his hands were heat-seeking missiles, designed to home in on all of Leah's hot spots...and the woman had a lot of them.

Sam had already exhausted himself with her three times during the night...and it still hadn't been enough. And that was after he'd jacked off in the shower last night like a randy teenage boy who couldn't control his impure thoughts. God, no wonder Leah practically ran out of the room. Surely, she had tired of him pulling her under him and rutting against her like a damn bull.

To be fair though, she hadn't turned him down once. He'd fallen asleep with his face buried in her vanilla-scented hair, and her warm, pliant body had been pressed tightly against his all night long. Hell, it would give any guy a boner.

Sam grinned. He'd spent hours exploring all the sexy curves of Leah's body and plunging into that sweet wet heat over and over again. It had been way better than anything he'd imagined.

But he hadn't meant for his hand to practically have its way with her this morning in his sleep-induced coma. Christ. He'd only woken up when he'd felt her body stiffen next to him. Even then, he still hadn't been fully aware of what he was touching until he curiously rasped his fingers over her again, and Leah squirmed in response. That was when his senses had shot to full awareness.

Before he could apologize or even so much as jerk his hand back, she'd moved away from him. He didn't want to make her even more uncomfortable so he pretended to be asleep. But the urge to pull her back into bed and kiss her breathless had been strong. Had he thought his admirable control would allow him to stop there, he might have actually done it. But he knew better than that.

After last night, he realized a simple truth.

I'm a fucking idiot.

Because there would be no winners in this game they were playing, and someone could wind up getting hurt. And that person most likely would be Leah. And she was all that mattered to him.

Okay, that wasn't entirely true. Somewhere along the way, he'd started to care what her family thought of him too. He didn't want them to hate him and didn't regret backing out on his and Leah's agreement. Her new plan to make her family believe he was a cheating bastard had been a good one. But damn it, he wanted her in his life.

Maybe that was just him being selfish. The last thing he needed was to put himself in a position where he'd break someone's heart.

When Leah had fallen asleep last night after round two, Sam had lain there staring up at the ceiling, listening to the raindrops tapping on the window and hoping the musical sound would silence the urge he had to wake Leah up and take her again. It hadn't.

Obviously, Sam could no longer trust his own judgment in relation to women. All of his relationships up to this point had had two things in common: how quick the relationship had begun and how fast each had ended. Yes, he was ready to settle down, but he wasn't willing to settle for the next girl who came along, no matter how much he liked her or how attracted he was to her. Call him crazy, but he wanted to be sure of his feelings before he got sucked into another crazy ride into marriageville.

And right now, he wasn't all that sure of anything anymore.

When it came to Leah, Sam felt . . . something.

It wasn't a confession of love though. He liked her. He enjoyed spending time with her. And he wanted to continue to see her naked, which in itself was a huge problem. People who are "just friends" shouldn't have a desire to see their friend without any clothes. So obviously, there were a few kinks in their friendship that he needed to work out in his head.

But he needed to be realistic too. He valued his friendship with Leah too much to let something as stupid as sex ruin it. Yes, he had some feelings for her, but he could ignore them. If they were going to stay in each other's lives, then maybe he should try to discourage any kind of romantic relationship between them. He obviously wasn't good at them anyway.

The memories of his past relationships still plagued him, and he didn't think he could bear it if Leah was one of them.

Maybe he could tell her that, even though he was attracted to her, he thought it was best to keep things platonic. She would understand that, wouldn't she? She had to. Because there was no way in hell he was going to let her walk out of his life.

It was the only way.

* * *

As Leah had expected, the early morning beach was deserted.

She kicked off the pair of sandals she'd borrowed from her mom and dug her painted toes into the warm sand. The sun hadn't been up long enough to heat more than the top layer of soil, but within a few hours, the surface would be blazing and definitely too hot to walk across barefoot. For now, though, it was perfect.

Leaving the shoes safely on shore next to the pier entrance, far out of reach of the rising tides, she ambled leisurely down to the water and dipped her toes in. As she waded out to the second sand bar, the balmy breeze wafted over her skin, amplifying the chill of the calm waves lapping at her legs.

From her previous trips, she knew it was easier to find sand dollars during low tide than any other time of day. The sand bar would only be knee-deep now, rather than the usual waist-high, and the water would be much clearer.

Unfortunately, she'd left her sunglasses in her purse back at the beach house.

Using her hand, she shaded her eyes from the bright sun, but the sparkling reflection on the water still made it hard to see the elusive sand dollars. Glancing up at the tall pier stretching out into the ocean, she formed an idea. The warning signs prohibited anyone from being under the pier, but with no one around to stop her, who would know?

She moved beneath it, where the wooden structure shaded a much larger area of water than her body did. The tide had already begun to rise so she worked quickly and efficiently, running her hands and feet beneath the gritty sand to uncover the sand dollars that had buried themselves below the surface. Lifting the hem of her shirt, she gathered the small brown sea urchins, one by one, and placed them safely inside the makeshift pouch.

Once a year, she'd take a dozen or so home with her to donate to her old kindergarten teacher, Mrs. Skinner. After bleaching and painting them with a glue solution to strengthen their fragile shells, the children in Mrs. Skinner's class would study them during ocean week—just like Leah had. On the last day, each child would paint a sand dollar and frame it, then take it home as a souvenir. Leah still had hers from years ago.

As she bent to pick up two more sand dollars, a faraway voice caught her attention. Righting herself, she glanced in the direction of the sound and saw Sam standing on the shore. He waved his arms in the air and yelled something, but she couldn't hear him over the distance. The pier almost seemed to insulate the roaring of the ocean in her ears.

He pointed frantically to something behind her, but before she could turn to look, something slammed into her, knocking her off her feet. She hadn't even had enough time to take a breath before the huge wave crashed over her, rolling her beneath its crest, and sweeping her under with its current. Her limbs flailed in the sea, hopelessly trying to regain her footing, but the force of the water continued to drag her along with it.

Leah's limp body stopped abruptly when her pelvis banged against a piling. She managed to wrap her arms around it, and holding on tight, she sputtered out salt water and gasped for a quick breath. The wave continued its warpath, the force of the tide still pulling on her body. Once the water around her settled to a calmer state, she released her grip on the tar-covered pole and struggled to stand.

Sam reached her within seconds and effortlessly lifted her to her feet, impressing her with his manliness. Boy, he was strong. "I tried to warn you about the coming wave," he said, checking her over for injuries. "Are you okay?"

Before she managed to speak, another large wave struck, following the path of the first one with almost the same amount of force. Sam positioned her back against the large round piling and placed his hands on both sides of her body, trapping her between his well-muscled biceps to keep her safely in place. She didn't mind.

His direct, unwavering gaze held hers. "Damn it, Leah. Answer me. Are you all right?"

"Yes," she whispered breathlessly, though her lack of oxygen had little to do with the ordeal she'd just experienced.

His eyes darkened. "Are you sure? You hit the piling pretty hard."

Yeah, no kidding. Leah blew out a slow, calming breath. "I'm fine," she said, though she winced as she rubbed one hand low across her abdomen where it still ached. "I'm pretty sure I took out an ovary though."

"But you didn't hit your head or anything important, did you?"

Anything important? She scowled at him. "I have news for you. I consider my ovaries *very* important, thank you very much."

Sam grinned. "Well, if you lose one, it's not necessarily considered life-threatening."

"Oh really? Do you want to be the one to tell my grandma I can't conceive your children? Trust me, it could be life-threatening."

He chuckled. "Okay, point taken. But you still have one good ovary left, don't ya?"

"What if that one doesn't work right?"

The corners of Sam's mouth lifted. "Then we'll get you an egg donor or talk to an in vitro specialist."

"What?" Leah shook her head furiously. "No way. That's way too expensive. We can't afford those types of medical procedures."

"Fine, then I'll knock you up the old-fashioned way."

"Not with a bum ovary, you won't."

Sam sighed with frustration. "Trust me, you'll live to ovulate another day. If my sperm has to send out a search party for your damn egg, I can guarantee you that one day you *will* be knocked up with my kid. Count on it."

Her mouth dropped open, and her eyes widened. "I, uh..." She didn't have a clue what to say to that.

Sam must've realized how it sounded though. "Oh. Sorry. I didn't mean...I was just playing along."

Of course he was. "Uh, yeah. I know." She fake-smiled so he wouldn't think she took his words to heart...even though she had. Damn.

He shook his head. "No, you really *don't* know," he said, his tone thickening with something that sounded much like anger. "That's the fucking problem." He started to say something else but stopped himself, as if he couldn't seem to find the right words.

She had no idea what he was talking about or why he was upset so she stood there staring at him for a full minute as the tide pooled around their legs. It was the most awkward sixty seconds in the history of awkward seconds, but he obviously had something he wanted to get off his chest. "You have something to say or not?"

"No." His voice came out rough, angry even.

"*No?*" she repeated.

"That's right. *No.*" A muscle ticked in his steel-like jaw as his intense eyes fastened to hers. After a moment, his gaze fell to her mouth, and he released a slow, uneasy breath. "Fuck it," he said. Then his hot, furious lips were on hers.

Leah froze mid-breath, unsure about what she did to piss him off. She considered stopping him long enough to ask, but he didn't give her a chance before his fingers tangled roughly in her wet hair, angling her head for better access, and his impatient tongue parted her lips.

By then, she no longer cared. She couldn't even form a coherent thought, much less ask him a question. Everything faded away. Their fake engagement. Her family. The sounds of the ocean slapping against the pilings around her. None of it mattered.

The only thing that mattered to her in this moment was...Sam.

Her hands flew to his bare chest, but without breaking the kiss, Sam grasped them and moved them to the base of his neck. Then he slanted his warm body more heavily into hers and rolled his hips in a subtle rhythm that hinted at the dangerous undertow of his desire.

Which only confused her more. Because as far as she

knew, friends didn't make out with friends on deserted beaches. At least she didn't think they did.

Even still, she couldn't bring herself to stop kissing him back. He'd locked lips with her before as a distraction. Then he did it once again to convince her family they'd made up. Maybe now he was kissing her because he was mad at her. She didn't know what she had done to anger him, but... well, she liked it. A lot.

Whatever it was she'd done wrong, she hoped she did it again soon.

Chapter Eighteen

Sweet and salty.

That was exactly how she tasted, and the fucking combination overwhelmed his senses. Because although Sam managed to pry his lips from hers, they only ended up on her neck, licking and sucking, as he continued on his path of self-destruction. There was a good chance he would demolish things between them—their friendship, particularly—and he didn't want that. But his mouth and hands just wouldn't listen to his head.

He wanted her. God, he wanted her.

Sam had been scared shitless when he'd watched her limp body slam into the piling, but even after he'd made sure she was okay, his thundering heart hadn't slowed any. Not for a second. Even now, it still hammered mercilessly against his rib cage, knowing she could have been seriously injured.

Then Leah arched her head back, exposing more of her throat, and the tantalizing scent of her sweet skin filled his lungs. More. He wanted more. He nibbled down her neck, biting and then soothing the ache with his tongue. She moaned deep in her throat, and the sound had him bracing himself with one hand on the pole behind her.

She wore a pair of faded jean shorts, showing off her luscious legs, and a loose, dark-colored top, which fell from her left shoulder. Her wet clothes clung to her curvy, glorious body, which fit perfectly against his. He needed to be inside her. Right fucking now.

Without thinking, he ran his free hand between her breasts and slowly down her abdomen to unbutton her shorts. Yet the moment his fingers reached her abs, Leah gasped a little and sucked in her stomach. Not in protest, but in surprise. She didn't make a move to stop him though.

Sonofabitch. Sam paused and blew out a breath. The last thing a self-conscious woman like Leah needed was a man trying to strip her bare in public. It didn't matter that the early morning beach was deserted and there was no one around but the two of them. Leah needed the comfort of a dark room, time to adjust to a man looking at her naked body, and enough privacy to feel safe and secure with herself, as well as with him. Not an embarrassment-inducing, half-dressed quickie in harsh daylight all because he wanted to claim her like a madman. Again.

If he had any chance of salvaging their friendship out of all of this, then his needs would have to wait. What she needed was far more important. He kissed her one last time for good measure, then pulled away. "We should probably get back now."

Her eyes enlarged to owlish proportions, and her lips pursed, as if a jellyfish had wrapped its tentacles around her leg and stung her silent. He wanted to explain why he'd stopped himself from moving forward, but it would probably only humiliate her more. So instead, he said, "I never did get my chocolate mousse last night."

It was a lame excuse, but one he hoped would buy him a little time to screw his head on straight before they headed for home.

They walked back to the beach house, then climbed the stairs and headed inside. Nancy sat alone on the sofa and lifted her head as they came in. "Leah, are you feeling well, darling? You look a little...flushed."

Sam grinned as Leah's eyes cut to him. "I'm fine, Mom."

"Are you sure? Maybe you should make an appointment with Dr. Singleton on Monday."

Leah shook her head. "I don't need to see a doctor."

"Maybe just for some bloodwork," Nancy said, ignoring her daughter. "He could even check you for diabetes while you're there."

"Oh, for goodness' sakes, Mom," Leah huffed. "I may be a little overweight, but that doesn't mean I have diabetes."

"Well, you won't know that for sure until you get checked out. All that sugar you consume is not doing you any favors. Besides, you stay cooped up in that bakery and hardly get any exercise. A physical wouldn't hurt."

Sam gritted his teeth. The only doctor Leah needed to see was a damn shrink, one who could help her deal with the only real problem the girl had: a deranged, melodramatic mother. And he, for one, was getting really tired of this lady's shit. "Nancy, you obviously don't know what the hell you're talking about," he said frankly, not giving a damn who liked it or not.

Shocked, Leah's mother stared wide-eyed at him, as if she were unsure how to respond. And he wasn't about to give her a chance to.

"Leah busts her ass in that bakery. Maybe you don't know

this, but she spends hours prepping before the doors even open, then runs back and forth behind that counter nonstop, while filling an endless supply of orders. Then, at the end of her shift, she cleans it all up and gets ready to do it all again the next day. Your daughter has a better work ethic than most of the men on my crew, and that's saying a lot because I have a damn good crew."

A pleased smile lit up Leah's face. "Why, thank you, Sam."

"You're welcome." He winked at her but couldn't stop himself from adding, "Besides, I *have* been keeping you pretty busy after hours, as well...if you know what I mean." He waggled his brows suggestively.

Ethan stepped out of the hallway and entered the living room. "Yeah, no shit. I had to listen to that headboard banging on the wall all night long."

"Oh my God." Leah's face reddened, and she rubbed at her temples as if she were trying to keep them from exploding.

Nancy blinked but didn't seem to know what to say.

Thankfully, Bill and his parents came through the front door behind them and hadn't heard a word of the uncomfortable conversation. "Hey, Sam, us men are planning on chartering a deep-sea fishing trip the last weekend of the month. You up for it?"

Leah waved her hand through the air. "Oh, that's okay, Daddy. Sam can't—"

"Sounds good," Sam said, cutting her off.

She inhaled a sharp breath and stared at him with a pointed gaze. "Oh, but sweetie, don't you have that thing you need to do that weekend?"

Sam shrugged lightly. "What thing?"

"You know, that *thing* you mentioned." Leah glared at him with fire in her eyes. "Remember?"

Nancy shrugged one slim shoulder and said, "Well, if he can't make it..."

Sam's eyes narrowed. "Of course I can make it," he said with a sly grin. "I don't know what Leah is talking about. I'm off that weekend. I'd love to join y'all for a fishing trip. Sounds great."

Bill gave a quick nod. "Good. It's settled then. I'll call you with all the details as soon as I set it up."

"Perfect," Sam said, daring a glance at his fake fiancée and putting her on the spot. "Right, baby?"

"Super," she said, an underlying sarcasm coloring her tone. "Oh, look at the time. It's getting late. We should probably head home." She turned an icy stare on Sam. "*Now.*"

Uh-oh.

Sam winced internally. Though she'd done a good job of covering her irritation in front of her parents, Leah's eyes shot fiery daggers at him. She was clearly pissed. Chances were good he was going to pay dearly the moment she got him alone.

Thank God her father followed them to the bedroom talking about the fishing trip while a seething Leah changed her clothes in the bathroom and they gathered their things. Otherwise, he might not have made it out of there alive.

When they returned to the living room with their bags, everyone rose from their seats and headed to the front door. Bill opened it and offered his hand to Sam. "We're not leaving here for a few more hours, but thanks for joining us this weekend, Sam. It's been...interesting, to say the least. Don't forget about our date with my patio door."

"Sure thing," Sam said, returning the firm handshake.

As Sam said good-bye to the rest of Leah's family, she walked out the open door, not bothering to wait for any more pleasantries to be exchanged.

"We'll see you soon," Sam promised over his shoulder as he hurried down the front stairs to catch up to a speed-walking Leah.

She didn't speak until they were in the vehicle with both doors closed and their seat belts fastened. Then she turned on him with both barrels fully loaded. "What the hell do you think you're doing? Are you fucking insane?"

He shrugged lightly, knowing that there was no right answer to that question. "Possibly."

"Oh God." She tossed her head back onto the headrest and blew out a long, irritated breath. "Jesus, Sam, I told you I couldn't keep doing this. Why in the hell would you willingly volunteer to go on a fishing trip with my dad?"

He wasn't sure how she was going to take it so he hesitated to answer. "You don't want to know."

"Oh, trust me, I do," she said, contempt rising in her sarcastic tone.

Sam dared to glance over at her. "You sure about that?"

She crossed her arms as she impatiently waited for an answer to her question. "Yes!" she shrieked.

He started the engine and put it into gear but didn't drive away. Instead, he grinned and said, "Because you need at least one sane person in your life."

She leveled a disbelieving gaze at him. "Are you kidding me? This comes from the guy who spent most of the weekend convincing my family that he was a fucking lunatic."

* * *

Confusion didn't cover it.

Leah had spent the entire weekend with Sam and her family, thinking she knew exactly how this vacation would end. But now that they were almost back to the bakery, she realized what a crock of bullshit that was. Her family didn't hate him at all. Actually, it was just the opposite. They all loved him more than ever.

Thanks a lot, Sam.

Now what the hell was she supposed to do?

Sam pulled the truck over next to the curb and parked under the Sweets n' Treats sign. "Honey, we're home," he said in a singsong manner. Wordlessly, Leah reached into the backseat of the truck's darkened cab, feeling around for her bag, but Sam grabbed it first. "I'll get it for you," he told her.

"That's okay. You've done enough, don't you think?"

He pulled her bag into the front seat and leveled a gaze at her. "Are you still mad about your dad inviting me to go deep-sea fishing?"

"No, I'm not mad about that at all," she said, pushing a strand of hair from her eyes. "I'm pissed that you told them you'd go. God, Sam. How the hell am I supposed to tell them that you broke up with me if you keep making plans with them?"

"Well, you don't have to tell them yet."

"Yes, I do. Maybe it's not a big deal for you because they aren't your family, but they are mine. I can't keep dragging this out and leading them on. I don't want them to get attached to you." *Like I am.*

"Oh, come on. They aren't attached to me. I'm just their newest plaything at the moment."

"Not even close. My family adores you, and I'm pretty sure you're going to get them in the divorce."

He shook his head. "Stop it. It's not going to come to that. We'll figure something out way before we get ushered down an aisle."

Leah opened her door and climbed out of the truck before adjusting the elastic waistband on her broomstick skirt. "I don't know what else we can do. We tried everything already. I'm just going to have to do what I'd started to from the beginning—tell them the truth."

Sam slid out of the truck and rounded the front bumper with her bag in hand. "No, you don't have to do that. I know you're upset that things didn't work out like we'd planned, but I'll fix this, I promise. I just need to..."

"What?"

He closed his eyes and breathed out hard. "I just need to think about all of this for a while. I'm sure there is a solution."

"Well, good luck with that," she said, reaching for her bag.

He held it away from her. "What, no invitation to come inside?"

She shrugged. "I didn't think you would want to." Especially after what had happened between them on the beach earlier in the day.

He grinned. "You owe me, remember?"

Leah squinted at him, not knowing what the hell he was talking about. Owed him? He could have taken her up against the pier, and he opted not to. She didn't owe him a damn thing.

"You promised me something sweet, remember?"

"What, when?"

"The day we arrived at your grandparents. You owed me for helping out Valerie, remember?"

Oh. Right. "So you're holding my bag hostage until I agree to make you a dessert? That's real mature, Sam."

His smile grew wider. "Is it working?"

She sighed, then motioned for the door. "All right, fine. I'll whip up something fast. Come on."

Leah unlocked the door and led the way through the

dimly lit bakery and into the back room, where she flipped the light switch on the wall next to the door. The fluorescents blinked on, and she set her purse down on a nearby counter, motioning for Sam to do the same with her bag. As always, Valerie had left the kitchen clean and organized after her morning shift.

She removed a ceramic coffee cup from the cabinet and a spoon from the drawer, placing both on the counter before heading to the dry ingredient pantry. Sam had leaned against the sink, waiting for her return, and he was standing in the same position when she came back carrying a handful of items she needed and placing them on the counter.

"What are you doing?" he asked, glaring suspiciously at the coffee cup.

"Making your dessert. Have you ever heard of a mug cake?"

"A what?"

She grinned. "A mug cake. It's a single portion cake made in a coffee mug. It only takes a few minutes to prepare and cooks in the microwave in seconds. I'll give you the recipe so you can make them for yourself once this thing with my family is finally over."

Sam's brows furrowed, but he remained silent. Guess he didn't like the idea of making his own desserts. Well, too damn bad. After tonight, she was done with all of this. No more lying to her family. And definitely no more torturing herself by pretending to be engaged to a man who didn't want her.

She was going to stop by her parents' house after work and tell them that she and Sam had gotten into a fight on the way home and he dumped her. And that would be it. End of story.

Leah measured out the dry ingredients and added them to

the mug one at a time. "Chocolate, right?" she asked, though she was already adding two tablespoons of unsweetened cocoa powder to the cup. She measured the wet ingredients and gave the concoction a good stir.

She pulled out a container of high-quality imported chocolates she normally used for melting and coating truffles or strawberries and dropped a couple of them into the center of the soupy brown mixture before carrying it over to the microwave.

A minute and a half later, the glorious scent of warm chocolate filled the room as she carefully pulled the mug cake out of the microwave with an oven mitt and set it down on the stainless steel table. She tossed the mitt aside and turned to face Sam. "Let it cool for a few minutes so you won't burn your tongue."

"Damn, that *was* fast."

"Well, yeah. That's kind of the point," she reminded him.

His eyes held hers. "You trying to get rid of me?"

God, no. I'm trying to keep from breaking my own heart. "No, Sam. I...I'm just being realistic."

"What the hell does that mean? Realistic about what?"

Jesus. He wanted her to say it out loud? "I'd really rather not discuss it. I know it's my own fault that it happened, but I'd rather let it go and save myself the embarrassment."

"What's your fault?" Sam asked, his brow quirking ever so slightly. "I don't think I'm following you here."

She lowered her head and rubbed at her face. Christ, why did she have to open her big mouth? "Look, I know you said not to read into anything that happened between us while we were role-playing for my family during this whole shebang, but...well, I did. It's not your fault though, and you don't have anything to feel bad about." Her eyes misted over, and her voice trembled as she added, "It's fine. Really."

His gaze darted back and forth between her watery eyes and pinched mouth, then his jaw tightened. "Obviously, it's not fine."

Leah turned away from him. "I said it's fine. Just leave it alone."

He sighed. "Come on, Leah. Why don't we just sit down and talk about—"

"Damn it, Sam!" she yelled, wheeling around to face him. Her emotions were running high, and she didn't want to have this conversation. "I said no."

With narrowed eyes, he strode toward her so fast and with such intent that she stepped back until the stainless steel table bumped against her ass. Sam stopped in front of her, his hands fisted at his sides. His assessing eyes searched her face, as if he was looking for an answer to an unasked question.

Mortification burned through her, and Leah's heart shriveled. She didn't know why he was staring at her like that, but she no longer cared. She'd had enough of him screwing with her head. With heat crawling up her cheeks, she tried to maneuver around him.

He placed his hands on either side of her, blocking her escape.

She sighed. "Jesus, Sam. What do you want?"

"You, goddamnit. I want you."

Chapter Nineteen

Sam hadn't meant to say it out loud.

But now that he had, he damn sure wasn't going to take any of it back. He *did* want her. And it was about damn time she realized it. Without warning, Sam grasped her waist and lifted her until her ass was firmly planted on the steel worktable.

She squeaked at the unexpected maneuver, and her eyes widened. "Um, here?"

"Right here. Right now," he said firmly, pausing long enough to give her a chance to deny him the pleasure of her body.

When she didn't, he strode over to the light switch on the wall and flipped off the overheard fluorescents. The room went dark, except for the yellow security light in the alley behind the bakery beaming through the uncovered windows.

Upon his return, he bent down to remove her sandals and tossed them onto the tile floor. Then he reached under the hem of her long skirt and slid his hands up her legs, taking the skirt with them. When his fingers reached her bare thighs, a shiver ran through her, and she tensed.

Sam stopped the motion. "Do you trust me?"

Leah nodded.

"Then close your eyes."

Warily, she did as he asked, and Sam reached for the mug at the end of the table. He dipped one finger into the center of the warm, sticky cake, then swept the melted chocolate gingerly across her bottom lip. The sweet scent of the chocolate filled his nostrils, and apparently hers, because she sighed at the heavenly fragrance and her mouth opened in invitation.

Sam teased her with his chocolate-coated finger, rubbing it lightly across her lips until her impatient tongue darted out and licked it. Then she took it into her warm mouth and greedily sucked away every bit of the remaining chocolate. His stomach muscles tightened, and his cock twitched in his jeans. *Fuck me.*

Wanting to taste the sugary residue on her lips, he bent his head and covered her mouth with his. She inhaled a sharp breath and gripped his biceps as if she were trying to steady herself as the erotic kiss took on a life of its own. He dragged his lips over hers again and again until, unable to help himself, the burgeoning frenzy had his hands moving to unbutton her blouse.

When she tensed again, his fingers slowed, and he pulled back to look at her. "I've already seen them, remember? Unless you've somehow grown a third breast since last night, they're going to look basically the same. "

She smiled. "I know. I'm just...nervous, I guess."

"You have nothing to be nervous about. Especially when it comes to your body. You're gorgeous, baby."

Her eyes lit up, and the tension in her posture seemed

to melt away. When she appeared completely relaxed, Sam lifted his hands once again and began unbuttoning her shirt. When all the buttons were undone, he slipped the garment off her shoulders and let it fall down her arms before tossing it aside. Then he reached around her and flicked open the clasp of her bra. Her bra loosened, but stayed mostly in place.

She shifted uncomfortably as he drew the straps down while he kissed her, hoping to occupy her mind with something other than her being half-naked in front of him. Then he eased the bra away from her, dropping it to the floor.

Sam dunked his finger back into the chocolate cake's gooey center, then painted it in a circle around her right nipple in slow, sensual strokes. After quickly sucking the leftover chocolate from his fingertip, he suctioned his mouth over her tightly puckered bud and rolled his tongue around it, chasing the sweet flavor.

God, that's good.

Leah clearly thought so too. She threw her head back, arching her body forward, as a deep moan vibrated from her throat. His hands roamed freely over her breasts as he switched between them with his lips and tongue, lavishing attention onto both. When he couldn't stand it any longer, he reached down between her legs.

Since her skirt was still riding high on her thighs, he easily slid two fingers beneath her damp panties. She gasped as he penetrated her, then again as he began working his thick fingers inside her. The heel of his palm applied pressure to her swollen clit as she squirmed relentlessly, thrusting and bucking against his hand. When her inner muscles quivered, alerting him to her impending orgasm, he removed his hand and nudged her onto her back.

He felt a shiver run through her as the cool metal touched

her skin, but he didn't plan on keeping her cold long. Within moments, he would be reigniting a fire under her that would have her body heated to a sweltering degree. And then he had every intention of continuing to fan those growing flames until she combusted.

Sam yanked her panties down her legs and discarded them over his shoulder. The scent of her arousal had his mouth watering, and he licked his lips in anticipation. He couldn't wait to taste her again. But before he even touched her, Leah did something provocative that he never expected.

She spread her legs.

His brow rose as he gazed down at her, taking in her glittery green eyes and the shy, impish smile she wore. Hell, the last time they were together like this, he'd practically had to use the Jaws of Life to get her legs open. Now she was willingly providing him access to her nether regions and, if he didn't know any better, was eager to do so. And it was incredibly fucking hot.

Lowering himself in front of her, Sam grasped her hips and brought her to his mouth. His tongue slid over her, teasing her slick folds and traveling in slow, lazy circles around her clit. She moaned loudly, but her body strained toward him as if she wanted him to apply more pressure. When he didn't, her fingers wove into his hair, gripping his head tightly to her body. Yep, definitely eager. And that enthusiasm only charged him with more excitement than before.

He wrapped his arms around her thighs and held her in place, taunting that sensitive bundle of nerves with hard flicks of his tongue while she trembled helplessly. The soft murmurs changed to panting pleas as her skin grew hotter and her breath bottomed out. *Oh, yeah. She's fucking close.*

For a moment, Sam considered standing and shoving inside her, needing to feel the clasp of her inner muscles as she accepted him into her warm body. But he had other plans right now. Parting her slick folds, Sam continued to torment her flesh until she screamed out his name and began convulsing uncontrollably.

As she came, the stirring of his primal needs clutched at his balls, making them ache. Sam tasted the aftermath of her pleasure and reveled in the flavor of her heat soaking his taste buds. He was never going to get enough of this. Of her. It wasn't possible.

Only when she dug her nails into his shoulders and her knees clamped around his head did Sam stop. He grinned triumphantly as he rose, wiped the wetness from around his mouth, and tore his shirt over his head. Not wasting a second of time, he pulled her to a standing position and spun her around, slapping her hands down on the table. "Don't move."

He jerked open his constricting jeans in order to free his rock-hard erection, and then pulled a condom packet from his back pocket. After ripping it open with his teeth, he rolled the condom on and bent his knees, poising his straining length at her entrance. Her wild response as she'd climaxed had heat swirling in Sam's gut, and his dick had hardened to the point of pain. He wanted to drive himself inside her and pound her flesh with his. Until they both came so hard that their eyes crossed.

With one powerful thrust, Sam buried himself as deep as he could go. As he filled her, Leah cried out and arched her back until her head lay on his shoulder. His teeth gently grazed her neck. "You all right? You want me to stop?"

"No. Not ever," she whispered.

Normally a comment like that from a woman would have made Sam cringe, but his dick throbbed in response. As crazy as it was, he rather liked the idea of staying buried inside her forever. He gripped her hips with both hands and ground himself more fully into her. She moaned.

Her soft center quivered around his rock-hard cock as he pumped into her, quickening his rhythm to a maddening pace. The strangled sounds escaping her throat pushed him to take more of her, but her undulating hips made the urgent need to spill his seed unbearable. Heat flooded his lower half, and he knew the dam wouldn't hold out much longer.

With sweat beading on his forehead, Sam tilted the angle of his penetration to a shallower depth in order to prolong the inevitable as long as he could. But it was as if her tight inner muscles latched on to him, trying to draw him farther inside her. When he finally felt the first ripples of her climax, he threw his head back and grunted his release as they both flew over the edge together.

Leah collapsed forward onto the table with her skirt still bunched around her waist. Sam loomed over her, hauling in deep, raspy breaths. Neither of them seemed all that worried about separating their connected bodies or doing anything other than existing in the moment of bliss they'd gifted to each other.

But after a moment, reality quickly set in.

Leah stirred and slid out from under him while awkwardly shoving her skirt down to cover her lower half. "There's a bathroom by the back entrance," she said softly, pointing in the direction he should go.

He hated when she did that. As if she were trying to get rid of him to maintain some form of dignity while she got dressed. Frustrating, since her rocking body was one of the things he loved most about her. *Wait…loved? Where the hell did that come from?*

Maybe she had the right idea, after all. He obviously needed a few minutes to himself to clear his mind.

Sam headed in the direction of the back door and found the small bathroom beneath the staircase. He went inside, closed the door behind him, and then rubbed a shaky hand over his face. What the hell had he been thinking taking her like that? Especially after she'd admitted to having feelings for him.

He disposed of the condom and shook his head. There was no way they could be friends with benefits now. Not when Leah would get hurt in the end. But he wasn't willing to give her up either. So now what the hell was he supposed to do?

As he washed his hands, an idea popped into his head that made him wince. But whether he liked it or not, he had no other choice. He needed to take sex out of the equation if he was going to keep Leah in his life. And if that meant going back to being just friends with her, then that's exactly what he would do.

Sam returned to the bakery kitchen to find it empty. "Leah?"

She didn't answer, but the creaking sounds coming from the ceiling above his head hinted at where he could find her. So he retraced his footsteps and climbed the stairs leading to her home over the store.

He'd never seen her place before, but the cozy one-bedroom apartment had an open floor plan which left the impression that it was more spacious than it was. A small but tidy kitchen connected to the dining room, where a little round pub table sat against a wall surrounded by three high-back chairs. The nearby living room held a sparse amount of furniture, but it all looked like solid, sturdy pieces.

Through an open door off the living room, Sam noted her bedroom and a light seeping from beneath the connecting bathroom door. So he walked in and sat on the edge of her queen-size bed, which was covered by a white down comforter and adorned with several throw pillows.

Moments later, the door crept open, and an already-dressed Leah stepped out of the bathroom, spotting him immediately. He must have been wearing a somber expression because she took one look at him and said, "If you want to put an end to all of this, I'll understand."

Sam's heart squeezed in his chest. "Leah, come here."

She did as he told her, sitting beside him on the bed. He turned his body to hers and gazed into her sad eyes. He knew what he needed to say, but the words were stuck in his throat and choking the life out of him.

So instead, he kissed her.

* * *

"Hey, Leah, are you up?" someone called from downstairs.

Leah's eyes popped open.

Valerie! Shit.

Leah quickly rolled over to find the other side of her bed empty. She gazed around the room, eyeing the floor for his clothes, but nothing of Sam's remained. Her stomach churned, queasy with the knowledge that he'd left her without so much as a good-bye. She hadn't expected it after spending long hours throughout the night pleasuring each other in every way imaginable.

"Yep, I'm up. I'll be down in a minute."

Leah flew out of the bed before Valerie could come up and see her sitting there in the nude. Her best friend knew damn well she would never sleep in the buff unless a man had spent the night. And even then, it was a questionable thing because she'd always put her clothes back on after she'd had sex with a guy.

Well, almost always, she thought, remembering how Sam had stripped her for a second time and had kept her naked and under him for the rest of the night.

She threw on her undergarments, a pair of jeans, and a T-shirt, then ran a brush through the tangled bird's nest on her head. She checked herself in the mirror. Yep, still had that freshly fucked look. Great. But she didn't have enough time before the bakery opened to do much about it. This would have to do.

She ran downstairs as fast as her feet would carry her, but Valerie had already disappeared from the kitchen. Noises from the front store room alerted her to her friend's whereabouts. Leah grabbed an apron from the hook on the wall and tied it around her waist. Then she spotted the stainless steel table and gasped.

The table. Oh, hell.

The mug cake was no longer there, but the memories of what took place on that work station had Leah sweating. Thankfully, Valerie hadn't been at work long enough to lay out the baking trays they usually placed there.

Grabbing a lemon-scented cleaner, Leah sprayed it liberally all over the table in a fine mist and began wiping it away with a clean rag.

Valerie flitted through the door, carrying flattened bakery boxes. "Wow, you look a little harried this morning. Everything okay?"

No, everything wasn't okay. Leah was wound up tighter than a loaded spring wondering why Sam had cut out on her without saying anything. "I didn't get much sleep last night." *Because I was having sex with my fake fiancé.*

"Was it *that* bad?"

Leah's cleaning rag froze in place. "Um, was what that bad?"

"The weekend with your family."

Oh. "Um, no. It was all right," she said, spraying more sanitizer and wiping the table down again. She could almost feel Valerie's laser-beam gaze drilling holes into the back of her head though.

"Okay, so what aren't you telling me?"

"Nothing," Leah said, focusing all of her attention on wiping down the table.

"Leah, you're such a terrible liar. Did something happen with Sam?"

Knowing Valerie couldn't see her face, she lifted the corner of her mouth into a smirk. She continued moving the cleaning rag in circles across the shiny metal, not bothering to answer her friend. It might be fun to keep her guessing the rest of the day.

"Oh my God! You had sex with him, didn't you?"

Leah stopped wiping and glared at her friend. How the hell did she do that? Was the girl psychic or something? She shrugged casually. "Maybe."

"You did! Okay, now you have to tell me all about it."

"No, I don't."

Her mouth drooped. "Oh, man. It sucked that much?"

"What? No, of course not. I'm just not going to discuss it. At least not while we're at work. It's bad enough I'm going to be thinking about it all day while I'm working," she said, gazing at the table and sighing.

Valerie leaned her hip against the steel worktable. "Why would you—" She paused, then followed Leah's gaze to the impeccably clean surface. "Oh gross," she said, moving away from it. "You're sanitizing your sex germs, aren't you?"

"Shh! Someone might walk through the front door and hear you say that."

Valerie laughed. "Oh man. No fucking way. You had sex in the bakery?"

"Damn it, Valerie. God. This is so embarrassing."

"Are you kidding me? It's not embarrassing at all. It's hot as hell."

Leah gave her a *yeah, right* look. "You just said it was gross."

"Yeah, but that's only because I have to touch that table, and now every time I do, I'm going to think of you and Sam having sex on it."

Blowing out a breath, Leah tossed the rag into the trash and washed her hands. "Sorry. I didn't know it was going to happen. It definitely wasn't planned."

"So what? Sometimes that's the best kind of sex." She shook her head. "But you are crazy, you know that?"

"Apparently," Leah agreed.

"Well?"

"Well what?"

"Oh, come on. You aren't going to make me beg, are you? Spill it. How big is Sam's dick?"

Heat flooded Leah's cheeks. "Why does it matter?"

"It doesn't. At least not to me. But after what Max said... Well, I can't deny that I'm curious."

"I don't know why Max told you that, but it wasn't at all true."

"Really? Maybe he had penis envy or something. Or maybe you just haven't been with enough guys to know the difference," Valerie said with a giggle.

Leah didn't know why she felt the need to defend Sam's package, but she did. "No, Max is just mistaken because... well, I'm pretty sure there is a donkey somewhere missing a dick."

"Holy shit!"

"Exactly what I thought." Leah walked to the pantry to pull out the large bag of flour they needed to get the doughnuts started.

When she returned, Valerie was still standing there with wide eyes and shaking her head. "Um. Wow."

"No kidding."

"Why would Max start a rumor like that about his friend? It just doesn't make any sense. It's not like they were competing for the same girl or anything."

"I don't know. I would have asked Sam, but we were a little busy at the time." She grinned at Valerie then cut the bag and dumped the flour into the heavy-duty mixer. "Come on, Val, are you going to stand around looking dumbfounded or are you going to get to work on the cinnamon rolls we need done before we open?"

Valerie laughed and reached for the large mixing bowls. "Okay, fine. But I have one last question. What was the chocolate mug cake sitting out on the counter for?" She giggled as flames of embarrassment licked up Leah's neck. "Never mind. I had a feeling I didn't want to know."

"Sam, uh . . . has a thing about sweets."

"Uh-huh."

"No, I'm serious. When it comes to chocolate, he's like a menstruating girl."

Val grinned. "After what you told me about his dick, I'd say he's nothing like a girl at all."

"Okay, stop it. And if he stops by, you better not act weird or anything. I don't want him to know we were talking about him."

"Wait, you mean he isn't still here?"

Leah shook her head. "God, no. Do you think I would be talking about his junk if he was upstairs in my bedroom?"

"What'd you do—rush him out of here before I arrived?"

"Um, no. Actually, he sort of left on his own...without telling me."

"So he just had sex with you and then left? That's a jerk thing to do."

Jeez. As if this couldn't get any more humiliating. "No, he stayed most of the night, but he was gone this morning before I woke up. I'm not sure what time he left. He didn't exactly say goodbye."

Valerie's lips turned downward, and her eyes narrowed. "So this was just a fling for him then?"

"I...I don't really know. It wasn't exactly the first time we had sex. Over the weekend, we had agreed to being friends with benefits, but I...don't think I can anymore. Not if he's going to come and go as he pleases. And I mean that in the literal sense." Leah sighed. "It makes me feel like I'm being used for sex so he doesn't have to face up to his commitment issues."

The scowl on her friend's face worsened. "I think he's a good guy so I'm going to give him the benefit of the doubt here and hope he had a damn good reason to run out on you. But if he doesn't, I'm going to seriously consider putting his donkey dick in that mixer and turning it on full speed."

Leah couldn't help but smile at Val's overprotective side, but inside she was cringing at what she was about to tell her. "Unfortunately, I have an even bigger problem than Sam leaving without waking me."

"What's that?"

She sighed, conveying her unhappiness. "What do you do when you fall in love with your fake fiancé?"

Valerie cocked her head, and her forehead wrinkled. "Oh, honey. You don't think he feels the same way about you, do you?"

"I honestly don't know what he's feeling, if anything.

Before this weekend, I didn't even think he was attracted to me so the whole friends-with-benefits thing came as a complete surprise. But now that I've been on the receiving end of his...um, benefits...I've fallen hard for him. I sort of mentioned it last night, but he's hesitant about serious relationships."

"Does he want to be with you?"

Leah shrugged. "I don't know. He didn't say."

"So ask him."

"What? Hell no."

"Why not? How else are you supposed to know what he's thinking?"

"I can't do that. I would like to think he wouldn't have had sex with me last night if he didn't feel the same way, but I honestly can't say for sure. He hasn't been real forthcoming about much."

"Leah, you need to go talk to him and find out where he stands after last night. You are a catch, and you shouldn't have to play guessing games when it comes to how a man feels about you. Just grow a fucking pair and go ask him already."

"B-but what if he doesn't reciprocate my feelings?"

"Then he's a fucking idiot, and we're going to tell everyone his dick is the size of a soda straw...whether it's true or not."

Chapter Twenty

Sam let out a string of curse words and threw the hammer out into the yard.

"Need a hand with that?" Bill asked, chuckling under his breath. "Or maybe I should just offer you my thumbs. You seem to be running out of yours."

Sam gazed down at his aching nub and gritted his teeth. "I've still got one good one left." But at this rate, he wouldn't have it for long.

Served him right though. He should have been paying more attention to what he was doing rather than thinking about spending last night with Leah.

Bill gestured to the patio chair across the table from him. "Why don't you sit down and take a break for a minute. You might work better if you cool off a little."

Aggravated with himself, Sam plopped down in the chair and wiped the sweat from his brow. The afternoon sun was still burning bright, and the heat was starting to get to him. Just like Leah had.

"You want to talk about it?" Bill asked, pouring a glass of iced tea from the pitcher on the table and passing it to Sam.

"No. It's nothing. Just something I'm trying to work out in my head." Sam took a big gulp of the sweet tea.

"I see. Well, if you need someone to talk to..."

Sam nodded. "Thanks. I appreciate it. I'm sure the problem will work itself out soon enough."

"And if it doesn't?"

"I know where to find you...and your thumbs." Sam grinned and then took another swallow of tea.

A moment of silence passed between them before Leah's father spoke again. "I like you, Sam."

"Bill, if you don't stop flirting with me, I'm going to tell your daughter on you."

He chuckled and pointed at Sam. "Right there. That is exactly what I'm talking about. You're a fun guy, and Leah hasn't always had that in her life. I see the way she is with you, the way she looks at you, and how happy she is having you around. The two of you fit together nicely."

Sam's blood ran cold. It was as if the man in front of him were a doctor who had just administered a heavy dose of guilt directly into his veins. Bill wouldn't be saying any of this if he'd known that Sam had been having sex with his daughter with no intention of turning it into a relationship. "Well, Leah's a great girl," he muttered quietly.

Her dad's eyes filled with pride. "Yes, she is. And she's also my favorite daughter."

Confused, Sam quirked a brow at him. "Isn't she your only daughter?"

"Well, yeah, but just because Leah didn't happen to have any competition in the daughter department doesn't mean she would automatically be considered my favorite. I've seen lots of parents who may love their children but can't stand the little assholes."

"Touché," Sam said, smiling.

"But Leah is a good girl. She's respectful and kind and hasn't got a mean bone in her body. She cares about the people around her, even when they don't deserve it. Like Gavin. When that little prick broke things off with her, I was dancing on the rooftops. She deserves someone better, a guy who will always come to her defense and appreciate her for who she is. Someone like you."

Sam didn't know how to respond so he just nodded in agreement.

Thankfully, Bill continued on without hesitation. "I have to tell you, Sam, when I first heard about her getting engaged, I wasn't the least bit surprised. I always knew Leah would one day meet that special guy who would love her for who she is. One who would put a ring on her finger as quickly as possible to keep another man from snatching her away." He cleared his throat, and a glossy sheen fell over his eyes as his emotions got the better of him. "Look, we didn't know each other at the time, and you may not have asked for my blessing, but I'm telling you...it's yours. You have it. I'd be proud to have you as my son-in-law."

Well, fuck. Now what the hell was Sam supposed to do?

This whole thing was supposed to be a quick solution to help get Leah out of an engagement that she was never really in to begin with. Instead they were screwing with these people's heads, and things were getting too far out of hand. And he had no one to blame but himself. If Sam hadn't opened his big mouth at Gavin's wedding, then none of this would have happened.

Learn to think things through, dumbass.

Under the circumstances, Sam did the only thing he could. He shook Bill's hand and muttered a quick, "Thanks. That means a lot." Then he quickly stood, retrieved his hammer from the yard, and got back to work on trying to remove Bill's old patio door.

Bill watched in silence as Sam pried off the weathered framework. He originally had planned on sending a crew out to do the job, which would have been much faster, but he couldn't risk one of his workers blowing his cover about being Leah's fiancé. None of them knew that Sam was engaged—fake or otherwise—to Bill's daughter. And he had no doubt the subject would come up. So he'd made up an excuse about being down a few good men and told Leah's dad that he'd do the job himself.

And Bill hadn't seemed upset about it. Actually, he'd smiled at Sam and said, "Good, it means I get to spend the day with my future son-in-law."

Sam sighed. He should have allowed Leah to end the engagement at the Water Gardens when she'd had the chance. Lord knows she tried. At least then he wouldn't be battling his conscience every minute of the day.

Like this morning, when he'd ran out on Leah without waking her. He was supposed to meet Bill early so that he could get started on the patio doors, but Sam had forgotten all about it.

Then again, he *had* been a little distracted last night... and a lot busy.

A devilish grin spread across his face. Yeah, Leah had kept him otherwise occupied for most of the night, and he'd enjoyed every fucking minute of it.

By the time he'd remembered the job, Leah had already drifted off to sleep. He'd hated leaving without waking her, especially since her luscious ass had been pressed so snugly up against him. But neither of them had gotten much sleep and she had looked so peaceful that he hadn't wanted to disturb her.

So instead, he had unwillingly torn himself away, dragged himself out of her bed, and thrown himself in the truck, hoping to get started on the job so he'd have one less thing to worry about. Leah, on the other hand, was the next thing on that list.

As if his mind had conjured her into a physical state, Leah rounded the side of the house. Her hair swayed in the slight breeze, and the scent of her perfume wafted to him, sending his heart racing. Her eyes met his as she reached the deck. "Oh. Um, hi," she said softly, then shifted awkwardly as if she didn't know what else to say.

And that only made Sam feel like more of an ass than he already did.

Irritated by his indecisiveness, he gave her a terse nod and said, "Hey." Then he went back to prying off the old framework, loosening it from the stucco.

"I didn't know you were here," she told him. "I was... looking for my mom."

"Here I am," Nancy said, stepping into the kitchen. Her voice was muffled behind the glass door. "I heard you knock, but I was upstairs on the phone."

Leah raised her voice so her mom would hear. "Well, I just stopped by to tell you that I received a thank-you note from Mrs. Newman. She said that everyone loved Gavin's wedding cake and that it was a huge hit. She's recommending my bakery to all of her friends."

"That woman doesn't have friends, dear. She has followers," Nancy said, wearing an amused expression. "But that's wonderful news. With her connections, I'm sure your bakery will be a huge success."

Sam grimaced and shoved open the patio door to make sure Nancy could hear him. "Leah's bakery is already a huge success."

"Yes, of course it is," Nancy agreed, giving him a lackluster smile. "In fact, we should celebrate and have dinner together."

Leah shook her head. "Oh no, that's okay. Tonight's not good for us."

"Actually, I was thinking we'd have dinner tomorrow night."

Leah glanced over at Sam, panic flashing in her eyes. "Um, no. I don't think so," she said hesitantly, as if she were trying to come up with a good reason for refusing.

But Sam saw an opportunity staring him in the face. As weird as it sounded, he needed to end his engagement to Leah before he ended up hurting her. "Sure, why not? We don't have any other plans for tomorrow. We'd love to have dinner with you, Nancy."

Leah's jaw hit the floor, but she didn't say anything.

"Terrific," her mother said. "I have a big surprise for the two of you so don't be late. Dinner will be at seven, and I'll make something special for the occasion."

Bill cleared his throat. "Um, Nancy, can I speak to you in the kitchen?"

"Sure," she replied as her husband joined her in the house.

Once Bill stepped through the doorway, Sam shut the door and started prying the last bit of framework from the wall to disengage the door.

Leah stepped over to him with a scowl on her face. "Um, what the hell are you doing?"

"I'm taking out your dad's old patio door," he said, motioning to the new French doors leaning against the wall nearby. Then he pointed to the glass door he was holding in place. "Hold on to this for me while I take the screws out of the bottom, will ya? It's not that heavy, but it's easier with two people doing this."

She put her hands against the door and held it up. "No, I mean what are you doing with my parents? Are you a glutton for punishment or something? Why would you agree to have dinner with them when I'd already turned them down?"

Sam reached for his drill. "Because we're putting an end to our engagement."

*   *   *

Leah loosened her grip, and the top of the door came halfway off the wall.

"Don't let go," Sam said, catching it before it fell on him. "Not until I get the bottom unscrewed and can grab the top from you."

She put her hands on the door again, holding it in place while Sam got to work on the screws. But she couldn't believe he was doing this to her again.

Sam had gone out of his way to stop her from ending their fake engagement at the Water Gardens. Why had he suddenly changed his mind? "What do you mean we're ending our engagement? You're the one who insisted that we keep the whole charade going."

"I know. But I realized that it isn't fair to keep messing with everyone's heads. It would be better to just end things now before we get in too deep."

Get in too deep? Then maybe he should have thought about that last night. Because she couldn't imagine him getting any deeper than *that*. What kind of sick game was this man playing with her?

She should have known better than to think Sam would get over his aversion to serious relationships. As if. He held on to so much baggage from his past that he'd probably never be able to commit to any woman. Or maybe it was just *her* that he didn't want to commit to.

He clearly liked her enough to have sex with her, but that wasn't saying much since two complete strangers could just as easily have gone home together. That happened all the time in bars. But she'd thought—or maybe she'd hoped—that she had meant more to him than that.

Apparently not. The devastating weight of that realization sat on her chest, making it difficult to breathe. "You know what, Sam? You're a real jerk."

She let go of the door, forcing Sam to shove his shoulder into it to keep it from falling. "Leah, wait—"

But she didn't. In a fit of rage, she cut around the side of the house and kept on walking until she made it to her car, where she climbed inside and slammed the door. After starting the engine, she pointed her car in the direction of the bakery and peeled out of the driveway. She'd barely pulled into the alley behind her store when her cell phone buzzed. She parked in her usual spot and glanced at the screen. It was a text from Sam.

I'll be at your place around 7 pm.

Her fingers hovered over the keys, itching to type something derogatory back to him, but she didn't do it. Maybe some of this had been her own fault. Was it possible she had talked herself into believing that Sam wanted something more from her? She didn't think so though, because when Sam looked at her, when he said things to her...it all felt real.

The phone vibrated in her hand, and her gaze fell onto a second text.

We need to talk about last night.

So that was it. Sam wanted to break things off with her. Leah threw the cell phone onto the floorboard and shook her head.

No, this wasn't her fault. It was all on Sam.

He knew she liked him. Standing in her bakery last night, she'd all but told him that she had feelings for him. He could have left. He could have called a halt to all of it then. But he hadn't. Instead, he had chosen to take advantage of her by having his cake and eating it too.

Literally.

But he didn't look at her that way. Or in any way, if she was being honest with herself. And she finally was. She'd meant nothing to him. Nothing at all. She closed her eyes as sharp pains tore through her chest, stabbing at her heart. It hurt to know how little he thought of her.

But she wasn't going to crawl into bed and eat another pint of Ben & Jerry's over losing a guy she never had to begin with. No fucking way. She wiped at her cheeks then took a deep, cleansing breath. She was done with feeling sorry for herself. She hadn't done anything to deserve the way he'd treated her, and she wasn't about to apologize for a damn thing.

When things had come to an end with Gavin, it had sent her into a tailspin, and she'd become a hermit, locking herself away for days at a time while her waist thickened from all the snacks she mindlessly reached for to soothe her broken heart.

Well, not this time.

She wasn't going to drive herself bat-shit crazy over what Sam thought of her or waste another minute of her time on a douchebag that couldn't see past her size or his own commitment issues. She was a good person, and no matter how big or small she was, she deserved better than that.

He could show up if he wanted, but she wouldn't be sitting at home waiting around for Sam Cooper. Leah was going to go out and have a good time...and forget all about the fucking jerk.

Chapter Twenty-one

The silence was killing him.

Not only had Leah ignored and avoided him for the past twenty-four hours, but she wouldn't even look at him since he'd picked her up to go to dinner with her family. When he'd arrived at the bakery, she had climbed into the cab and then spent the rest of the drive staring out the passenger window. Even the humid Texas climate couldn't defrost the solid block of ice sitting next to him in the passenger's seat.

She hadn't answered his texts or his phone calls yesterday, and when he had gone by the bakery after work, she either hadn't been home or had ignored him pounding on her door. So he'd been more than a little surprised to receive a text from her this afternoon asking him to pick her up at six thirty. Either way, he was glad dinner was still on with her folks. All of this had to come to an end now or he was going to lose Leah from his life. And he couldn't let that happen.

She was clearly still upset with him for agreeing to have

dinner with her family in the first place. If only she'd just say so. That way they would clear the air before going inside and having her parents notice the standoffish vibes flickering between them.

"Are you still mad?" Sam asked, trying to get her to speak to him.

"Yep," she answered flatly.

"Do you want to talk about it?"

"No."

He sighed. "Are you only going to keep giving me one-word answers?"

"Possibly."

"Well, it's going to seem really strange that you aren't talking to your fiancé. You know you're going to have to at least have a conversation with me at some point tonight."

"Nope."

"Oh, come on. I already apologized. I didn't mean to thrust myself into an awkward situation with your family."

She pushed her hair off her shoulder, crossed her arms, and glared at him.

"Okay. I didn't mean to do it *again*. Happy now?"

"Hardly."

Sam sighed. At least she was talking to him. Even if she still resembled a statue with her tight-lipped mouth and stiff posture. The only thing relaxed on her were the faded Levi's she wore. Then he realized something. "Do you know you wear a lot of black?"

"Yep." A wry grin cradled her cheeks.

He gritted his teeth, then finally asked, "Why?" *Ha! Let's see her give me a one-word answer for that.*

"Because they don't make anything darker."

Anger swept through him, and his eyes narrowed. "Bull-shit. That's your mother talking, not you."

Her gaze lifted to his, and her cheeks flashed with heat. "Maybe so, but she's right, ya know? Black is slimming."

"Yeah, but that doesn't mean moms always know best... even when they think they do."

She snorted. "My mother would disagree with that statement."

This wasn't his idea of good conversation, but at least Leah was talking to him again in complete sentences. "That's because your mother disagrees with everything when it comes to you. Why don't you stand up to her already?"

"Why? What good would it do? It won't change anything. She's been like this for years. Besides, I'd rather my mom comment on my weight than to put her nose into my business matters, which is the fun new thing she's been doing all week," she said, a hint of sarcasm tainting her tone. "You know, ever since you went on your tangent about how hard her daughter works."

He had unknowingly sicced her mother on her by telling Nancy she didn't know a damn thing about what Leah did at the bakery. He didn't doubt what he'd said about her was 100 percent true, but he hadn't meant to cause Leah any grief over it. "Surely your mother knows what a smart, savvy businesswoman you are by now."

She groaned. "Yeah, right."

"No, I'm serious, Leah. You run your own company at twenty-seven years old, and from what I hear from my crew, everyone in town loves the new bakery. Hell, almost every one of my guys stops in your store each morning before coming to work."

Leah's chest visibly swelled with pride. "Really?"

"Yes, really. Some of them have even been late because the lines have been so long. You're slammed every morning, and I'm constantly threatening to fire my guys unless they bring me a chocolate-topped doughnut."

"Oh, stop it." She rolled her eyes. "Even you wouldn't do something that sadistic for sweets."

"Wanna bet? I had three of them just this morning, and it wasn't because I paid for a single one." He grinned, quite proud of himself for coming up with the strategy.

She glared at him. "Oh, hell. Now I'm feeding you without even realizing it?"

"Well, I had to do something to satisfy my sweet tooth. I would have raided your walk-in cooler last night, but *someone* wouldn't open the door or answer their phone."

Leah shrugged lightly. "I was busy."

Busy being pissed maybe. "What about today? I went by the bakery three times."

"Sorry you missed me. I had some errands to run."

"Uh-huh," he said, eyeing her. "Well, I'm pretty sure Valerie thinks I'm a stalker now. And since I fixed a loose cabinet door for her while I was there, you owe me another dessert."

"What? You can't make me pay up for things you fix when I'm not even there. You'll have to collect from Valerie."

"Nope. You're the bakery owner so that makes it your responsibility. I expect you to pay your debt...in chocolate. And unlike your father, I do break knee caps. So you might want to think twice about your refusal to cooperate." He grinned at her, hoping she would loosen up a little.

A vague smile flitted across her lips. "We'll see."

Sam slowed, then veered onto her parents' paved circle drive. He followed it until he rolled to a stop in front of their white stucco home. The freshly manicured lawn and meticulously groomed hedges resembled consecrated burial grounds and would have inspired jealousy in any cemetery's landscaper.

Shutting off the engine, he glanced over at Leah, who was reaching into the backseat for the bakery box she'd brought with her. "What's in the box?"

"A pie."

His brow rose. "Chocolate?"

"No, it's cherry." A coy little smirk pulled at the corner of her mouth as she opened the door.

Sam shrugged, his mouth still salivating at the thought of tasting another one of her desserts...even if it wasn't chocolate. "It'll do." They climbed out of the truck's cab and started up the sidewalk. "So you're done being mad at me, right?"

"No, I'm not," she said as they reached the front door. "But right now, I just want to go inside and get this over with. And I'm warning you, if you back out—"

"I won't. Trust me. By the end of tonight, this will all be over, I promise." He thought that would make her happy, but something very different flashed in her eyes then dissipated. Something that closely resembled...sadness? "Leah, maybe we should talk before we go in—"

The front door flung open, and Nancy stood there in a fancy red dress. "Right on time," she said, smiling. "Come on in. Dinner is almost ready."

Since he'd parked around back when he'd been there installing the new French doors, Sam hadn't seen much beyond the kitchen. So as they stepped inside, he gazed around the open space of the pristine living room, noting the oriental rugs, polished antique furniture, and expensive-looking paintings decorating the wall. On the mantel above the fireplace, a wooden stand cradled an old revolver and a glass case held an elaborately designed golden egg.

Let the games begin, he thought with a grin.

Sam turned to Nancy as she shut the door behind Leah. "Nice collection," he told her, making Nancy's face beam with pride. Then he added, "Looks like a thrift store in here."

Her hand flew to her chest as she gasped in horror at the insult. But before she could say anything, a deep chuckle resonated from somewhere behind him. He spun on his heel as Bill entered the room, wearing pressed black slacks and a white dress shirt. "I've been telling Nancy that for years," he said, stretching out his hand. "Good to see you again, Sam."

"Same to you, old man."

Bill firmed his grip around Sam's hand and pulled him forward. For a second, Sam considered that he might get punched in the face. But instead, Leah's father leaned in close. "I just want you to know I had nothing to do with it," he said, before releasing Sam's hand.

Sam wasn't sure what any of that meant, but he didn't get the chance to ask before Ethan came down the stairs. "Hey, kid. Still rocking that shirt, I see."

Ethan looked down at his yellow shirt in confusion and then glanced back to Sam. "This isn't the same one."

"Oh, really? My bad. Still a good color on you though."

Ethan's eyes widened. "You've got to be freakin' kidding me!" He glared at his mom and then quickly exited the room...probably to go change his clothes.

Leah stood off to the side, biting her bottom lip, as if she was trying to keep from laughing.

"My goodness," Nancy exclaimed. "What in the world was that all about?"

Bill shook his head. "We should probably get that boy tested for drugs."

"Oh, I'm sure it's just normal teen angst," Leah told him, defending her poor brother. "His hormones will level out...eventually. Do you want me to go up and get him to come back down for dinner?"

"Uh, no. That's okay, honey," Nancy said. "I'll take him up a plate later. We don't want to hold up dinner waiting for him." She motioned with her hand. "Bill, I've already placed the wine and crystal on the table. Would you pour each of us a glass, please?"

"No problem," Bill said, then shuffled toward the dining room.

The women headed for the kitchen so Sam followed them. Leah's mother checked on dinner while Leah set the pie box down on the counter and leaned against it.

Nancy turned her gaze onto Sam. "I hope you brought your appetite with you, Sam. We're having herb roasted chicken, steamed asparagus, baby carrots, and a mixed green salad."

After a few moments, Nancy lifted and proudly held out a silver platter of food that looked like it had been plated and arranged by Martha Stewart herself. Then she shifted her eyes onto Leah. "I made this meal special for you, honey, keeping your dietary restrictions in mind, of course."

Leah sighed. "Mom, I don't have any dietary restrictions."

"Ah, well, that seems to be the problem, doesn't it?" Nancy stated as she carried the platter toward the dining room.

Sam mentally cringed at Nancy's irritating insult. The only problem he could see was an unsupportive mother badgering her grown daughter about her weight. *Diet-friendly menu, my ass. We'll stop for a cheeseburger on the way home.*

But when he glanced over at Leah and saw her looking back at him with heated cheeks, Sam gritted his teeth. He was damn tired of Nancy humiliating her daughter and getting away with it. Enough was enough.

Leah apparently noticed the way his jaw tightened because she wasted no time in grabbing the salad bowl and stack of white plates and making a beeline for the dining room, as if she was trying to head her mother off at the pass.

But it was too late. Nancy was already returning through the doorway.

"I grabbed the salad and the plates already," Leah informed her.

"Thank you, dear. But I still need to grab the silverware. I know you're used to grabbing take-out and eating fast food with your fingers, but we don't do that here. We aren't cavemen."

Sam's lips pressed together as he bit his tongue, but his narrowed eyes zeroed in on Nancy. Like a pissed-off bull, he was definitely seeing red...but it had nothing to do with the color of her dress.

Leah must've realized it, probably from the way he was flaring his nostrils. When her mother tried to maneuver around her, Leah stepped in her path and shoved the salad and plates into her mom's arms. "I'll get the silverware!" The words flew out of her mouth, fast and forceful, as if she was afraid Sam would say something to Nancy about her demeaning comments.

Her mother nodded and turned back to the dining room but stopped in the doorway. "Sam, dinner is on the table. If you would like to join—"

"Hold your goddamn horses, Nancy. I'll be there in a minute."

Surprised by his gruff tone, the woman paused and blinked at him, as if she wasn't sure what to say. He grinned at his small win, knowing that a pushy woman like Nancy probably didn't back down from many things.

But then another figure filled the doorway next to her. "Samuel Ryan Cooper!"

Oh, shit! "Mom?"

* * *

Leah swayed in stunned silence.

Mom? As in Sam's mother? No, that wasn't possible.

But Sam regained his composure and stepped toward the woman. "W-what are you doing here, Mom?"

A tall man with gray streaks in his hair stepped out of the dining room. He looked like an older, handsomer version of Sam. "I think the better question is why are you speaking to Nancy in that tone of voice. I raised you better than that, young man."

Sam grinned sheepishly. "I was ... uh, just kidding around with her."

"Well, it sounded disrespectful," his mother chastised. "I believe you owe her an apology."

"You're right," Sam agreed, then turned to Nancy. "I'm sorry. I hope you will forgive me."

She smiled. "Of course. But only if you forgive me for sneaking your parents into town without telling you. I thought it would be a nice surprise."

What the fuck, Mom? Leah's mouth gaped open. "Wait. Mom, how are you responsible for his parents coming in? You didn't even know them."

"Oh, they were easy enough to track down once Sam gave me their names and told me where they lived. So I called his mother and introduced myself. We had a lovely chat. And when Sharon mentioned she wanted to come for a visit, I thought it might be fun to surprise the two of you."

Sam shook his head. "I...don't know what to say. I mean, I'm definitely surprised." Then he reached for his mom and hugged her. "It's great to see you." When he released her, he shook his father's hand and gave him a manly thump on the back.

His mother's gaze landed on Leah. "So you must be the elusive woman I've heard so little about," she said, wearing a good-natured smile. "I'm Sharon, and this is my husband, David. Our son is in big trouble for keeping you all to himself."

"I'm Leah," she said, extending her hand. "It's nice to meet you both."

Nancy clapped her hands together. "Well, now that introductions are out of the way, I think Sam has something he wants to announce to his parents."

Sam pulled at his shirt collar with one finger. "No. Nothing I can think of."

Nancy giggled. "Oh, Sam, stop kidding around and tell them the good news already."

His mom's brow rose. "Okay, what am I missing here?"

"It was just something I was going to mention. But it can wait until after dinner," Sam said, trying to buy himself some time.

"Samuel..." his mother said, her tone sounding much like a warning.

He wiped away the sweat beading on his brow. "Okay, fine. I was just going to tell you that Leah is my...f-f-f...." The word died on his lips.

Oh, fuck me. "I'm his fiancée," Leah blurted out.

Sharon's eyes widened, and her mouth hinged open.

Leah hadn't meant to shock the woman, but Sam

obviously had a hard time saying the word, and she couldn't take it any longer. Besides that, she wasn't entirely sure that he wasn't going to call her his "friend," which would have tipped off her own parents about the fake engagement.

"You're getting married?" Sharon said, blinking at her son. "I . . . I can't believe it."

Sam shrugged casually. "Yeah, I can hardly believe it myself."

"I mean, I had a feeling something like this was going on, but when I didn't see a ring on Leah's finger—"

"Oh, that's because it's at the jeweler's getting resized," Leah cut in. "We'll have it back soon."

"I see. Well, congratulations to both of you then. I think it's wonderful news."

David squeezed his son's shoulder. "It's fantastic! We should make a toast, don't you think?"

Leah's mom grinned. "The wineglasses are already filled. Why don't we go sit down at the table before our dinner gets any colder? Leah, would you be a dear and get the silverware, please?"

Everyone started for the dining room, while Leah grabbed the silverware from the kitchen counter. As she turned to head back to join the others, she ran smack dab into Sam's chest. "What are you doing? Why aren't you with the others?"

"Leah, we need to talk."

"About what?"

"Look, I know we said we'd end this tonight, but . . ."

What? No! "Sam, don't you dare say it. You promised."

He hung his head and sighed. "I know. But that was before I realized my parents were here."

"So?"

"So you saw my parents' reaction to what I said to your

mom. If I pull that kind of shit while they're sitting there, my mom is going to have a heart attack and my dad is probably going to take off his belt and smack me with it."

"Damn it, Sam. Then give your mom an aspirin and stuff a pillow in the back of your pants and take it like a man."

"Leah..."

"God, I can't believe you're doing this to me again."

"Hey, it isn't my fault. It was *your* mom who invited my parents into this whole mess. Blame it on her."

"Don't even go there with me. If you hadn't started this fake engagement to begin with, then your parents wouldn't be involved in it. This whole thing is your fault."

Sam scrubbed a hand through his hair. "You're right. I'm sorry. I shouldn't have said that about your mom. Once my parents leave, we can figure out how to end all of the insanity and get back to our normal lives. Until then, we're going to have to keep playing the happy couple. Think you can do that?"

Frustrated, she closed her eyes and took a deep breath. Unfortunately, Leah didn't have a choice. Or did she?

Yeah, she had a choice all right. Whether Sam liked it or not. *He can't back out on me again, damn it. I won't let him.*

Chapter Twenty-two

Sam and Leah settled into their side-by-side chairs and waited for his father to finish toasting their engagement. When he was finished, Leah's dad took his place at the head of the table and began carving the roasted chickens, while Nancy passed Leah the salad bowl with a big smile.

Sam was sure it was supposed to be a subtle hint, but Leah ignored it, probably used to dealing with that kind of crap from her mother. Leah only took a small helping before passing the salad bowl to Sam, who crinkled his nose at it. The ugly brown dressing didn't look very appetizing and was probably just as diet-friendly as everything else on the menu.

Once her dad had finished cutting up the two birds and sat in his chair, they took turns passing around the silver platter until everyone's plates held a serving of herbed chicken, steamed asparagus, and baby carrots.

Sam stabbed his salad fork into a chunk of red leaf lettuce

dripping with the brown ooze and glared at it warily. "What kind of dressing is this, Nancy?"

Leah's mother dabbed politely at her mouth with a white linen napkin before answering. "It's a new version of a balsamic vinaigrette. You're going to love it. It's low in calories, fat, and carbs."

Sam cringed inwardly, but before he could respond, Leah blurted out, "So is semen. At least that's what Sam keeps telling me."

Oh, Jesus. She did not just say that! The entire room went still, except for Leah, who speared a carrot on her fork, popped it into her mouth, and grinned her ass off as she chewed.

Sam rubbed his hand across his face, avoiding his parents' expressions. His father coughed a little to stifle a strained chuckle, but by the way his mother's fork had clanged clumsily against her plate, Sam imagined his mom sitting there with wide eyes and an open mouth.

He had a feeling he knew exactly why Leah was smiling like that, and it wasn't a good one. Normally, Leah would never say something so inappropriate, especially in mixed company. But since she had, only one reason came to mind.

Sam slumped over his plate and continued eating. If he pretended he hadn't heard what Leah had said, maybe it would discourage any more conversation for the remainder of the meal. God, he hoped so.

But of course, he couldn't get that lucky.

"Sorry we took so long getting the silverware," Leah offered. "Sam had something he wanted to discuss with me."

"And it couldn't wait until after dinner, son?" his mom asked.

Sam didn't even get a chance to answer her.

"No. He's impatient like that at times." She shrugged nonchalantly. "It's my own fault though. Sam keeps telling me when he says jump, I should ask how high. I just never learn." She smiled politely at them, though both sets of parents stared at her as if she'd sprouted two heads, one on each shoulder.

Sam scowled at her. "That's, um, not exactly what I said, sweetheart."

"Well, I would hope not," his father stated, snorting at his son like an overprotective bull guarding a herd of females. "That kind of sexist attitude has no place in the world today."

"Oh, no. Sam isn't sexist, David. He believes in women being complete equals. That's why I open doors for him, instead of the other way around. He even trained me to leave the toilet seat up."

Sam's stomach soured. He pushed his plate away from him and crossed his arms. "Is it time for dessert yet?"

Leah grinned. "See how impatient he can be?" She stood and stacked her dinner plate on top of his.

His mom stared at Leah's plate in confusion. "But, honey, you have barely touched your food."

"I know, but Sam wants his pie. And what Sam wants, Sam gets," Leah stated plainly, as if she were his obedient submissive or something. "I'll just grab it from the kitchen."

Christ.

"I'll help," Sam said, scrambling out of his seat.

Once they were out of their parents' earshot and standing in front of the kitchen sink, Sam leaned in and whispered, "What the hell are you doing?"

Leah squinted at him. "I'm getting the pie you wanted," she whispered back.

Sam sighed. "No, I mean, why are you making me look like such a jerk?"

The dishes clanged together as she set them in the sink. "Well, maybe you don't want to go through with the original plan, but I do. I can't keep doing this. It's ending tonight, whether you like it or not."

"The plan was to make *your* parents hate me, not make mine disown me. Besides, *I* was supposed to do it. Not you."

"Does it really matter?" she asked, stretching up on her tiptoes to grab the dessert plates on the top shelf.

He leaned over her from behind, pressing his body against hers. His cock pushed against her ass, which had him holding his breath. Once he'd pulled the plates down, he set them on the counter. "Hell yes, it matters. You're making me look like a chauvinistic prick."

"Me?" She laughed and shook her head as she turned and plucked forks and a pie server from the silverware drawer. "Hardly. You did that on your own when you smacked my ass and started making sexual remarks about me to my dad while we were on vacation."

"Maybe. But my parents hadn't been there for any of that."

Leah stilled, and her eyes narrowed. "So it's okay to do all of this to my parents, but yours are off limits? I don't think so, Sam."

He sighed wearily. "Look, that's not what I meant. I know you want to put all of this to rest, and we will. Just not tonight."

"We're just going to have to agree to disagree," she stated, stacking the plates and utensils on top of the pie box.

When she started to lift them, Sam said, "Here, let me get those for you."

"I've got them," she said hastily, then hurried toward the dining room.

Apparently, she didn't need or want any more favors from him.

As they rejoined their parents, his dad took one look at her and then glared at Sam. Most likely because he had come back empty-handed while Leah had carried everything in. That wasn't Sam's fault, of course. But it's not like he could defend himself without telling him that they'd been arguing in the kitchen.

Leah set the stack down and opened the box, containing the presliced pie she'd stolen from her own bakery. Using the pie server, she began placing wedges of the pie on small dessert plates and passing them around the table.

Sam closed his lips around his first bite and moaned appreciatively with a sound that was purely orgasmic in tone. Leah glanced up at Nancy, who was staring at him in horror. "What can I say? He loves my desserts," Leah explained, taking a bite of her own slice of pie.

"I do," Sam agreed. "I could eat your cherry pie all night long, if you'd let me."

Leah choked, then quickly reached for her glass of wine.

Sam hadn't meant what he'd said to come out sounding so...sexual. Now that it had though, he couldn't help but grin at Leah's shocked expression. Served her right. But when he noticed his dad's red face and how his hand fisted on the table, Sam decided to cool the sexual remarks. His parents were probably horrified enough with the things Leah was saying about him.

Great. He's going to have some major explaining to do after tonight.

He couldn't let things spin farther out of control than they already had, but there was no way to stop Leah from saying whatever the hell she wanted. And that knowledge only pissed him off more.

Once they'd finished dessert in silence, Nancy suggested they move to the parlor. Sam couldn't believe her snooty ass even called it that. It was a goddamn living room, if you asked him.

"Leah, why don't you and Sam make yourselves comfortable on the settee," Nancy said, motioning to the prissy-looking love seat with the ugly-ass flowers. "Sharon and David can sit on the one across from you, Bill will sit in his recliner, and I'll sit over here in my reading chair."

Sam rolled his eyes. Now they had assigned seats? What the fuck were they—kindergartners? And did this pretentious woman have to have a fancy name for almost everything in her home? What was wrong with just calling it a sofa or a couch? He dragged himself across the room and sank down next to Leah.

"So tell me, Leah, what drew you to my son?" David asked, making conversation. "Was it his dynamic personality?" He leaned back and smiled at Sam with genuine pride.

"Not really," Leah replied. "I'm pretty sure it was the size of his package that did it for me."

"Leah!" Nancy exclaimed, shaking her head. "I swear. I'm not sure what's come over you tonight. The god-awful things that are coming out of your mouth are . . . Well, it's just not like you to say such things."

A grin spread across Leah's amused face. "Hey, I'm not the one asking the questions here. I'm just answering them." She gestured to Sam. "If you ask him what he liked about me, I'm pretty sure he'll say he liked my big boobs."

Sam closed his eyes and breathed out heavily through his nose. Okay, so her breasts *had* been the first thing he'd noticed from across the bar the night he met her. But he'd damn sure never told Leah that. And it wasn't at all what drew him to her. Not really. "Actually, it was your eyes," he said, gazing at Leah as he spoke the truth. "The moment I saw those gorgeous emeralds up close, I was a goner."

His mom smiled at him, and his dad nodded in approval. But Leah cocked her head, as if she was trying to figure out whether he was making it up on the spot. He wasn't. Then a glossy sheen fell over her eyes. She blinked it away.

He placed his hand on hers, but she stood up quickly. "It's getting late. I should probably get home and go to bed. Bakery hours start early."

"Leah..."

"Sam, can you please just take me home?"

* * *

Yawning, Sam plopped down in the chair inside the small construction trailer, kicked his feet up onto the solid oak desk, and leaned his head back until it was cushioned by the top of the chair. Then he closed his eyes.

It was noon, and most of the guys had already clocked out for their lunch break. But Sam didn't want to go to lunch. What he wanted was to take a damn nap. He hadn't blamed his parents for being upset with him for not explaining what the hell was going on. But he'd promised to call them later in the week and give them some answers. Maybe by then he'd actually have some.

He'd spent the entire night tossing and turning, and then he'd gotten up earlier than normal so his parents wouldn't miss their flight. The airport was only a thirty-minute drive from Granite, Texas, but they'd left the house early to avoid any rush-hour traffic. Thankfully, there hadn't been any. But Sam had spent the rest of the morning fighting exhaustion and couldn't wait for this workday to be over.

He would have taken his lunch hour to go talk to Leah,

but he didn't think that an hour was enough time to re-solve everything between them. Not after she'd become emotional last night and had wanted to go home. He would have tried to talk to her then, but with his parents in the truck, that would have been an awkward conversation, for sure.

As it was, the ride to her house had almost been unbear-able. Leah had sat in silence the entire way, not looking at him even once. When they'd arrived, she slid out of the truck, pausing only long to tell his parents that it'd been nice to meet them. Then she'd walked inside.

The trailer door flung open, and Max climbed inside. "Hey, you just get back from lunch?"

Sam opened one eye and glared at him. "No, I didn't go to lunch today. I had to get up really early to take my par-ents to the airport, and now I have too much work to catch up on."

"Really? Because it looks like you're taking a nap."

Sam chuckled. "Yeah, trying to. What's up?"

"Just clocking back in, boss. So where were you this past weekend? I went by your apartment every single day, and you were gone each time."

"I went out of town."

Max's brow rose. "Really? With who?"

"A...friend."

A sinister grin lifted the corners of Max's mouth. "Does this friend have boobs?"

"Does it matter?"

Max's smile stretched wider. "Thought you were done with women."

Sam rolled his eyes. "I was just taking a short break."

"And now your break is over? Or are you still going to try to convince me that there's nothing going on between you and Leah? Because, at this point, I'm pretty sure I'm not the only one whose head you're fucking with here."

Sam's eyes narrowed. "I'm not fucking with anyone's head."

"Oh yeah? Did you tell Leah how you feel about her?"

His eyes narrowed, and his jaw tightened. "I already told you—"

"Right. Nothing's going on. I've heard it all before, buddy. And you're full of shit, you know that?"

Sam had had about enough of Max butting his nose in where it didn't belong. What the hell did that asshole know about relationships anyway? The idiot rarely ever made it past more than one night with a woman as it was. And the last thing Sam was going to do was sit around discussing his feelings like he and Max were a couple of teenage girls.

This was a construction site, damn it. Not a girls' bathroom. If he had the power to do so, Sam would have revoked Max's man card on the spot.

Besides, Sam couldn't talk about something he didn't fully understand himself. And his feelings for Leah were definitely at the top of that list.

After everything that had happened between them, being just friends was no longer an option. It would never work. He wanted her too damn much to allow any opportunity for another guy to come into the picture. The very thought of another man putting his grubby hands on her body made Sam want to take out a hammer and break someone's fingers.

That wasn't love though. If you asked him, it sounded more like a male dog marking his territory. But since when had Leah become *his* territory?

Probably since the night you announced her as your fiancée, dumbass.

But what did any of it mean? He liked being around Leah.

Hell, he actually liked everything about her. And that damn sure included having sex with her. Was it possible he had fallen in love with her?

Hell if I know.

Apparently, he'd never been in love before. Not truly. Because if he had, he should be able to recognize the symptoms. And right now he was clueless.

Either way, the only person he wanted to discuss his feelings with was Leah. He needed to see her, which he planned to do the moment he got off work. Until then, he wanted Max to shut the hell up and leave him alone. "Can you stop keeping on about Leah already? I've had about enough of your shit. I said we are just friends, and I meant it. Now drop it."

"Getting awfully defensive for a guy who is trying to convince me you don't have anything going with her."

"What do you want me to do—recite a fucking love poem for you? Look, I did you a favor that first night. You asked me to be your wingman so you could hook up with her friend—a feat you failed at, dickhead. But I did my job as your friend. So now do yours and leave it the fuck alone already."

A thump came from outside the door.

"What the hell?" Max asked, getting up to check out the noise. He shoved open the trailer door, glanced around, then closed it again. "Maybe a bird flew into the door."

Sam sighed heavily. "Okay, if you're done harassing me, you can get back to work now. We have to finish this job within the week or heads are going to roll. And it will be yours, not mine."

"All right, fine. I'm going." Max punched his time clock on the wall. "But I'm just saying, if you're done with Leah, I know a few guys who might be interested in tapping that."

Fire blazed through Sam, and his hands fisted on the desk. "Careful," he warned, his threatening tone filling the small space around them.

Max grinned, raising his hands in surrender. "Okay, okay. Damn. A little territorial for a guy who says he isn't into the girl."

"Get the fuck out of my office before I fire your ass."

Chapter Twenty-three

Leah couldn't believe she'd been so stupid.

After last night's embarrassing disaster, she'd done exactly as Val had suggested and gone to talk to Sam about their "relationship." She'd even brought him a box of chocolate éclairs from the bakery to use as an ice breaker. But when she'd heard Max's voice inside the construction trailer, she decided to wait for him to leave before entering. All because she hadn't wanted to make him uncomfortable by putting him in the middle of an awkward situation between her and Sam... *That bastard.*

She hadn't meant to eavesdrop on their private conversation. But the moment her name had popped out of his mouth, she couldn't stop her ears from perking up and tuning in. It had hurt to hear Sam say he wasn't into her, especially after he'd spent the other night with her convincing her otherwise. His callous words had taken her breath away and stopped her heart from beating as if he'd reached inside and tore it from her chest.

He took one for the fucking team. That was basically what he'd said, after all.

Leah had been so shocked to learn that Sam had strung her along from the beginning for his buddy's sake that she'd accidentally dropped the box of pastries onto the ground outside the trailer door. The loud thump had drawn their attention, but she managed to swipe the box off the ground and hide out on the side of the trailer before Max had thrown open the door.

When he went back inside and shut the door behind him, Leah had hightailed it out of there as quickly as possible, stopping only long enough to toss the crushed bakery box into a nearby Dumpster. Then she'd climbed behind the wheel of her car and sped out of the parking lot. She wanted to put as much distance as she could between her and the hurtful words that had fallen from Sam's lips. Between Gavin and her mother, she'd already heard enough of them to last her a lifetime.

Damn it, Sam. Not you too.

She shook her head as she swiped away a fat teardrop that landed on her puffy cheek. She'd been nothing more than a third wheel for Valerie and Max the night they had all met, and Sam had only entertained Leah to keep her busy while his friend had tried to hook up with her friend.

And she'd fallen for it. *God, I'm so stupid.*

The asshole had actually been honest with her from the get-go. Well, sort of. He'd told her the truth when he'd said she wasn't his type, he wasn't interested, and he didn't want a relationship. So why the hell hadn't she listened to him?

Friends with benefits. Christ. He'd all but told her everything she needed to know by that statement. And if she had taken what he'd said at face value, then she wouldn't be driving back to the bakery with tears in her eyes and a heart as crushed as those damn chocolate éclairs.

Sam hadn't made any public declaration to Max about what had taken place between them. And there had never been any mention of him having feelings for her either. In fact, it was just the opposite. He'd adamantly denied it all.

And that was just fine. Because the last thing she wanted to do was get involved with another asshole who didn't appreciate what she had to offer.

* * *

After getting off work later than he'd expected, Sam ran home for a quick shower and a change of clothes. He could have used the sink to wash the dried wood glue off his hands, but his sweat-soaked shirt and varnish-stained jeans were not suitable attire when a man was planning on telling the woman in his life that he wants to pursue whatever the hell this thing was between them and see if they had a future together.

It was well past closing time when he arrived at Sweets n' Treats. Locked up tight, the bakery was dark, and it appeared no one was home. Sam walked around the building to the back entrance and banged on the door as well, but there was still no answer. Leah's car wasn't there, and she wasn't answering her phone either.

Where the hell is she?

He'd texted her and said he would be coming over, but since she hadn't replied, he wasn't even sure if she had seen the message. Sam drove out to her parents' house, which only took him about fifteen minutes. Their inside lights were on, but Sam didn't bother to stop since Leah's car wasn't in the driveway.

He wondered where else he could look for her but didn't have an idea where she would be at this time of night. Valerie's house, maybe... but he didn't know where she lived so he couldn't go beat down her door. Too bad he didn't have her phone—

Sam grinned. He didn't have Valerie's phone number, but he would bet his life that Max did. Or would at least know where she lived. Pulling over on the side of the road, Sam fished his phone out of his pocket and tapped Max's name.

The phone rang only twice before someone picked up and loud country music blared in the background. Max had to raise his voice to talk over it. "Hey, buddy. Good timing. I was just about to give you a call."

Sam groaned. "If you were going to call and harass me some more about my relationship with Leah, then you can go fuck yourself," he said playfully to his friend.

Max chuckled. "Nope, that wasn't it. But you can deny it all you want, that's fine by me. I was just going to call you and let you know that the girl you have no feelings for whatsoever is here at Rusty's Bucket... and she's not alone."

"Leah's there? With who... Valerie?"

"Nope. She's with some guy. And they're looking pretty damn cozy, if you know what I mean."

Fuck.

Hot rage swept over him, and he contemplated stopping off at the job site to pick up his hammer. Because if that guy laid a finger on Leah, he would have no problem getting kicked out of Rusty's a second time. "I'll be there in ten minutes," Sam said, ending the call abruptly.

He held the steering wheel in a death grip as he swung the truck around in a wide, illegal U-turn, then stomped the gas pedal to the floor. Sam didn't know what the hell was going on or why the fuck Leah was out with another guy, but he was damn sure about to find out.

Sam made it there in six minutes flat.

It was just past dark, and Rusty's Bucket was lit up from one end to the other with flashing neon lights. Old beer signs sat in the dirty windows of the rickety old bar. There weren't many cars in the parking lot, but more than he'd expected for a Thursday night.

The only one he cared about though was the red sedan—Leah's car—sitting front and center. How the hell had he not seen it when he'd passed by there on the way to her parents' house?

He entered through the side door and glanced around the room until his gaze landed on Leah sitting alone. Thank God.

As he started for her, she leaned over the table, reaching for a bar napkin, and her snug jeans stretched tight across her lush ass. Sam's dick twitched at the sight, but he also couldn't help but notice that his eyes weren't the only ones watching her. Several men lounging at a table in front of her had craned their necks to glance in Leah's direction.

But the moment he stopped behind her and she settled back in her chair, Sam understood why the men's eyes had been glued to her. The low-cut blouse she wore barely kept her ample breasts contained, and the deep amounts of cleavage she showed off had given the other men an eyeful of what he'd spent a whole night playing with.

He didn't know which pissed him off more.

Sam moved around to her side, where she could see him standing next to her. "I've been looking for you."

Unimpressed, Leah straightened in her chair and pushed her hair off her right shoulder. "Well, you found me."

His brows furrowed at her distant tone.

"Did you want something else?" she asked, her voice as remote as her eyes.

He wasn't sure why she was being so cool with him, but he damn sure wanted to figure it out. "We need to talk."

"Okay, I'll try to give you a call tomorrow."

Sam's hand balled into a fist. "It's important, Leah."

She turned to face him and hooked her arm around the back of the chair. "Okay, then shoot. What did you need?"

He glanced around and sighed. "Maybe we could go talk somewhere a little more private."

"Sorry, I can't right now. I'm here with someone."

Sam gritted his teeth. "Yeah. So I heard. What the hell is this all about, Leah?"

Before she could answer, someone approached from behind him and said, "Excuse me, pal."

A young guy stood there with two beers, one in each hand. He maneuvered around Sam and plopped down in the chair next to Leah, pushing a drink her way. "Here ya go, sweetheart."

"Thanks, Jason."

When Sam continued to stand there, the man glanced up at him and then back to Leah. "Who's he?" he asked.

Sam grinned. He couldn't wait to see the expression on this jackass's face when Leah told him Sam was her fiancé.

"Oh, I'm sorry," Leah said, waving her hand through the air. "I guess I forgot my manners. This is Sam Cooper. He's just a friend of mine."

Friend? Not fucking hardly. The last time he checked, friends didn't go down on each other and spend the rest of the night seeing who could give each other the most orgasms.

"Nice to meet you," Jason muttered, offering his hand.

But Sam ignored him. He was too busy eyeing Leah and

trying to understand what the hell was going on in that mind of hers. He didn't know why she was sitting with this clown after the two of them had been sleeping together, but he'd damn well had enough of the games.

"Excuse us for a moment," he said, grasping Leah by the arm and dragging her from her chair before she could protest. He pulled her toward the front door of the bar, hoping to get her into the parking lot before she stopped him, but she jerked her arm free in the middle of the bar.

"What the fuck do you want from me, Sam?"

He glanced around at all the faces staring at them and spotted Max standing off to one side. Then he turned his attention back onto Leah. "I want to know why you're giving me the cold shoulder. What the hell's wrong with you tonight?"

She crossed her arms and glared at him. "That's just the thing, Sam. There's not a damn thing wrong with me. It may have taken me some time to realize it, but I'm not the problem here. Men like you are."

His eyes narrowed. "What are you talking about?"

"I'm talking about your inability to see me for who I am, rather than a number on a scale. You may not know this, but my worth is not measured by my hip size."

"You know damn well I'm not that kind of guy, Leah."

"Yeah right, Sam. You don't have to pretend anymore," she said sharply. "I get it. You were just doing Max a favor by being his wingman." She glanced up toward the ceiling, as if she was thinking, and then held up one finger. "Actually, I believe you called it your *job*. Isn't that what you said?"

Sam recognized his words immediately and put together the sequence of events that led to this very moment. *Fuck me.* His heart sank in his chest, and his stomach twisted.

She'd obviously overheard the conversation he'd had with Max, and he cringed as he recalled exactly what he'd said. "Leah, if you'll just let me explain—"

"Oh, I've heard enough already, don't you think? Enough to know exactly where I stand with you. And that's fine, but I wish you'd had the balls to tell me yourself instead of embarrassing me like you did."

"Damn it. Leah, what I said to Max, it wasn't about you. It was more about me not wanting to tell Max about us and the way he kept on pushing—"

"I don't care. I'm not interested in hearing anything else you have to say. You have some nerve sleeping with a girl, screwing with her head, and then talking shit about her behind her back."

"God, it wasn't like that, I swear. Damn it, Leah, I care about you."

She shook her head in disbelief. "I heard how much you cared for me. You were too embarrassed to even tell Max that you had gone away with me for the weekend, much less that you slept with me."

"Leah, listen to me. I didn't want to tell Max about us because I was waiting until I talked to you first. I would have eventually said something to him."

She rolled her eyes. "Well, it's too late. I'm not interested in only being with someone behind closed doors. I don't want or need a secret admirer, and I refuse to be your dirty little secret."

"Goddamnit, stop it and listen. It wasn't like that, and you know it."

"I don't know any such thing. As far as I'm concerned, that's exactly what it was like. But this is who I am, Sam. And I'm happy with myself...even if you don't like it. I don't want your pity—and definitely don't need another sympathy fuck. You can keep it. I'll wait around for someone who is proud to be with me, fat or not. Sure, I'll probably lose weight eventually, but it won't be for you, Gavin, or any other guy, and it sure the hell won't be for my mom. It'll be for *me*."

Sam's stomach soured, and the acidity bubbled up into his throat. "Leah, please."

"What? You can't handle being rejected by the fat chick? Afraid your friends will have an opinion on that too?" She shook her head, disgust showing clearly on her tight lips. "You know, I may be bigger than some girls out there, but that only means I have an even bigger heart. And it won't be wasted on a shallow asshole like you."

Leah turned and simply walked away. His stomach lurched with regret, and his chest ached from the acute pain of her absence. He didn't blame her for being pissed. She'd obviously been hurt and embarrassed by what he'd told Max earlier in the day. But he needed her to know the one thing he hadn't been aware of until this very moment.

He loved her, damn it.

That he knew for sure now. Because only losing someone you loved and wanted to spend the rest of your life with would hurt this fucking much.

Max stepped up beside him and nodded toward the direction Leah had gone. "You going after her?"

"No," Sam said, cringing at his own answer.

It took everything he had to stay put and not run after her while begging her forgiveness. But no matter how badly he'd screwed things up with Leah, he refused to deprive her of the one thing she had needed most of all: self-confidence.

That damn sure didn't mean he would give her up for long though.

Chapter Twenty-four

Leah pulled up in the circle drive out front of her parents' home and turned off the engine. She dreaded the idea of going inside but didn't have much of a choice. It was her birthday party after all.

Still, birthday or not, she had no interest in attending a party where all eyes would be on her. Especially since she planned to tell her family the truth about Sam at last. Since they were no longer on speaking terms, she would just have to face her family alone. *Thanks for that, Sam.*

It had been over a week since she'd last seen him, and she couldn't believe he hadn't so much as called to apologize. Not that she planned to accept it or anything. Or even answer her phone. But he could have at least acted like he felt bad about the whole thing. Instead, he had let her walk away without saying a single word.

Guess she'd been right all along. He hadn't cared at all.

Now she just needed to figure out how to break the bad news to her family. She'd considered telling them that Sam had broken up with her, but that was hitting a little too close to home. Because although they hadn't actually dated for real, it was a breakup of sorts. He probably wouldn't refer to it as that, since he obviously didn't give two shits about her, but that was the way she looked at it.

Oh well. She was tired of lying to her family anyway.

Sure, telling them the whole thing was a ruse would be embarrassing as hell, but it was about time she finally stopped worrying about what other people thought and worried more about herself. Besides, nothing could compare to how mortifying the whole situation with Sam had been standing in the middle of the bar.

Thank God it was all over. Well, except this one last thing.

Time to face the music.

Sighing heavily, Leah climbed out of her car and lifted a large white bakery box from the backseat before kicking the sedan's door shut with her foot. When she reached the front door of her parents' home, she balanced the cake box in one arm while she fumbled the door open and stepped inside.

The house was eerily silent, as if no one was home.

"Mom? Dad?" she called out, though no one answered.

Leah walked into the kitchen and set the box down on the counter. She was about to go check the dining room when she heard murmurs coming from the patio. *Ah, so that's where they are.*

She hesitated, dreading the moment she would have to face up to the lie she'd been living for the past two weeks about her fake engagement. But it was time to come clean about everything once and for all. It would suck, but it was nothing compared to how bad Sam had made her feel. She had gotten through that though, and she would get through this too.

Leah turned and started toward the patio, but her feet froze in place.

The single back door of her childhood home had been replaced by a pair of fancy French doors made out of clear glass framed in solid pine. But that wasn't what had her feet stalling beneath her.

Through the glass, she spotted Sam on the back deck, sitting at the table with her family surrounding him, looking as comfortable as ever. He pulled the sleeves of his white Henley shirt up his forearms and smiled as he reached for the open beer on the table in front of him. Before bringing the bottle to his lips, he said something to the others that she couldn't quite make out, though they all roared with laughter.

Lava flowed through her veins, and her eyes lit with pure fire.

Though she didn't think he was talking about her, it pissed her off that he was even there, much less that he was entertaining her family with the same easy charm he'd used on her. She marched over to the newly installed French doors and threw them open, loudly banging them against the inside wall.

Everyone's eyes shifted onto her, including Sam's. The new red dress she wore suddenly felt even tighter with his eyes glazing over and scrutinizing every curve the way he did. "What the hell are you doing here?" she sneered.

He seemed to snap out of his trancelike state. "You're here. Good. Excuse us for a minute, folks," Sam said to the others, rising to his feet and moving quickly toward Leah. "I need a minute alone with my fiancée."

"Well, then you better go find her... because we both know you aren't talking about me!"

Her mother blinked at Leah's harsh tone then shook her

head. "Now, Leah, don't say things like that. Nothing Sam's done could be so bad that you want to back out of marrying him."

Leah rolled her eyes so hard they hurt. "Back out of it, my ass. We were never—"

Before she could finish what she was saying, Sam tugged her into the kitchen, slamming the doors quickly behind them. "Stop. I didn't tell them."

"Well, you obviously told them something," she accused.

"Only that I had done something that upset you and we were having a lovers' quarrel. But I assured them I would make it right, and that they didn't need to worry about it at all."

"What the hell is wrong with you?" Leah leaned on the counter with both hands, trying to figure out why the hell he'd do such a thing. "God, Sam. I'm telling my parents the truth today. Are you purposely trying to make this more difficult for me?"

"No, Leah, I'm not. But before you say a word, just promise that you'll hear me out. Please. Give me to the end of the party. If you still want to tell them the truth, I won't like it, but I won't try to stop you."

"Well, I don't give a shit what you like. It's over. There's no point in dragging it out any longer. I know where I stand and—"

"No. You don't."

"The fuck I don't," she said with a biting tone. "It was all perfectly clear. And you know what, Sam? I'm not even upset that you don't want me. I just wish you'd have told me so before having sex with me. What a joke that was. Biggest mistake of my life."

Sam's eyes narrowed, and his jaw tightened. "Why is it that you'll make excuses for everyone else in your life to mistreat you—your mother and Gavin, in particular—but you won't let up on me for one second and let me explain why I said what I did?"

"Because their words never hurt me as much as yours did!" Her voice cracked, and her eyes clogged with tears. Cringing, she turned away. Damn it. She hadn't meant to say that to him. It was the truth, but she hadn't wanted him to know what kind of power he held over her.

"Leah?" When she didn't answer him, Sam stepped around her and tilted her chin up, using his thumb to wipe away a tear from her cheek. His eyes softened, and he leaned down to touch his lips to hers.

"Don't," she said, moving away. She wouldn't be able to stand him kissing her again, knowing that he didn't feel the same way she did.

He started to speak, but the French doors opened and her dad poked his head in. "Everything all right in here? Is it safe for us to come in now?"

She gazed up at Sam, and his eyes pleaded with her to give them a few more minutes, but she didn't want to hear any more of his excuses. "It's fine, Dad," she said glumly.

As the family piled into the kitchen, Sam glanced at the bakery box on the counter. "Did you bring that with you?" When she nodded, he added, "It looks good."

She knew what he meant, but she wasn't in a real charitable mood at the moment. "It's a box," she said dryly.

"I meant what's inside the—"

"Yeah, yeah, I know," Leah said, rolling her eyes so hard they probably resembled the spinning reels of a slot machine after the lever had been pulled. "You have an addiction to sweets. We get it." She shook her head in irritation and reached for the dessert plates. "Who wants a piece of the stupid cake?"

Her brother laughed. "Damn, Sam. You must have really done something bad to put this big of a bug up her ass."

"Ethan Martin! Watch your mouth," their mother warned.

"Just sayin'," Ethan said, grinning widely.

Leah had had enough of this. She just wanted to get it over with and move on with her life. Like ripping off a bandage. Get through the pain quickly so that she could start to heal. She pulled the box over to her and threw open the lid, revealing a dark chocolate cake with elegant swirls of icing decorating the top.

Her mother glanced over, and her mouth hinged open. "Oh. I thought you were going to make a carrot cake for tonight."

"I didn't want a carrot cake," Leah said firmly. "I wanted a chocolate cake. And since I was making it and it's my birthday, I made the one *I* wanted to eat."

"Okay then. Well, don't eat too much of it. You don't want to put on any more weight than you already have before we start shopping for wedding dresses. It's going to be hard enough to find one in your size as it is."

Leah stared at her point blank. "Mom, knock it the fuck off."

Her dad's eyes widened, Sam grinned, and her brother stifled a cough. But her mother's hand flew up and covered her mouth. "My goodness, Leah. What in the world?"

"I've had enough of your insulting comments and demeaning remarks. You've been picking at me for years, and I, for one, am damn tired of hearing it. One slice of cake won't kill me, nor do I need your constant reminders about how overweight I am. I own a mirror, and I have eyes. You don't need to constantly point out my flaws."

"I—I'm sorry you feel that way," she said, folding her hands in front of her.

Leah shook her head. "No, you aren't doing that to me either. That's not an apology, and I'm not going to sit here and let you make me feel bad about myself anymore like your mother did to—"

When her mom winced, Leah stopped talking. She hadn't meant to bring any of that up, especially since she knew it would upset her mother. And it had.

Her mom's eyes misted over, and a deep-rooted pain surfaced in them as her chin quivered involuntarily. "It's okay. You can say it . . . like my mother did to me."

Leah cringed. "I'm sorry, Mom. Grandma died a long time ago, and I know you don't like talking about the past."

"No, it's not the past that bothers me. It was her. Always her." She wrung her hands together. "You have nothing to apologize for, Leah. I, on the other hand, do. I'm sorry, honey. I . . . guess I didn't realize how much I sounded like her. After she died, I swore I would never treat my children the way she had treated me, but it seems I've been doing just that."

"No, it's nothing like what you went through. Dad told me stories about how cruel Grandma was to you, and I hate that you grew up that way. But you aren't like her. You just sometimes say things that . . ."

"Aren't very nice," her mother finished for her. "And that's what makes me just as bad as her. She was a cruel woman, but it was never my intention to make you feel bad about yourself. I don't want to do that to you. I love you, Leah, and I'm very proud of the woman you've become . . . even if I don't always show it."

Tears pricked Leah's eyes. "I love you too, Mom. And I know you're proud of me. I just wish you would tell me more often, rather than dwelling on my imperfections. I just want my mom to accept me for who I am."

Stunned, her mother sat there staring at her daughter for

a long moment as if she was finally realizing something. "It's...exactly what I wanted too." She dashed at the moisture beneath her eyes, then glanced over at her husband. "Bill, would you please set up that appointment for me to see the therapist you mentioned? I think I would like to talk to her after all."

"You bet," Leah's dad said, placing a supportive hand on her shoulder.

Leah moved closer and wrapped her arms around her mom. "I'm proud of you, Mom."

Her mother obviously hadn't been told that much in her life because it took her a second to hug Leah back. "I'm proud of myself too. For raising a beautiful daughter—inside and out."

After a few minutes of hugging and wiping their eyes with the tissues Bill passed to them, Ethan rolled his eyes and said, "Okay, enough with the mushy stuff. Let's eat some stupid cake already."

Sam eyed her brother's orange shirt warily. "Don't you want to change your shirt first? I thought you said you didn't like that color."

Ethan's jaw dropped open. "God, Mom! Why? Why do you keep doing this to me?" He stormed toward the stairs and disappeared around the corner.

"Maybe I should make an appointment for Ethan too," Bill said, making the others laugh. "I don't know what's come over him lately."

"Must be those damn teenage hormones," Sam said, grinning at Leah.

She didn't smile back though. It hurt too much seeing him there with her family, knowing she loved him and he didn't love her back. "Mom, Dad...can you give me a minute alone with Sam?"

"Sure, honey," her mother said, then headed for the living room with her husband on her heels.

Once they were out of earshot, Leah spoke. "I just wanted to forewarn you that I'm going to tell them the truth. You don't have to stick around though. You can slip out the back door and leave without any of them even knowing you're gone."

"I'm not going anywhere, Leah."

"Sam, it's okay. I don't need you at my side when I tell them. Besides, I don't want my dad to take a swing at you."

"Why not? We both know I deserve it after the way I treated his daughter."

Pain surged inside her, but she shook her head. "No, you don't. You can't help the way you feel any more than I can."

"Will you at least open my presents before you throw me out?" He walked over to the far counter and lifted two boxes, setting them in front of her.

She gazed at the white boxes tied with pink satin ribbons. "You didn't have to get me anything for my birthday."

"Open them," he encouraged.

She smiled and slid the ribbon off the first box, then flipped open the lid. Inside was a pair of shoes—the same kind of sandal she'd lost at the beach. "How did you..."

"Know what shoe size you wear?" he asked, grinning. "You left your old sandal in my truck."

"No, I mean, where did you find them? I must've hit every store in Texas and couldn't find them in stock anywhere."

"Maybe you should've tried Florida."

"Huh?"

He chuckled. "I asked my mom to help me locate them. She found them in a store near her and shipped them to me."

Leah squinted at him. "Why would she do that after the way I acted in front of them?"

"They liked you. Thought you were a bit crazy, but I explained to them that you had a few too many glasses of wine before we arrived to dinner that night."

Leah's head spun. "What? No, I didn't."

He shrugged. "They don't know that."

She wanted to ask him why he would come to her defense, but before she could ask the question, Sam pushed the other box in front of her. "Open this one."

She hesitated, then yanked on the ribbon, letting it fall off the box before opening it, revealing something she would never have expected from Sam. Her breath caught in her throat, and her eyes watered, making her vision blur.

"It's chocolate," he told her. "That's what you said you wanted, right?"

"Y-you made me a cake?"

"With my own two hands."

Yep, she could tell. The lopsided cake had sunk in toward the middle, and crumbs littered the uneven clumps of ugly black frosting. But somehow it was the most beautiful cake she'd ever seen. And she knew that box had looked familiar. He obviously had gotten it from the bakery. *Damn it, Valerie. Stop supplying the enemy with ammo.*

"I...don't really know what to say," she said, swallowing hard. "Thank you, Sam. You didn't have to—"

"I wanted to. Mine may not look or taste as good as yours, but it was my first time making a cake. I'm sure I'll improve each year. No matter what, my wife isn't going to make her own birthday cake ever again."

She sighed. "You can stop with the wife stuff. My family can't see or hear us from the living room."

"Good."

Without warning, Sam wrapped his long fingers around her neck and bent his head, slanting his mouth across hers. She shuddered as he held her against him, feeling the warmth of his body seeping under her skin.

But she didn't want him to touch her. Not anymore.

She needed to stop all of this. Now. Because the dull ache in her chest was only becoming worse after being around him for even a short period of time. Maybe they could eventually be friends, but that would have to wait until her feelings for Sam no longer existed. And judging by the way she struggled not to kiss him back, she didn't think that would ever happen.

Leah backed away from him, and he let her. She didn't know why he'd kissed her but didn't get a chance to ask him before he spoke. "I have one more present for you," he told her.

"No, Sam. No more presents. I think you should leave now."

"I already told you I'm not going anywhere," he said, his eyes glittering.

"You have to. This isn't going to work. We can't be friends."

"God, sweetheart, that's what I'm trying to tell you. I don't want to be friends with you."

She blinked at him. "But you said—"

"I know what I said. I said a lot of shit that wasn't true. The stuff I told Max? All bullshit. For men, construction crews are the equivalent of women's bathrooms. But I was trying to figure out where we stood, and he wouldn't leave me alone. I was tired of his constant harassment. I'm sorry…for everything. I've been burned in the past and didn't want to fall into another quickie relationship that wouldn't last. But none of that had anything to do with you, I swear."

"I don't know what you want from me, Sam. You expect me to believe it had nothing to do with me, yet you couldn't even tell your best friend about us. I find it all a little hard to swallow."

"I don't expect you to believe anything I say. I plan on proving it to you. That's what this is for." Sam pulled a small black velvet box from his pocket and set it in front of her. "Open your last present."

Her heart pounded wildly. *Is that what I think it is?* It couldn't be.

She gazed at him warily then turned her attention to the black box, lifting it from the counter. With her fingers trembling, she raised the lid and spotted a large diamond engagement ring glinting under the kitchen lights. Puzzled, she turned back to Sam, who had knelt down beside her. Her eyes widened. "W-what the hell are you doing?"

"I'm proposing to my fiancée."

She glanced around, making sure the others were still in the living room. "Sam, stop it. This isn't funny."

"It's not meant to be funny." He took her hand. "I should have told you this sooner, but I fell for you, Leah. I didn't mean to. Hell, I even tried to stop it from happening. But the more involved I became, the more I realized the desserts you make aren't the sweetest thing about you."

"Sam…"

"Let me finish, please. You're kind, considerate, funny, and real. More real than any other woman I've ever met. Not to mention unbelievably sexy."

Heat crawled up her neck and pooled in her cheeks. "Sam…"

"Shh! I'm on a roll, sweetheart." He winked at her. "Leah Martin, somewhere along the way, I stopped pretending. I fell in love with you. Do you hear me? I love you. I don't want to be friends with you. I want you to be my wife...for real this time."

A tear tracked down her cheek. "You mean that?"

"Every last fucking word."

Her heart beat faster, but she paused. "Wait a minute. Is this your way of keeping yourself in desserts for the rest of your life?"

He couldn't seem to stop himself from grinning, but said, "Even if you never made me another dessert for the rest of our lives, I'd still want to marry you and spend the rest of mine with you."

"Do I still have to pay you for any work you do in my bakery?"

Sam's smirked, and his eyes did that funny smoldering thing again. "I think we could work out some kind of payment arrangement that would be mutually satisfying."

Feeling the heat of his gaze on her, Leah blew out a long, slow breath. "Then I guess we're getting married. But do me a favor and let me make our wedding cake."

Sam laughed. "I thought you'd never ask." He rose swiftly, dipped her in his arms, and gazed deeply into her eyes. "God, I love you, Leah."

Her heart swelled, filling with more happiness than she'd ever known. "I love you too."

Then he kissed her. Really kissed her. His tongue thrust inside her mouth, and she returned the favor, needing to taste him once again. By the time he pulled back, they were both panting softly. "Want to go burn some calories together at my place? I'd really like to get my hands under that dress."

"Only if we can take the chocolate cake with us."

He righted her, chuckling. "Which one?"

"Both," she said seriously.

Sam winked at her. "That's my girl."

Her mom stepped into the doorway, the clatter of her shoes on the tile drawing their attention. "Honey, your father said he knows a caterer who will probably give him a discount, but he's wanting to know how big this wedding is going to be."

Leah and Sam exchanged knowing looks. Then she smiled and said, "I think I can speak for both of us when I say size doesn't matter."

Alison Bliss continues her contemporary romance series about three curvaceous heroines finding love, with humor and heart...

Look for *On the Plus Side,* available in May 2017.

A preview follows.

Chapter One

Valerie Carmichael needed a drink. A strong one. Because it was the only way she envisioned herself getting through the night.

Then again, maybe if she drank enough, the alcohol would sour her stomach and give her a good excuse to bail out and take the first cab home. Sadly, that option sounded the most appealing.

An elbow nudged into her side, bringing her thoughts back to the crowded bar. "I can't see anything through all of these fucking people," Brett said, scanning the room with his eyes. "Come on, let's go to the other side so I can get a better view."

Sighing, Valerie trudged behind him without a word.

When Brett had asked her to attend the grand opening of the new bar in their hometown of Granite, Texas, she'd hesitated to say yes. Sure, she was curious what the inside of the recently remodeled bar looked like and had no doubt the place would be jam-packed with handsome, available men. But it was still the last place on earth she wanted to be.

She knew better than to hang out in bars with her older and only—*thank God*—brother. Every time she'd done so in the past, the nights had always ended the same way. Brett would spend the entire evening hovering over her like a rabid pit bull, daring any single guy with a glint in his eye to look her way. And eventually, one of them would.

At least one brave soul, brimming with liquid courage, would be dumb enough—or drunk enough—to risk approaching her while Brett stood guard. Then the potentially suicidal man would quickly find out what a hot-tempered, cockblocking asshole her brother could be. It was inevitable.

Because Valerie turned heads. She always had.

Oh, she wasn't silly enough to believe she looked like some gorgeous supermodel with a lean, trim figure or anything. She definitely didn't. But she had a pretty face, banging plus-size curves, and a lively personality. And that was good enough for her. Valerie was just... Valerie. And damn proud of it.

Unfortunately, that noteworthy self-confidence of hers was akin to a powerful magnet, drawing unassuming male moths to her female flame. Which meant, as with any heat source, there was always a chance someone would get burned. And with Brett around, odds were in her favor that it wasn't going to be her.

As they made their way across the room, Brett's muscular frame easily parted the sea of people, giving her plenty of walking space to follow behind him without bumping into anyone. But even then, she only made it ten feet before a masculine arm circled her waist and pulled her back against a hard body. "Hey, baby. Wanna dance?"

Valerie winced. *Another guy with a death wish. Lovely.*

No, wait. She recognized that voice, didn't she?

Glancing over her right shoulder, she stared directly into

Max's playful eyes just as Brett whipped around and shoved Max away from her. "Get your fucking hands off my sister, jackass."

Max released her and held his hands up in surrender. "Whoa! I was just playing around with her. No need to get pissy about it, buddy."

"I'm not your goddamn buddy," Brett sneered, fire flashing in his eyes as he stepped toward Max.

Valerie scrambled into her brother's path to keep him at bay. "Stop it! He's just a friend of mine, Brett. You don't have to go all caveman on him."

"Then tell your *friend* to keep his damn hands off you." Her brother shot Max one of his blue-eyed Taser glares, which usually sent most men retreating.

But Max wasn't like most men and continued to stand there, as if he were throwing down a challenge of his own. One Brett was clearly willing to accept, since he started for Max.

Jesus. Here we go again. Valerie readjusted her position and placed her hands on Brett's chest to stop him. "Knock it off right now. Damn it, you promised to behave yourself tonight. If you can't control yourself, then I'm going home." She almost hoped Brett would throw a punch just so she had a reason to leave. *Sorry, Max.*

"Me?" Brett asked innocently, his eyes widening. "I didn't do anything...*yet.*" He zapped another threatening look in Max's direction for good measure.

Valerie shook her head, annoyed with the whole situation. "Why don't you just go ahead without me, and I'll catch up to you in a little bit?"

Her brother didn't move.

God, why did I come out tonight? Me and my bright ideas. "Damn it, Brett. Just go already. I'll be fine. I want to talk to Max." Her brother planted his feet, as if he planned to wait for her, so she added, "Without my bodyguard present, if you don't mind."

Brett gritted his teeth and set his jaw but eventually stalked away. Once Valerie was sure he wasn't coming back, she turned her attention to Max and sighed. "Sorry about that. My brother's a little...intense."

"Who, that guy? Nah." Max's sardonic tone wasn't lost on her, but then he shrugged. "No big deal, Val. You warned me that your brother was an asshole. If I had known he was with you tonight, I wouldn't have grabbed you like that."

She grinned. "You're such a liar."

The corner of his mouth lifted into a tiny smirk. "I know."

Though they'd met only six months before at Rusty's Bucket—a seedy local dive bar that made this place look like an upscale Vegas cocktail lounge—she'd had Max's number from the beginning. And she wasn't referring to his telephone digits...though she had those too.

Upon meeting Max, Valerie had quickly figured out two things about him. One, he was a decent guy, even though he was a bit of a troublemaker at times. Two, he hadn't been remotely attracted to her. Which was fine with her, since she hadn't been interested in him either.

She hadn't lied when she told Brett that Max was just a friend. Nothing romantic had ever evolved between them and never would. At the time, they had each unknowingly used the opportunity to set up their best friends, Leah and Sam, by feigning interest in each other.

And it had worked! The lucky couple were now engaged and living together in Sam's apartment while his construction crew built their new home not far from Leah's bakery, Sweets n' Treats. Within three weeks, Leah would have her intimate beach wedding and be moving into her glorious new home with the man of her dreams.

And Valerie couldn't be happier for them.

Especially since Leah moving in with Sam had left her one-bedroom apartment over the bakery available for Valerie to rent, thus making Leah not only her best friend and employer, but also her landlord. At least for the past month.

"I'm surprised to see you here tonight," Max said, steering Valerie toward a surprisingly vacant seat at the small side bar in the corner. "Leah said you weren't coming."

"I didn't plan to," she said, noting how strange it was that there were plenty of seats in the area around them while the rest of the bar harbored wall-to-wall people. She slid onto the black, vinyl-covered stool as Max stationed himself next to her. "I know it's hard to believe I'd miss it though."

"No kidding. Since when do you not enjoy the bar scene, party girl?"

Okay, so maybe I'm not the only one who got someone's number.

Grinning, she ignored his question and glanced around the room. "So where are Leah and Sam? I thought they'd be here by now."

"They're here," he confirmed. "They headed over to the main bar to get a drink. The bartenders over there are much faster than this one is," Max said, gesturing to the young man standing idly behind the bar. "If you want something to drink, you better tell me quick. If he has to make more than one drink at a time, you'll die of thirst before I can save you."

Normally, Valerie would have ordered a beer, but the shiny metallic bandage dress she wore showed off her feminine side and wasn't really the kind of outfit a lady would drink a beer in. *Hmm. Something colorful and fruity, perhaps?* Besides, the hard liquor would probably help ease some of the tension she'd felt creeping up her spine since she'd entered the building. "Um, how about an appletini?"

"A what?"

She grinned. "An apple martini."

Max nodded. "You got it. Coming right...er, scratch that. You might get it soon, if you're lucky." He grinned, then leaned over the bar and repeated the order to the young bartender.

The barkeep nodded in acknowledgment but seemed a bit unsure of what to do. When he finally made the decision to reach for a glass, it took him three tries before he found the one used for martinis. Even as he chilled the glass with ice, he moved so slowly and deliberately that Valerie wondered if he was pacing himself so he didn't pull a muscle in his hand. If he didn't learn to speed up, the thirsty bargoers would eat him for breakfast. Because, chances were, it would take him until morning to finish making one drink. *Jeez.*

While they waited for her drink, Max and Valerie lingered at the bar counter chatting about their friends' pending nuptials. Since they were the best man and maid-of-honor, Max and Valerie would soon be walking down the aisle together. Of course, she wouldn't dare word it that way to her brother or he'd jump to conclusions and blow a gasket.

After a few minutes, Sam and Leah emerged from the dense crowd, each holding a beer bottle in their hands. Leah blinked at the sight of Valerie sitting with Max. "Val? What are you doing here? You said you weren't coming."

Valerie shrugged. "I changed my mind."

"Are you feeling okay?"

"Yeah, sure. Why?"

"When you said you didn't want to go out, I assumed

you were sick. You *never* turn down a night out. Actually, you're the one who's always asking me to go." Leah placed her palm lightly against Valerie's forehead. "You sure you don't have the flu or something?"

Valerie laughed and pushed her friend's hand away. "Oh, stop it. I just didn't feel like getting dressed up. I'm getting tired of the whole bar scene."

Leah squinted with disbelief. "Since when?"

Since three weeks ago when I found out this place was opening. Valerie gazed longingly at the bartender, who was using a jigger to carefully measure out the vodka for her cocktail. Damn, she could really use that drink about now. She sighed inwardly. "I'm fine," she told Leah. "I was tired, but the mood passed."

"Good," Sam said cheerfully, clasping a hand on his buddy's shoulder. "Then maybe you can help us keep Max out of trouble for one evening. Lord knows he needs all the help he can get."

Max just grinned.

"Already on top of it," Valerie replied. "A few minutes ago, he met my brother."

Leah's eyes widened. "Oh, no. Brett's here? I can only imagine how well that went over."

"Yep, exactly what you're thinking. It didn't. But I managed to send Brett away for the time being. I'm sure he's still watching me from some dark corner though." She leaned over to Max and loudly mock-whispered, "If you want to keep your arms attached to your body, I wouldn't make any sudden movements in my direction."

They all laughed, probably because a truer statement had never been spoken. As the chuckling died down, the young bartender finally slid a green-tinted apple martini on the counter in front of Valerie. *Thank goodness.*

Max reached for his wallet and nodded across the room in the direction Brett had wandered off. "Think I can get away with paying for your drink, smart-ass? Or should I consult your brother first?"

She smiled up at him, her eyes twinkling with mirth. "Oh, no. You don't have to ask his permission for that." Then her gaze followed the same trail Max's had. "Always feel free to pay for my—"

Valerie's heart stopped, along with her lips. *Oh God.*

Across the room, Brett stood there talking to a tall, dark-haired man who had one thumb hooked in the front pocket of his jeans while he leaned comfortably against the wall with his right shoulder. She couldn't see the other guy's face, but she didn't need to. Valerie recognized all six feet, two inches of him.

Jesus. I don't think I can do this.

"Can't do what?" Leah asked, puzzlement filling her voice.

Shit. Had she said that out loud?

Valerie winced. Her friends probably thought Brett's ridiculous brotherly behavior had been the motivation for her wanting to stay home tonight…and that was partly true. But she hadn't told them the real reason—a bigger reason—for wanting to avoid stepping into the new hottest bar in town. And that reason not only had a name, but he was the owner.

Logan Mathis.

"Val?" Leah placed her hand on Valerie's shoulder, pulling her out of her thoughts and right back into her noisy surroundings.

She immediately lifted her drink and downed the martini in one gulp, then rubbed a flat hand across her queasy stomach. "I *can* do this," she whispered in encouragement to herself.

Sam and Max were no longer paying attention and were busy having a heated football discussion, but Leah raised one suspicious brow. "What the hell are you talking about?" she asked before her gaze fell on the empty martini glass. "How many of those have you had?"

Valerie glanced across the room again at the man who had her insides tied in knots and sighed heavily. "Not nearly enough."

Leah's gaze immediately followed the invisible trail of bread crumbs Valerie had left behind. She grinned and pointed across the bar. "Hey, isn't that—"

"Logan Mathis," Valerie groaned, not bothering to hide the contempt in her voice.

"Yeah, that's the one. He was your brother's—"

"Best friend."

She nodded. "Yep, but didn't he move away like—"

"Eight years ago."

Leah pursed her mouth in annoyance. "Okay, how about you actually let me ask the question before you answer it?"

Despite the way her stomach was churning, Valerie couldn't help but grin. "Sorry. Go ahead."

"Isn't he the guy you had that huge crush on back then?"

Valerie blinked rapidly. "Wait. H-how did you . . ."

"Oh, come on," Leah said, rolling her eyes. "You didn't really think you fooled me, did ya? You mooned over the Mathis boy every chance you got. And the way you always wanted to tag along with the two of them, though Brett frustrated the hell out of you most days. It was obvious."

Great. Just great. Valerie closed her eyes and rubbed at her temples before looking back at Logan. He had shifted his position and was now leaning with his back against the brick wall, which gave her a clear view of his face. Her mouth went dry. *Good Lord. Could he possibly get any hotter?*

He had the same brooding brown eyes as before, but his muscled frame had filled out and taken on a more rugged appearance. A five o'clock shadow now graced his chiseled jaw but gave his face more depth and dimension.

His clothes, however, were a bit misleading based on the Logan she remembered. The neutral-toned flannel shirt permitted him an almost respectable, approachable look that was probably good for his business. But then she noticed that he'd only slightly tucked in the front of the shirt, enough to showcase the noticeable bulge beneath his belt buckle. As if he were putting his manhood on display.

There's the Logan she remembered. *That damn subtle arrogance of his.*

Leah eyed her warily. "So that's why you're acting so weird tonight? You still have a thing for Logan?"

"No, I don't," Valerie answered quickly.

"Oh, my God. You do! You're practically sweating right now," Leah accused, grinning her ass off. She peeked over at him again. "Hmm. Well, he does look good."

"Really? I haven't noticed," Valerie said, keeping herself from taking another peek.

Leah looked more confused than ever. "But haven't you seen him since he got back into town?"

"No. I've been...busy. I had all that unpacking to do, ya know? And I'm pretty sure that opening a new bar required a lot of his attention."

"Val, you moved into my old apartment a month ago, and I helped you unpack everything the first week you were..." Leah paused. "Hold on. Did you say he opened a new bar? As in *this* bar?"

"Um, yeah. It's his place."

"I didn't know that. I guess all this wedding planning has kept me distracted and out of the loop. I'm surprised you didn't mention it thou…" Leah paused then threw back her head and cackled. "Oh, I get it! So that's why you didn't want to come out tonight. You're avoiding him." When Valerie bit her lip, Leah grinned wider, apparently enjoying the role reversal they had going on. Then she eyed Logan from across the room once more. "I never thought I'd say this to you, Valerie, but payback is a real bitch."

Before Valerie could stop her, Leah waved her hand in the air, snaring Brett's attention. He immediately recognized his sister's best friend and nodded to her before leaning toward Logan. Brett's mouth moved with inaudible words that had Logan's head spinning in the girls' direction.

Valerie leaned back quickly so that Max's body blocked her from view as Logan glanced over. "Leah, what the hell?" She peeked around Max's shoulder in time to see Brett start in their direction… with Logan on his heels. "Damn it, Leah! Why the hell did you do that?"

"Because I'm your friend. There's no point in avoiding him. It's like ripping off a bandage. Just get it over with already."

"Damn it, Leah…"

"Don't be mad. Besides, Granite isn't that big of a town, and you were bound to run into him sooner or later anyway."

"I was good with later."

Leah giggled, then tapped Sam on the shoulder, interrupting his conversation with Max. "Why don't the three of us go grab another round of drinks from across the room? Brett's coming over here, and I'm pretty sure Valerie is going to need a refill… or possibly ten."

"What?" Valerie blinked at her. "Now you're leaving me all by myself? Gee, thanks. Some friend you are."

"I'm doing you a favor. You'll thank me for it later. Besides, you wouldn't want me standing here grinning like a fool when he walks up," Leah said with a wink. "Let me know what happens though. I'm dying to hear how all this plays out." Then she flitted away, taking Sam and Max with her.

Traitor. She'll be lucky if I tell her anything at all.

Brett and Logan wove their way through the crush of people invading the bar, and with every step they took in her direction, Valerie could feel the room growing considerably smaller. Unwilling to make eye contact, she turned her body to the bar and stared straight ahead. Adrenaline raced through her veins, and her nerves surged with anxiety. *Yep, definitely going to throw up.*

But the moment the air pressure surrounding her changed, she knew there was an overbearing male presence standing behind her. It was as if she could feel the tension rolling off Logan in waves.

Unfortunately, she couldn't put it off any longer. Straightening her posture, she sucked in a calming breath and crossed her legs, allowing her short skirt to ride up her thighs a little more than was polite. She planted a big smile on her face, spun around on her bar stool, and looked directly at Logan's unsmiling face. He had always towered over her much shorter frame, but somehow she'd forgotten how impossibly small he could make her feel with just one simple look.

Logan's eyes met hers head on, and his lips curved. "Well, well. If it isn't Princess Valerie."

*   *   *

Logan Mathis hadn't seen Valerie Carmichael since he'd skipped out of town eight years ago, but the moment he'd come face-to-face with his best friend's kid sister, he couldn't help himself. He'd called her the one thing he knew would get a rise out of her.

And boy, did it ever.

Just like in the past, Valerie jutted out that perfect pointy chin and narrowed those piercing ice blue eyes. But instead of shrieking at him like she used to, Val did something he hadn't expected. She lifted one brow in a prominent arch, as if daring him to find out just how much of a princess she really was. *Interesting.*

Her cool, assessing eyes flickered over him. "Logan," she stated calmly, though her pitch held an undeniable amount of irritation, "I heard you were back in town. What happened? Houston got tired of you and decided to kick you out?"

The young Valerie he remembered from years before had always been pretty and blooming with personality, but this girl, this *woman*, sitting in front of him had an air of confidence he hadn't seen before.

He smiled at the hostile edge to her tone, but as his gaze landed on the exposed flesh of her upper thighs, he began feeling a little antagonistic himself. "Yeah, guess that's what happens when a guy makes his way through all their women."

Brett laughed and slapped him on the back. "Good one, bro." Then he nodded toward the empty glass on the bar. "Looks like you're empty, Val. Want another one of those...uh, whatever the hell that thing is?"

A smile tugged on her red-painted lips as she swept her long, wavy blond hair off her right shoulder. "It's an apple martini. And yes, I'd love another." She leaned toward her brother and lowered her voice to almost a whisper. "But you might want to order it from the main bar across the room."

Logan didn't need to ask why. He knew Derek wasn't as

fast as the other bartenders he'd hired, which was exactly why he'd started him out at the small side bar, where he wouldn't see as much action. But he seemed like a good kid and had the desire to learn. He'd get faster in time. Probably.

But leave it to Valerie to point out the one weakness in his staff. At least she hadn't been loud about it. Didn't matter anyway. Brett was so preoccupied by a redhead who walked past that he didn't even question why he'd have to get their drinks at the main bar. He just nodded and said, "All right. I'm going to grab a beer while I'm there. Logan can keep an eye on you while I'm gone."

"I don't need a babysitter," she said, rolling her eyes.

Logan considered doing the same. It was as if Brett expected women-eating sharks to start circling if he left his sister alone for even a minute. Then he noticed a guy standing a few feet away with his eyes trained on the hem of Valerie's barely there dress. *Okay, so maybe Brett has a point.*

Shifting his position, Logan used his own body to block her legs from view. Unfortunately, that meant he was practically standing over her, which only gave him a better view of her never-ending cleavage. His gaze focused between her breasts and slid all the way down to where hardened nipples poked through the thin fabric.

"You want something, Logan?"

Oh, yeeeah. It took him a moment to realize he still hadn't answered Brett's question out loud. "Uh, no. I don't drink on the cock...I mean, clock." *Shit.*

Brett chuckled. "You sure you haven't been drinking, buddy?"

"I'm sure," Logan said, forcing his gaze away from Valerie. "Just give the bartender your name, and they'll put your drinks on my tab. I've already told them to expect you to—"

Brett snorted. "You aren't comping our drinks, jackass. You can't make money by doing shit like that. First night on the job and you already suck as a businessman." When Logan opened his mouth to argue, Brett held up one hand. "I'm serious, dude. Don't make me kick your ass in front of everyone."

Logan grinned. "You could try."

Once Brett disappeared into the crowd, Logan turned back to Valerie, keeping his eyes on hers. His gaze begged him to shift lower, but he wasn't about to let that happen. Even if she was wearing a sinfully tight dress.

Actually, if you asked him, it wasn't really a dress. More like a sparkly, figure-flattering scrap of spandex that outlined the shape of her curvy-ass body. The torturous, low-cut hem practically screamed at him to slide some part of his anatomy under it.

His hands wouldn't have been his first choice, but the nerves in his fingers twitched anyway. The last thing he needed tonight was to see her prancing around in shit like that.

"Nice dress," Logan said, clenching his jaw, though he managed to keep his tone casual. "Where'd you get it—the fabric store?"

She grinned, as if his backhanded compliment pleased her. "I bought it online." She stood, which brought her much closer to him than before, and smoothed her hands down her sides. Her eyes glittered under the flashing neon lights. "Do you like it?"

"Not much to like," Logan said gruffly.

"Well, that's basically the point, isn't it?" Valerie giggled in that sexy, girly way that made a man's balls draw up inside him.

"I'm surprised your brother let you wear that. I figured he would have wrestled you to the ground to keep you from walking out the door in something so low-cut."

"Oh, please. Brett doesn't have a say in what I wear. I don't live with him."

"That hasn't stopped him in the past."

Valerie sighed. "That was a long time ago, Logan. Believe it or not, I'm fully capable of picking out my own clothes. I don't need his approval. Or *yours*." She leaned forward, licking her plump lips, and whispered, "Maybe you haven't realized this yet, but I'm not a little girl anymore."

His stomach tightened. *You can say that again.* But he also knew Brett better than anyone. "How many times did you change before you passed inspection?"

Her lips curved. "Only once. Brett said the first dress would have gotten me arrested...or possibly him."

Damn it. Now Logan wanted to see that one too. It didn't really matter which one she wore though, since he was pretty sure both would look fan-fucking-tastic lying on his bedroom floor. He'd never find out, of course, but he couldn't help grinning for being right about her brother. "Yeah. I thought so, princess."

Her lips pursed as if she were mildly annoyed, but she recovered quickly. "So what are you doing back here anyway? The way you left town so fast, I was sure you'd never step foot within the city limits again."

"I came back to open a business. Or did you forget that you're sitting in *my* bar wearing next to nothing?"

"Yeah, but you could have opened a bar anywhere."

Yep, he could have. But he didn't. "So?"

"So why here?"

"Why not?" he asked, deflecting the question.

She gazed at him curiously and shrugged. "Seems like an

odd choice, that's all. Houston is a much larger city. Why would you want to open your business in a small town like Granite?"

Damn. Couldn't she just leave it alone already? "I'm from here, Val. And my mother still lives here, remember?"

"Of course I remember," she said, lifting one inquisitive brow. "I guess I'm just surprised *you* do. Your mom comes in the bakery all the time. I've probably seen her more in the past month than you've seen her in the past eight years."

Ouch. Okay, that stung. But what really pissed him off most was that she was right. He hadn't come home. Not even once. And although he had his reasons, he wasn't willing to discuss them with Valerie. Ignoring the jab, he gave her one of his own. "Yeah, your brother told me you were working in your friend's bakery now. How many people have you poisoned with that endeavor?"

"None yet," she said, giggling. "But I'm certainly willing to make an exception in your case." She grinned again.

God, she had to stop doing that.

The way her sensual mouth curved with that secretive little smile of hers had always driven him up the wall, but it was flat out lethal when paired with the delicate scent of her perfumed skin hovering in the air around him. Sugared oranges and sweet coconut. Like the blond goddess had bathed in a pool of ambrosia. It was enough to drive a man insane.

He needed to wipe that sexy grin off her face before he did something stupid like lean over and kiss it away. "I'm not surprised," Logan said, leaning forward and inhaling deeply. "But then again, I've always been the exception. Haven't I, princess?"

His comment had her temper flaring in those catlike eyes

of hers, deepening the color. She crossed her arms, which only succeeded in pushing her breasts higher. "God, must you keep calling me that?"

He shrugged lightly. "It suits you."

Her eyes held his. "Why? Because my brother would love nothing more than to fit me with a chastity belt and lock me away in a tower somewhere? Or is it because you've always thought of me as a royal pain in the ass?"

Stunned, his mouth hinged open. He hadn't expected her to be so...direct. When had that changed? In the past, she'd always been sly with the subtle overtures she'd sent his way. Not that they'd ever gone unnoticed or anything. At least not by him. But even then, he'd done the only thing he could. He'd ignored them. Because if Brett ever found out his sister had made flirty passes at his best friend, Valerie would have found herself locked away, all right. Never to be seen or heard from again.

Would serve her right.

Either way, Logan had no intention of telling her the reason behind the nickname. That was his business, and if she didn't like it, tough shit. Let her think whatever she wanted. "Both," he lied.

Her eyes narrowed slightly, but her smooth, silky voice held the drugging sensation of hot, sweaty sex. "Well, I can see you're still the same cocky jerk you've always been."

Unable to resist, he stepped closer to her. "Sweetheart, you have no idea how *cocky* I can be."

Logan knew better than to say something like that to her, but her sultry eyes played tag with his and forced all rational thought out the window. And watching her tongue dart out to swipe across her full bottom lip only made things worse. An image of him taking her back to his office, bending her over his desk, and finding out exactly what was under that damn slinky-ass dress had his dick hardening almost to the point of pain.

But then he spotted Brett making his way through the crowd with a drink in each hand and cringed inwardly. *Sonofabitch.* Logan quickly moved away from her and ran a frustrated hand through his hair. *Damn it. What the hell am I doing?* He'd gotten so caught up in their exchange that he hadn't realized he was toeing a very dangerous line, one he wasn't willing to cross.

Brett was the closest thing to a brother Logan would ever know. Which meant that no matter how eye-catching the guy's sister was and no matter how many times she flung herself in his direction, Logan wouldn't risk giving up a life-long friendship for one night of pleasure. It wasn't worth it.

His gaze traveled down to her crossed legs, and he imagined those strong, sexy thighs gripping his hips as he shoved into her. He swallowed hard. *Damn, it would be one long-ass night with a whole lot of pleasure though.*

As Brett approached, he scowled and handed Valerie a half-full green apple martini. "Here, take this fucking drink. Do you know how hard it is to walk through a packed bar with one of those things?" He pulled his shirt away from his body, showing them a wet spot that had darkened the front. "I spilled it on myself twice, and that fruity shit is sticky."

"I've got a box of T-shirts with the bar's logo on them in the back," Logan told him. "I'll get you one, and you can change into it."

"Thanks, man. But only if you let me pay for the shirt."

Logan grimaced. As if he wasn't already feeling guilty enough about accidentally flirting with the man's sister, Brett had just unknowingly twisted the knife. "Damn it, Brett. You don't have to pay for the fucking—"

"Don't go there with me, Logan. I said I'm paying for it."

Brett's straightened his posture, as if to show how firm he stood on the idea. "If you have a problem with that, then I'll just go home and change. Up to you."

Logan sighed. "Fine, get your shirt from Paul. He's the head bartender. He can ring you up and grab one from the storeroom."

As he watched Brett head out in search of Paul, Logan shook his head. *Stubborn asshole.* Then he grinned because the big, lovable jerk knew the dire situation Logan was in and was obviously damned determined to help in any way he could.

Logan needed money. And he needed it now.

"Want to explain what that was all about?" Valerie asked.

The sound of her voice alone had Logan furrowing his brow. He needed to get away from her before he did something stupid. "Nothing. It's just a damn T-shirt."

"I wasn't talking about the shirt. I was talking about...the way you were looking at me before my brother walked up."

His eyes drifted over her face, and his throat tightened, but he said nothing.

Valerie smiled, as if the thought of silencing him had shifted the winds in her direction for a change. She slinked over to him with a feline grace that disturbed the air around him and held a man's attention.

"What's the matter, Logan?" Her sharp eyes focused on him with an intensity that heated his blood and made his heart hammer against his rib cage. "Cat got your tongue?" The words hissed past her parted lips and sizzled in his ears.

He'd love nothing more than to stroke Valerie's...ego and see how many times he could make her purr. But he didn't have time for games. Especially not with *her* of all people. She was off-limits. A distraction. One he didn't need or want in his life.

Logan took a step back. "I've got to get back to work. Why don't you go find your friends and let one of them babysit your ass for a while." Then he turned and stormed away.

He hadn't meant to be so harsh and imagined her staring after him in confusion, but he refused to look back. One minute, he'd been flirting with her, then the next, he'd come to his senses and snapped at her . . . like it was her fault. *God, I'm a fucking idiot.*

Maybe it was better this way. Safer even.

Logan remembered all the times she'd flaunted herself under his nose, teasing and taunting him. And memory served him well. She'd damn near tortured him back then, and he wasn't about to let it happen again. He'd just do what he had done years before—avoid her . . . even if it was difficult to do since the girl was impossible to ignore.

He wasn't going to look at her, think about her, or imagine what she looked like naked. Been there, done that. And all it had ever done was get him into trouble. He knew better than to get anywhere near Valerie, and he was washing his hands of her. For good this time.

Dismissing all thoughts of her from his mind, Logan crossed the room and searched for Brett. He found him standing at the main bar, waiting to get Paul's attention. Along with about twenty other people crowded around the bar with money in hand.

Logan sighed. He'd been afraid of that.

Grand opening night was the worst time to be understaffed, but it couldn't be helped. Logan had hired the only three bartenders he could find on short notice—Paul, Derek, and James.

Paul and James both seemed to know their way around a bar, working fast and efficiently, but Derek was younger and didn't have the same level of experience as the other two. At least his pours were accurate and the cocktails were well made.

Though some of the customers were moving away from Derek's section to order their drinks from a waitress or traipsing over to the main bar to order for themselves, there wasn't much Logan could do. If he hadn't been forced into opening the bar sooner than he'd expected, he would've had time to find another qualified bartender or two. *Lesson learned, for sure.*

Logan stopped beside Brett and caught him scoping out a brunette wearing a tube top at least two sizes too small for her ample breasts. "Hey, Romeo, put your tongue back into your mouth before you step on it."

Brett grinned. "I think I just died and went to heaven."

Chuckling, Logan said, "Yeah? Well, then where do you want me to bury your body?"

"In her cleavage."

Logan shook his head at his buddy. Some men acted like such fools when it came to women. All they thought about was sex. Thank God he wasn't perverse like that.

Brett watched the woman join a group of her friends, then smirked. "So where do you want to be buried?"

Logan sighed. *Balls deep in your sister.*

ABOUT THE AUTHOR

Alison Bliss grew up in Small Town, Texas, but currently resides in the Midwest with her husband and two sons. With so much testosterone in her home, it's no wonder she writes "girl books." She believes the best way to know if someone is your soul mate is by canoeing with them because, if you both make it back alive, it's obviously meant to be. Alison pens the type of books she loves to read most: fun, steamy love stories with heart, heat, laughter, and usually a cowboy or two. As she calls it, "Romance...with a sense of humor."

Fall in Love with Forever Romance

TOO HOT TO HANDLE
By Tessa Bailey

Having already flambéed her culinary career beyond recognition, Rita Clarkson is now stranded in God-Knows-Where, New Mexico, with a busted-ass car and her three temperamental siblings. When rescue shows up—six-feet-plus of hot, charming sex on a motorcycle—Rita's pretty certain she's gone from the frying pan right into the fire...The first book in an all-new series from *New York Times* bestselling author Tessa Bailey!

SIZE MATTERS
By Alison Bliss

Fans of romantic comedies such as *Good in Bed* will eat up this delightful new series from Alison Bliss! Leah Martin has spent her life trying to avoid temptation, but she's sick of counting calories. Fortunately, her popular new bakery keeps her good and distracted. But there aren't enough éclairs in the world to distract Leah from the hotness that is Sam Cooper—or the fact that he just told her mother that they're engaged...which is a big, fat lie.

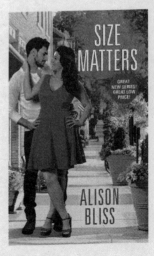

Fall in Love with Forever Romance

MAYBE THIS TIME
By Jennifer Snow

All through high school, talented hockey player Jackson Westmore had a crush on Abby Jansen, but he would never make a move on his best friend's girl. He gave her the cold shoulder out of self-preservation and worked out his frustrations on the ice. So when Abby returns, newly divorced and still sexy as hell, Jackson knows he's in trouble. Now even the best defensive skills might not keep him from losing his heart…

LUKE
By R.C. Ryan

When Ingrid Marrow discovers rancher Luke Malloy trapped in a ravine, she brings him to her family ranch and nurses him back to health. As he heals, he begins to fall for the tough independent woman who saved him, but a mysterious attacker threatens their love—and their lives. Fans of Linda Lael Miller and Diana Palmer will love the latest contemporary western in R.C. Ryan's Malloys of Montana series.

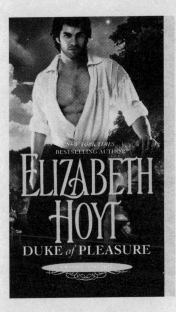

DUKE OF PLEASURE
By Elizabeth Hoyt

Sent to defeat the notorious Lords of Chaos, Hugh Fitzroy, the Duke of Kyle, is ambushed in a London alley—and rescued by an unlikely ally: a masked stranger with the unmistakable curves of a woman. Aif has survived on the streets of St. Giles by disguising her sex, but when Hugh hires her to help his investigation, will she find the courage to become the woman she needs to be—before the Lords of Chaos destroy them both?